RE

He enveloped her in his arms, with a hold that was half-tough, half-tender. The rough material of his jacket scratched her shoulders, but Brianna didn't care. It made the velvet of his lips seem even smoother against her own. They were cool from the evening air, but held the promise of warmth to come.

She gave herself up to that promise, her own lips melting under his. He touched, tasted, savored. She gave. Much too soon it ended. Trevor pulled away, straightened his jacket and gazed down at her.

"Ah, my sweet. I've been wanting to do that since you walked in tonight." He touched his lips to her chin and murmured against her skin, "Don't expect an apology, my little Rebel."

She stared up at him and said the only thing she could say—the truth. "I didn't ask for one."

The low growl deep in his throat was her only warning before he drew her back into his embrace. The jolting of the carriage wheels, the hard seat, the brisk air all ceased to exist for her. The only thing of importance was his strong arms around her.

She raised her head to meet his next kiss. This time he was neither gentle nor searching. His lips plundered hers, demanding all she could give. North and South no longer remained—only the sensations that swept through her body in waves. Enveloping fire. Breathlessness. Desire.

JOYCE ADAMS

REBEL MINE

ZEBRA BOOKS
KENSINGTON PUBLISHING CORP.

ZEBRA BOOKS are published by

Kensington Publishing Corp.
475 Park Avenue South
New York, NY 10016

First Printing: July, 1993
Printed in the United States of America

To my husband for loving and believing,
and To Mom, my mother-in-law, for her
never-ending encouragement.

Chapter One

June, 1861

He was up to something again. Brianna Devland knew it as sure as she breathed. This time she intended to catch her twin red-handed. Laughing softly, Brianna nudged her horse with her knees and rode closer to the overgrown boxwood hedge.

She'd teach Ethan to keep secrets from her and let her take the blame. The last time her golden-haired twin came home knee-walkin' drunk, Aunt Harriet nearly woke up half of the capital. Tonight, Brianna intended to see he stayed out of trouble.

As if the very word trouble had conjured them up, a cluster of blue-coated soldiers rode out of the far side of the woods. She spotted them easily in the early twilight.

Brianna stood in her stirrups to peer around the leafy boxwood—the cultured Southern belle of an hour ago now gone. She watched as Ethan pulled his bay to a stop in the clearing and waited. Whatever was he doing? Everyone knew a group of Yankees was sure trouble. Hadn't the secessionist ladies of

Washington learned that in the two months since the Yankees started the war?

"There's the damned spy!" The shout echoed in the night, raising the gooseflesh on Brianna's arms.

As she watched, the troops broke out of the brush and surged in a group after Ethan. Her twin spun his horse around and kicked the bay into a gallop, the bluecoats on his heels. Across the field, one soldier raised his rifle. Brianna stared in horror.

"Ethan," she called out. "Here."

He jerked on the reins, turning the horse in her direction. Moments later, man and rider sailed over the far side of the hedge. As they crested the top, a shot rang out.

"No!" Brianna threw out her arm, trying by will to stop the lead ball. Her stomach tightened into a knot of fear.

Ethan jerked in the saddle, then crumpled forward. At the same moment a searing fire jolted through Brianna's shoulder. As in the past, she felt her twin's pain. Her breath rushed out in a gasp so intense she almost fell from her mount. Grabbing the horse's mane, she gripped until her knuckles whitened.

Less than twenty feet away, Ethan's mount slowed to a walk, then stopped, sides heaving. She had to reach Ethan. Nothing else mattered. She kicked her filly into a gallop.

Within seconds she reached the other horse, bent low, and grabbed the dangling reins. "Ethan, hang on."

Pulling the bay behind, she urged both horses on. If she could only get to the far side of the hedge, they had a chance. Beyond the brush lay a hidden trail that few knew about. She pulled the reins tighter, drawing the other horse closer.

Brianna glanced over her shoulder. The blue-coated riders had been thrown off by Ethan's jump. As she urged the horses on, the bay pulled back, and her filly stumbled, almost throwing her.

"Bree . . ." Ethan's cry trailed off, and Brianna knew even before she looked back that he'd lost consciousness.

They'd never make it this way. She couldn't handle Ethan and two horses and outrun the Yankees. Despair threatened. She fought it off. She'd get them both out of here.

Yanking back on the reins, she pulled her horse to a stop and jumped down, thankful for the breeches she'd borrowed from Ethan's room. A stinging slap sent the little filly galloping down another trail. She stared after the horse a moment; she could only pray the soldiers wouldn't follow her home. There was little choice—she'd have to worry about that later.

Brianna steadied Ethan's slumped body, then mounted behind him, closing her arms tightly about him. A wet stickiness seeped onto her wrist, and she bit back a cry. She glanced over her shoulder to assess the distance between them and their pursuers. The Yankees were closing in.

She sent the bay charging for the far side of the hedge. Shouts and thundering hooves echoed behind her. A shot cracked in the gathering dark, and Brianna flinched before letting out her breath. Thank God the soldiers weren't close enough for the musket's ball to reach her. Another shot cracked—this one closer. Where was that trail?

Digging in her heels, she begged the stallion for just a little more. Fear and desperation were tangible things snapping at her heels like a rabid dog. A shot whizzed past her to thud into a nearby tree. She swallowed down her cry. She'd see Ethan out of here safe, she vowed.

Ahead several feet, a tall birch jutted out, and Brianna almost shouted. The trail. Praying that the blue-coated riders would miss it in the gathering darkness, she turned the stallion down the narrow path, unmindful of the branches that grabbed at her arms.

As she reached a fork in the trail, a thought struck her. *Her frantic ride was leading the Yankees right to them.* Damnation, what a fool thing to do. Reason returned with a sudden calmness. She slowed the bay and listened, holding her breath. Distant sounds of pursuit echoed in the night.

Brianna fought the urge to kick the stallion into a gallop. Instead, she pulled him off the path. A short distance to her right lay a thick clump of brush and surrounding birches. Dismounting, she led the horse into the midst of the undergrowth. Perhaps she could throw off the soldiers. She steadied Ethan's unconscious form, then drew the horse closer, soothing him. She held the stallion's head close as she'd once seen Ethan do to prevent a betraying whinny.

Around her the woods grew loud as the sounds of night creatures intensified in the stillness. The horse shifted, and Brianna tensed, holding him tighter. He stilled. She peered through the brush, trying to see in the dark surrounding them. Not a breath escaped her as she listened for the soldiers' approach.

At the sound of hooves, she jumped, then tightened her grip on the stallion. *Please,* she begged him, *stay quiet.*

Around her the sounds of men and horses filled the night. She stood rigid, willing Ethan's bay to be still. Her palms grew clammy, and sweat trickled down her shirt in spite of the growing cold.

The voices drew closer, then receded. Brianna released a shivering breath. Perhaps. . . . Above her, Ethan moaned. She jerked her head up. Had the troops heard him?

She stared up at Ethan in horror. As he shifted his head, she threw out a hand, clamping it over his mouth. His breath was warm against her palm. *Forgive me,* she begged silently.

At a movement on the trail, she froze.

"See anything?" a man called out.

"It's no use. We lost him," another answered.

A horse nickered, and Brianna gritted her teeth. She attempted to hug the bay closer and keep one hand over Ethan's mouth. Her arms ached with the effort. She wanted to scream out her frustration at the Yankees, but she stayed silent as the men tramped around.

"Might as well get back to the captain," a man shouted.

Yes, please go away. Her arms throbbed, yet she held them steady. Hardly daring to breathe, she stood in place, waiting. Ethan's shallow breath warmed her hand. The woods around her teemed with noise. She thought she heard footsteps receding, but didn't dare move yet.

After what seemed like hours, the chill night air penetrated her senses, and she shivered against the growing damp. What was this cold doing to Ethan? Another thought held in her throat, choking her. Was he still drawing breath? Forcing herself to find out, she raised her fingers over his nose. As a light flutter of air brushed against her fingers, she sagged against the horse's side. Ethan still breathed. But for how long? His breath seemed so slight. His twinkling blue eyes, a match to her own, lay closed now. She had to get help.

On tiptoe Brianna led the horse out of the brush, almost sure she'd hear a shout at any moment. Surely the Yankees were gone by now, she prayed. She peered through the darkness around her. *Please let it not be a trap.*

Her stiff muscles screamed out as she pulled herself up behind Ethan again. She walked the horse at a slow pace for a distance, too afraid to make more noise. Once on the trail, she gripped the reins and urged the bay into a canter. She hugged her twin closer.

As if her nearness had revived him, Ethan raised his head and looked over his shoulder. "Fine mess I've dragged you into."

"Shh. I'll get you out."

"Brianna," Ethan gasped, then coughed. "Go to Rose . . ."

Mrs. Greenhow? The merry widow who, some

whispered, had her own spy ring? The thoughts chased each other across her mind.

"Our only hope." Ethan sagged forward.

His words echoed in her mind like a dirge. *Our only hope.*

Did they even have that? Desperate, Brianna guided the horse through the woods, following the winding trail, her thoughts prodding her onward. Could they escape the soldiers?

Ethan's body grew heavier, and Brianna clamped her hands over her wrists, the reins between them. Her twin, a spy? How long? Guilt struck her as sharply as a piercing arrow. Why hadn't she known? Or guessed? She should've. Ever since Papa's illness had forced him to leave the Senate and return home to Tennessee in March, Ethan had become more secretive. He'd been furious at having to stay in Washington with Aunt Harriet.

Questions stalked Brianna as surely as the Yankee troops. Why had Ethan done it? She steadied his limp body, gritting her teeth as her muscles cramped.

"Not much longer, boy," she whispered her encouragement to the tiring horse.

Brianna followed the narrow pathway, silence enclosing her like a heavy woolen cloak. She plodded on. She'd almost begun to fear they were lost; then the woods thinned. Hope soared when she spotted the unfinished dome of the Capitol in the distance. Washington. They'd outrun the bluecoats. She picked her way carefully, avoiding Pennsylvania Avenue, and watching for any other people about—especially soldiers.

Before a two-story brownstone looming dark and forbidding in the night, she drew to a stop. Not even a dim candle offered welcome. Was she doing the right thing? She clamped her hands together, holding Ethan closer. He'd told her to come here.

Raising her chin in determination, she urged the stallion forward. At the back door, she pulled the horse up and dismounted. The reins locked in her fist, she stepped forward and rapped on the door.

A light flickered; then the door swung inward suddenly.

"What in tarnation?" Rose Greenhow held a candle up to Brianna's face.

Brianna blinked against the sudden light.

"Child, what are you doing here?"

"It's Brianna . . . Brianna Devland." She found her voice thin and unsteady. She pushed on. "Mrs. Greenhow . . . it's Ethan. He . . ." She gulped. "He said to come here."

"What in—"

"He's been shot," Brianna blurted out.

"Oh, my stars!" Rose Greenhow shot a glance to the horse, then quickly looked around. "Get ahold of him and we'll carry him inside."

As Brianna seemed frozen in place, the woman gave her a shove. "Hurry. Do you want to bring the soldiers down on us?"

At the word "soldiers," Brianna jumped into action. Together they carried Ethan into the house.

"In here." Rose nodded to a servant's door. "We'll put him in Wilkens's room. He's gone for a day or two."

Ethan stirred, moaning.

"Quick, ease him down," Rose ordered.

Brianna lowered Ethan to the small bed.

"Stay with him, child. I'll send for a doctor—one I trust," Rose assured her.

"Ma'am?" A servant hovered in the hall. "Want I should go for—"

"Yes." Rose met the man at the doorway. "But first, there's a horse outside. See it's well hidden."

"Only one horse, ma'am?"

"I couldn't handle both horses," Brianna explained, looking up at Rose. "I set my filly loose in the woods."

"Very well, child." Rose strode over to lay a calming hand on Brianna's shoulder. "I'll take care of everything."

Rose turned away and crossed the room again. With a soft swish, she stepped outside, pulling the door behind her. It stayed partially ajar.

Rose turned back to the servant. "As soon as you fetch the doctor, go to the Devlands' and find the other horse."

"Yes, ma'am."

Brianna listened numbly as footsteps sounded, then faded away. She brushed back Ethan's hair from his forehead and smoothed his brow. He was so cold. She pulled a blanket about him.

"Bree?" he murmured, then moistened his lips, and called louder, "Bree?"

"Shh. I'm here." She leaned closer so that he could see her.

"Got to get to . . ." He struggled to sit up and

sagged against her.

"No, Ethan. We're at Mrs. Greenhow's. Now lie still. You're hurt."

"You could say that." His chuckle turned into a raspy cough. "Where are we?" He caught her hand. "Rose's?"

Brianna nodded and squeezed his hand. "She's sent for a doctor. Lie still and I'll go check . . ." She stood.

"No." Ethan pulled her down, his grip surprisingly strong in that moment. "Bree, no time left now."

His words froze her as surely as a winter storm. He was wrong. She wouldn't let him die. "Ethan—"

"Listen to me, Bree." He paused for breath. "Up to you now." He grasped both her hands in his, drawing her closer.

As a warm stickiness eased between her fingers, Brianna caught back a gasp. A single tear rolled down her cheek.

"The Code." Ethan paused to gather his strength. "Rose will . . . teach you how to—"

"You'll teach me yourself when you're better."

Saving his breath, he shook his head. A lock of blond hair tumbled forward to be held fast by the sweat that now streaked his brow.

Brianna gently brushed it back. "Ethan—"

"My room . . . in my red cravat . . . Vigenere Code." He coughed, and a trickle of blood colored the corner of his mouth.

Brianna wiped it away. Worried, she glanced at his chest. So much blood—it kept spreading, darkening his shirt. She forced herself to look at his face instead.

"The Confederacy's cipher," he whispered.

"I—" Brianna's words died in her throat. Ethan, a spy.

She gazed down at her twin. She could see more—that his boyish manner was only a facade to deceive. He'd convinced even her. How long had he been leading a double life—friendly to the Yankees at parties, and carrying their secrets to the Confederacy?

"Tell Rose . . ."

"You'll tell her yourself." Brianna bit her lip to fight back the tears. "She'll be back here soon."

Ethan shook his head. "No, Bree. Too late. We both know it. Tell Rose . . . need you now. Rose . . . will explain all."

He gripped her hand, and she held to him tightly, ignoring the crusted blood between his fingers and the tears trickling down her chin.

"Bree . . . promise . . . promise me you'll take my place." He sagged back, weakened by the effort the words had cost him.

Her, a spy? No. She couldn't do it. "Ethan, I—"

He struggled to breathe, tightening his grip on her hand. She could feel his desperation giving him strength. She brushed her tears away. Ethan couldn't die. He just couldn't.

"Promise . . . me?" he implored.

She swallowed down her denial. She couldn't refuse him. Not now. "Yes, Ethan. I . . . you have my word," she whispered.

He nodded, then coughed again. This time his hand came away red. "Bree . . ." He paused. "Letter . . . third . . ." He fell silent.

"Ethan?"

At her anguished cry, he blinked his eyes open. "Shh . . . you'll wake the house." He smiled and touched her damp cheek. "Don't cry." He dropped his hand back to his side. A moment later, he tensed. "Beware . . . spy . . ."

His voice faded, and she had to lean forward to catch his hoarse words.

". . . the . . . jackal." His lashes fluttered, then lay still.

"Ethan!" Brianna cried out. His hand tightened its grip on hers, then stilled. A terrible coldness penetrated through her.

She gathered him to her as if by holding him close enough she could infuse his body with her own lifeblood. Tears ran unchecked down her cheeks, dampening the blond head resting on her breast. She rocked him gently back and forth.

"Oh, Ethan," she murmured, kissing the top of his head. "Why? Why?"

Brianna fell silent. *Damn Yankees.* Keeping the South in the Union wasn't worth Ethan's life. *Damn them all.*

The door swung inward, and Rose stepped into the room. "Brianna?"

Silence greeted her, and she called again. "Child?"

Brianna looked up at the other woman, then gently laid Ethan back on the bed. "They've killed him. The Yankees killed Ethan." The words fell hard and cold into the room, matching Brianna's heart.

Rose quickly crossed to the bed, bent over Ethan, and listened for a heartbeat. She straightened and faced Brianna. She eyed the younger woman silently, measuring her. Pretty, intelligent, guileless—she'd be perfect. Even more effective than Ethan.

"I'm sorry, child. He's gone. I'll take care of everything."

"He told me to come here." Brianna stared blankly at the wall.

"It was good that you did."

A terrible numbness engulfed Brianna. She wrapped her arms about herself. "He's been spying. I never knew."

"Shh."

"How did he . . ." Brianna clenched her hands into fists. "Who recruited him?"

"I did," Rose answered calmly with pride.

Something in Brianna snapped. "You!"

She stared at Rose with growing comprehension. This was the woman her twin had been sneaking out to see. Poor Ethan hadn't stood a chance.

"You caused this! You killed him just as sure as the Yankees."

Rose grabbed Brianna by the shoulders. "No. Ethan loved the South. He believed in the Cause. The Yankees killed him—don't you forget that." She turned her loose and stepped back.

Brianna stared at her.

"Hate them, Brianna, not me. I didn't force him. I loved Ethan, too."

Brianna quelled her bitterness. Rose was right. No one could ever force Ethan to do anything. Perhaps the other woman had cared for him.

"Child? What of your promise?"

"My promise?" Brianna questioned, then narrowed her eyes at Rose. "You heard? You were listening?"

"I came back to the room. I could tell he was . . ." Rose paused delicately, "I didn't want to disturb your final time together."

Brianna blinked back the fresh tears that sprang to her eyes. "Thank you."

"Tell me, do you intend to honor your promise?"

The words hung in the room, challenging her. Brianna clenched her hands together. To Ethan honor had meant everything. Could she respond any differently?

"Child?"

Brianna opened her mouth and sucked in a deep breath. "Yes," she answered.

Rose stared at the dry-eyed girl a moment. "I will arrange everything. Ethan will be . . . taken care of," she spoke softly, observing Brianna.

"He—"

"Everyone will be told he left to join your father in Tennessee."

"But—"

"Act as if nothing is wrong. When people ask, tell them your father's condition has worsened, and that Ethan left to be with him. Because of the war you are staying on with your Aunt Harriet. Do you understand?"

"Yes," Brianna agreed. The only outward sign of her inner turmoil was her firmly clenched jaw.

"Your aunt will be the only one besides us who knows the truth. Tell her what happened. Harriet can be trusted."

"Mrs. Greenhow?" Brianna met her stare bravely. "Tell me about the Vigenere Code."

Rose nodded her approval. "Tomorrow will be soon enough for that. Go home and try to get some sleep. You will have to work hard for the next month. There is much to learn."

Brianna clenched her hands tightly together to stop any giveaway tremble. Like Ethan, she would have to grow up behind her own facade. "I'm ready."

"Yes, I believe you are." Rose reached down and drew Brianna to her feet.

"I won't fail him," Brianna vowed.

"I know you won't." Rose released Brianna's hands. "Come back here tomorrow. From now on, you'll be known as the Rebel Fox." With those final words, she led Brianna to the door.

Chapter Two

July, 1861

Major Trevor Caldwell leaned against the tall pillar, crossed his arms, and concentrated on the blonde waltzing around the ballroom. She moved with the grace of a butterfly, sampling the favors of one partner after another. So this was Brianna Devland. The name fit—almost as well as the creamy gown that barely covered her attributes.

He continued to watch her. She was every bit the temptress he'd been expecting, but somehow she'd surprised him. In spite of her blatant flirting, an aura of innocence surrounded her. Or was it because of it? Could this child-woman be one of the sesech ladies? More important, was her brother, Ethan, the spy he sought?

She laughed up at her partner, her head thrown back. Red-gold curls trailed across one shoulder and came to rest over her breast. Trevor's loins tightened.

A gay tinkle of laughter like a crystal spring reached out to him. Her partner's hand slipped to her waist, and Trevor stiffened. She eased away from the eager young man. Trevor relaxed against the pillar. Why should he care if the young pup held her waist—a waist Trevor was sure his own hands could span. He desired to try it and feel her beneath his palms.

He pulled his thoughts up sharply. There was an abundance of willing women in the capital city. Willing Union women who weren't suspected of harboring sesech sympathies. What did Brianna know of her brother's whereabouts?

Her twin's name was on his list of suspected Confederate spies. Although Trevor had only been in Washington a few days, he'd already heard much of Miss Brianna Devland. Her name was on many men's lips.

Did she know the truth behind her brother's disappearance? If she did, her movements around the room held a dangerous meaning.

She danced with young, low-ranking officers. Most of them gangly youths away from home for the first time. All with information to impart to an attentive, beautiful woman. This was no normal butterfly. She moved with a reserved, but underlying purpose.

Perhaps it was time he sampled Brianna Devland's charms for himself. Trevor straightened away from the pillar and stepped forward.

He was watching her again. The Yankee officer's very presence had commanded Brianna's attention from the first glance. He couldn't be ignored. His towering height, hair the color of midnight, and the way he'd watched her with hungry eyes couldn't be denied. Those dark eyes had followed her like a dog eyeing a juicy platter of meat. She did not enjoy the feeling. What did he want with her? Under that uniform was no gentleman.

Brianna shook her crinolines and skirts free of the grains of colored sand that clung to them, wishing she could free herself of the Yankee as easily. Deliberately she watched the sand fall. The multicolored granules sprinkled to the floor, reminding her of the earlier beauty of the dance floor's intricate sand design. It had been destroyed the instant the first dancers swept across the floor. Destruction came so easily to these Northerners. As natural as breath.

Brianna flipped open her fan and waved it back and forth. The summer evening suddenly seemed overly warm. She turned her head and met the impudent stare of that annoying Yankee officer across the room. His blue uniform proclaimed him her enemy. Her hand stopped in midair, motionless. His finely chiselled features kept him from being handsome, but there was something. . . .

Even though they hadn't touched, she felt as if they had collided. She drew a breath into air-starved lungs and spun away.

"Brianna, you're looking lovely tonight, my dear."

She jumped at Rose Greenhow's greeting. "Ah . . . thank you, Mrs. Greenhow. It's a wonderful party, isn't it? What a beautiful gown."

Rose stroked the lace on the bodice of the richly colored silk that could be called anything but plain brown. Her eyes narrowed on Brianna. "Is something wrong?"

"Yes. No," Brianna corrected. What could she say?

That the sight of a man disturbed her? She glanced back at the wall, but he was nowhere in sight.

"Oh, I do believe I see Secretary Seward," Rose exclaimed. She snapped her fan open, and a coquettish smile graced her face.

Brianna followed Rose's gaze to the secretary of state with his ever-present cigar in his large mouth. His head with its silver hair and broad brow seemed oversized, and was carried thrust forward as if it were too much for his small neck to hold up.

Rose tapped her shoulder. "Don't let his looks deceive you. He's still got some snap left in his garters."

Brianna bit back an unladylike chuckle. The merry widow reminded her of a hungry fox stalking a chicken coop. Rose should have been named the "Rebel Fox" instead of her.

Rose took two steps, then stopped. "Oh, my dear, you will be sure to stop by for tea tomorrow? I'm sure we'll have much to talk about."

"I'd be delighted." She knew Rose was referring to the information she hoped Brianna would gather tonight and deliver to the messenger tomorrow night.

"Oh, here comes Lieutenant Stratton." Rose smiled. "Be nice to him, dear."

Inwardly Brianna groaned. She'd already endured one dance with the clumsy young officer. He'd been shy and silent. However, rumor had it that his regiment might be moving south soon. She smiled at his request for a dance and let him lead her out onto the floor.

Across the room, she spotted the dark-haired officer striding toward her. She missed a step, and her partner trod on her toes. Before she could recover the rhythm, he whirled her around, and she lost sight of the stranger.

The strains of a waltz carried through the ballroom, above the hum of voices, and Lieutenant Stratton stepped on her foot for the third time.

Brianna held back a sharp retort and smiled up at him. "How do you like Washington?"

He mumbled a response.

She eased closer, knowing she was putting her new slippers in danger, and asked, "I'm sorry, with this loud music I didn't hear you."

"I haven't been here that long."

"But you're so popular with the ladies, I thought you had been in town for some time."

"No, ma'am."

"But the other girls here like you, too. In fact, we'll all miss you when you leave."

"Lieutenant? Will you introduce me to the young lady?" The deep voice behind her stroked her. It was velvety soft, yet slightly rough like a cat's tongue.

It had to be the Yankee officer. Her persistent watcher. That voice could belong to no one else, she was sure. Though it didn't seem as coarse as most Northerners'.

Brianna looked up and stopped in midbreath. She met *his* stare again. Her first thought was that his eyes weren't dark after all. They glowed with a golden sheen to their green depths, like a sleek cat in the forest. Gooseflesh spread across her shoulders.

She missed the lieutenant's answer. Suddenly her hand was in *his*, and he was speaking again. If she hadn't been trying to get information from the lieutenant, she'd be in danger of being fascinated by this man.

"My pleasure, Miss Devland," he said, his voice lowered, just for her ears. "Major Trevor Caldwell, at your service." He bowed over her hand, his lips grazing her flesh.

The gentlemanly act, when performed by him, carried a blatant sensuality. Breathing ceased to be a natural action. Odd, she'd never had to work at it before. She fought to draw air into her lungs—and succeeded.

"Major." She inclined her head. Thankfully her voice sounded normal, if a bit stiff.

A couple danced past, staring at the trio. Brianna bristled. They were causing a scene, and she felt a fool for her part. She'd practically gawked at the man. It was time she put the daring Yankee in his place.

"Major"—her voice was as cool as a summer smokehouse—"as soon as the lieutenant and I finish our dance—"

"Trevor," he cut in. "And this is our dance." With a natural aura of command, he pulled her away from the young man and into his own arms.

Shock and anger surged in Brianna. Now she'd never get that troop information from Lieutenant Stratton. She choked back the words that surfaced and fixed an icy stare at her new partner. It bounced right off his self-confidence. Convention required that she avoid an embarrassing disturbance. She'd carry this off with grace.

"As you wish, Major." She stressed the title.

He eased closer and whispered, "Trevor, please."

Brianna stiffened and drew away, forcing a respectable distance between them.

Trevor looked down, and a grin spread across his face. The silk strained over her bodice. He marvelled at what miracle allowed the minx to draw a deep breath without a natural disaster occurring. He forced his gaze back to her face. He should at least pretend to be a gentleman . . . tonight.

Feeling his eyes on her, Brianna glanced up at her partner. The intensity of his gaze startled her, and she felt the heat of a blush creep up her cheeks. None of the other men's stares had caused her to react so. Brianna swallowed down her unease and met his gaze squarely.

She cleared her throat. "Have you been in Washington long?"

That was a safe enough question, and one of the first ones Rose insisted she ask each new partner. Not that Brianna expected this man to fall at her feet and reveal any information. But right now, it was the only question she could think of.

"Obviously not. I just met you tonight, otherwise I would think my time here had been wasted so far."

Brianna raised her brows at the obvious flattery. Somehow the words held a ring of truth. Oh, he was good.

"You're not planning on leaving us to return home like your brother, are you? There'd be many a broken heart left behind, Brianna." Her name was a mere whisper on his lips.

Brianna gasped and tensed in his arms. The question had been spoken so innocently. But was it? What did he know? She forced herself to smile up at him. Hair as dark as black velvet brushed his forehead. His was a strong face, and he exuded power. The only thing to soften the effect was a thick, dark mustache over sensual lips. Trevor Caldwell would make a formidable enemy.

He stepped closer. "Whatever made you stay here in Washington without your family?"

"But I am with family. I'm staying with my aunt."

Brianna inclined her head to the corner where Aunt Harriet held court from a comfortable chair, her wooden cane propped across her knees. Her red hair glinted brightly. Tenderness gleamed in Brianna's blue eyes.

"Papa didn't want her left alone at this time." She turned her head back and met Trevor's stare boldly. "And he didn't want me involved in the war, so I'm staying here."

It sounded so reasonable, so believable. Brianna almost laughed. Her words gave away no hint of the abandonment she felt. Or the pain of Ethan's loss. Sometimes she felt as if her twin were still there—still alive.

Across the room, Brianna caught sight of Rose Greenhow. A deep frown marred her face. Rose waved her fan at Brianna and shook her head in warning.

The gooseflesh prickled across Brianna's shoulders, and she shivered against the sudden premonition it brought. For a minute the breath tightened in her throat, almost choking her. Rose had warned her against talking with the newer officers until she had checked on them. One of Rose's sources had passed on the news that the Union was intensifying their search for any Rebel spies.

Was that what Trevor was doing? He seemed to irritate and charm her in turn. He had been so different, his charm obvious but sincere, that Brianna had forgotten all of Rose's instructions. She'd babbled away to him. How could she have been such a fool? But she hadn't really said anything revealing, had she?

The music came to an end. However, Trevor continued to hold her in his arms. Her heartbeat raced, and she closed her eyes, hoping to slow it down.

"I'll call on you tomorrow, Brianna."

A warm flush spread through her, then was rapidly replaced by a chill. The last thing she needed was a determined Yankee major hanging around her.

"I'd rather you didn't, Major Caldwell."

He smiled. "The name is Trevor. Until tomorrow."

"I told you—" Brianna stopped. He'd already strode halfway across the floor, leaving her alone in the middle of the room with her mouth open. Damn him!

She raised her chin, turned away, and walked in the opposite direction. His parting words returned to haunt her. Was this what a real fox felt like when he heard the baying of the hounds and knew the hunter was not far behind? Was Trevor the hunter? Or only a conceited Yankee?

* * *

In one angry move, Trevor Caldwell swept his arm across the table, sending the sheets of paper to the floor. The information in the report was about as useless as it could be.

A lone page teetered on the table's edge, taunting him. He grabbed up the paper, crumpled it in his fist, and threw it against the wall. If the general agreed with Captain Lewis's report and recommendations on the Rebel Fox, the Confederate spy would escape and crawl back into his hole again.

The war was not going as well or as quickly as expected. If they didn't stem the daily flow of information to the South, things would worsen. Was he the only one who could see that? The fools in Washington were even allowing correspondents to report new troop strengths in the newspapers. Those same newspapers found their way across the lines to Richmond—even to Jeff Davis himself.

Trevor slammed his hand down on the table. These Confederate spies had to be stopped, as well as the Washington sesech ladies who aided them.

He'd been given a list of three suspected spies. Two men were here in Washington, but young Ethan Devland had vanished a month ago. He'd bet pretty Brianna knew more than she was telling. However, if she knew something, he would have expected her to be more reticent. Her sassy blue eyes taunted him still. The memory of the feel of her in his arms heated his blood even now. He grabbed up a paper.

The headlines of the *Washington Star* blared their news at him. Hell, the Confederates had probably read the paper before him.

He dropped his head in his hands. The situation was worsening. With the defeat at Bull Run, the tide of the war had turned against the Union. Too many lives—friends' lives—had been lost on that battlefield. All because of the Confederate spies. In the last month, one name had come up again and again.

He spat the words out. "The Rebel Fox."

The name left a bitter taste on his tongue. He clenched his jaw. He would uncover this spy. As his teeth ground together, he forced himself to relax his jaw.

Picking up a two-day-old copy of a Washington paper, he scanned the headlines. Another regiment had moved into the Capital. He turned to the want advertisements. If he was right, the answer to his problem lay in these pages. All he needed was one piece of information disproving the report General Scott valued so highly.

He spread the *Evening Star* across the table and focused on it with grim determination. Time swept past, the room growing dim as he read the columns over and over.

Twenty minutes later, Trevor shouted and slammed his hand on the page. From his pocket he withdrew a folded sheet of paper containing the smuggled copy of the latest Confederate code. He laid the pages side by side and set to work.

When he unscrambled the coded words he could scarce believe them. Before him lay the instructions for the Rebel Fox to meet a courier outside Washington tonight. With a whoop of victory, Trevor grabbed the newspaper and strode out the door.

The echo of his boots on the wood flooring followed him down the hall. At the general's office, he barely came to a halt before pounding on the door. Dragging a hand through his dishevelled hair, Trevor attempted to bring some order to the unruly strands before he faced his commander.

At a barked order to enter, Trevor opened the door and strode to the desk. The man behind it took center stage. His back ramrod straight in spite of his advanced years, he sat proudly in his version of the Union uniform with its eagle-covered brass buttons and velvet cuffs and collar. General Winfield Scott had been described by many as crusty. Secretly, Trevor agreed.

He gave a sharp salute. "Sir."

"What is it? Speak up, boy."

Trevor winced at the term. His grandfather and the general had served together in the Mexican War. It had been long ago, but the general still persisted in referring to Trevor as "boy."

"General, the Rebel Fox is in the capital."

"Impossible," General Scott growled the word. "Our reports place him south of Richmond." He slammed his huge hands on the desk top, indicating his unwillingness to discuss the matter further.

"Those reports are false."

"Damnation, Major." General Scott struggled to his feet, resting his large weight on his hands.

Trevor faced him squarely. Damned if he'd back down. The two men glared at each other.

"They're wrong." Trevor spoke with deadly conviction.

"Humph."

"Read this." He tossed the decoded message onto the desk.

General Scott looked down at the paper. After reading the words, he sank into his chair. "You're sure?"

"As sure as I breathe."

The general fingered the paper in silence.

"Put me in command of the Rebel Fox's capture, sir. I'll deliver him to you before summer's out." Before the general went on the retired list, Trevor added silently.

"You sound damn sure."

"I am. I've already got someone in place. A counterspy." Usually he didn't trust informants, but this one needed money in the worst way.

The general laughed. "Good work. He's yours—but before winter."

Trevor smiled. If his plan worked, tonight he would have his spy.

The dark wig itched, and Brianna fought the powerful urge to yank it off. A mental picture of her long, blond hair and dye-stained skin flashed in her mind. She dropped her darkened hand to her side in disgust. The disguise of a former slave always made her nervous. She could imagine a dutiful countryman trying to return her to her master. How much protection would the hollow log she sat on offer?

At the sound of footsteps, she snapped her head up and stared into the moonlit night. She'd delivered the coded message and left the courier half an hour ago. She should be alone. A twig cracked, and she knew she wasn't.

Brianna dove into the hollow log. She feared she was about to find out just how much protection it offered. Dank, musty air engulfed her, and she wiggled a hand up to cover her nose. Feathery threads crept across her fingers. Was it a cobweb or a daddy longlegs? She flicked it off with her thumb and shuddered, refusing to think of what other creatures might be sharing her log.

Outside, voices carried in the night, a horse whinnied, and Brianna lay still. From the sounds around her she'd narrowly missed a Union patrol. This portion of the woods was supposed to be safe. A niggling thought surfaced and grew. She'd been betrayed—just like Ethan. But by whom?

Around her the men tramped back and forth in the woods, searching. The dampness from the log seeped through her, and Brianna shivered. She thought she felt something slither down her leg and held back her scream. How long before the woods fell silent she didn't dare guess, but finally the noise and soldiers left.

Gingerly, Brianna crawled out of the log. She brushed at her arms and legs, dislodging heaven only knew what. Satisfied that nothing still crawled on or clung to her arms or skirt, she started off walking toward town. Suddenly a night creature skittered across her path, and she bolted into a run. She didn't slow down until she passed the clearing beside town.

Brianna sagged against a lone tree, breathless. Putting a hand to her throat, she tried to calm her breathing. Her escape had been terrifyingly close. Where had that patrol come from? It hadn't been there the last time she'd delivered a message across the lines. She wiped the sheen of sweat from her forehead. Her fingers came away sticky. Damn—the temporary dye was running.

She had to get to Rose's house soon. Hiding from the patrol had made her late, and Rose would be near frantic by now.

The moonlit street was empty, so Brianna gathered up her skirt and dashed across the rutted lane. Intent on haste, she didn't hear the horse and rider until they were almost upon her.

At a shout, Brianna whirled around. Horse hooves pawed the air above her head. She jumped to the side and fell hard. For a moment everything went dark around her.

Then Brianna opened her eyes and stared into the face of Trevor Caldwell. It was a dream—it had to be—or a nightmare.

Chapter Three

Brianna closed her eyes tightly. Maybe when she opened them again he'd be gone—a haunt—an apparition. She didn't believe in ghosts, but maybe just this once. She hoped there were spirits.

Tentatively, Brianna peeked at him. Damnation. The man bending over her was real all right.

The sharp cheekbones, firm sensual lips, and rough stubbled chin belonged to no ghost. The Yankee blue uniform pulled taut across wide shoulders and outlining muscular thighs was not imagined. The smell of leather, horse sweat and pure man was real enough. Her gaze dropped lower before she stopped herself. Quickly she looked up. Her heart pounded within her breast.

Major Trevor Caldwell, over six feet of barely leashed masculinity, leaned over her. The daring hunger was missing, but she knew it was still there—buried just under the surface. It was waiting to pounce on her. She recalled his actions of last night. No doubt about it. The major was more trouble than she cared to think about.

Brianna slumped back against the cold earth, snapping her eyes closed again. *Don't let him recognize me, please,* she begged. She could almost feel the weight of the shackles pressing into her skin. *Please, let him think me a servant. Let the dark dye work.*

Plans of escape chased each other around her head. Try as she might, she couldn't entirely ignore the feel of his hands on her arms. What would those hands feel like—she cut the thought off. Escape, she told herself. Wait, her body answered.

His hands eased up her arms to her shoulders. Brianna gasped.

"Girl?"

She'd know that voice anywhere, even in pitch darkness. She pretended unconsciousness. Perhaps, if he didn't look too close, her disguise would work.

"Girl? Wake up." Trevor grimaced at the young charge on the ground.

She was filthy. Her dark hair lay in mats, cobwebs intermingled with the tangles. The streaks of dirt that covered her face hid her features. If she didn't awake, would he have to carry her to aid? He couldn't very well leave her. Something about her tugged at him.

At the sound of approaching riders, Trevor stood, one hand on his pistol. Two men galloped in from the east, moonlight glimmering off their uniform buttons and sword hilts. As they neared, he recognized his men. When he called out, they pulled their mounts to a halt and saluted.

"Anything to report?" Trevor asked.

"Nothing, sir," one soldier answered.

"Maybe that Rebel spy ain't come back from his meetin', sir," the other man added.

A shaft of fear stabbed Brianna. These men were part of the trap laid for her. Was Trevor behind it? It was obvious the men were reporting to him.

Brianna watched as Trevor pulled out a pocket watch, tilted it to the moonlight, and read the dial. Now or never, an inner voice prompted her.

Taking advantage of the distraction, Brianna sat up. As if he'd sensed her movement, Trevor turned back to her at once.

"Massah . . . sir," Brianna pitched her voice higher. "I's fine, sir." Her voice broke.

"Girl?" He took a step forward.

Brianna sprang to her feet. "I gots to get home. Thank . . . thank you," she stammered, trying to imitate Aunt Harriet's young maid.

"Wait—"

Before Trevor could step closer, Brianna grabbed her skirt in one hand and quickly stepped back out of arm's reach. When neither he nor his men came forward, she spun around.

Brianna ran as if the devil himself were after her. Thinking of Major Trevor Caldwell, she feared it might be so. She dared a look over her shoulder. He stood silhouetted against the night. She didn't need daylight to see the irritation on his face. She knew it was there.

The intensity of his stare reached out to her across the distance that separated them. A strange mixture of excitement and trepidation swept over her. She knew they'd meet again. Her stomach tightened.

Brianna grabbed her skirts once more, turned, and dashed across a deserted, rutted lane. She thought she heard the clip of horse hooves pursuing her and quickened her pace. She ran through the streets of Washington, heedless of any curious stares she drew. Her side hurt, but she pressed on. The imposing picture of Trevor Caldwell standing tall in the moonlight haunted her even more than if he'd been an apparition.

Trevor took a step after the fleeing girl. Something had scared her; that much he knew for sure. But what? She'd been so filthy, he'd felt sorry for her. He wouldn't miss the few coins he felt inclined to give her. However, to do that he'd have to catch her. He was pulled up short by a shout behind him.

"Major?"

Trevor spun around. Irritated at the interruption, he snapped a response.

"Sir, we were wondering if you wanted us to keep searching for that Rebel spy?"

Trevor balled his hands into fists. He'd been so caught up in the plight of the girl that he'd allowed himself to forget the mission. Damn the girl. What was it about her that had accomplished the seemingly impossible feat of drawing his attention from capturing the Rebel Fox? Something nagged at the back of his mind like the slow, steady dripping of water. He wondered where the girl had run to and why. As he mounted his horse, he spared one last glance, but she was long gone.

Brianna slowed when the back of Rose Greenhow's brownstone came into view. She quelled the urge to throw herself at the door and pound on it until it opened. Instead, she knocked on the back door in the rat-a-tap-tap signal Rose had taught her.

Brianna leaned against the stone wall and gulped in deep breaths of air. Her mouth was so dry, her chest ached. The stone wall was cool to her overheated skin, and she pressed against it, resting her cheek on the blessed coolness. She was safe.

The breeze ruffled her wig and tugged at the edges of her ripped blouse. Brianna raised a hand to tuck the tattered material together. She must look a sight. A picture of Trevor, crisp and clean in his Yankee uniform, sprang unbidden to her mind. She brushed it aside. He'd been out to trap the Rebel Fox—her.

A click startled her, and she jerked her head up, checking for danger. A sigh of relief gushed out as the door opened slowly. A familiar chubby face peered out at her. Wilkens's mouth formed an "oh," and he stared at her as if she were a ghost.

Brianna offered the butler a weak smile. Thank goodness she didn't have to explain her disguise to Wilkens. He'd been there when Rose had applied the dark, washable dye to Brianna's face, arms and hands.

"Miss Brianna." Wilkens threw the door open wide. "What happened to you?"

As she took a step forward, a cramp of pain gripped her calf, and she cried out. She sagged back against the wall.

Eyes wide with fear, the butler hollered for Rose.

"No," Brianna tried to silence the alarm. "It's nothing."

She threw out her arm to stop Wilkens, but to no avail. He ignored her protests. The door swung closed as he rushed off to get the mistress of the house. Brianna scowled at the door. What else could go wrong? On second thought, she didn't wish to know. She rubbed her leg with both hands, kneading out the painful cramp. The door swung open suddenly, and she looked up.

"Oh, my stars," Rose Greenhow gasped, covering her mouth in dismay. "Wilkens, bring her in. Then go fetch the doctor."

Brianna stepped forward, limping slightly. "No." Her voice rang out clear.

The butler froze in midstep.

"I am fine. Really," she assured them both. "It was only a pain in my leg from running."

"Well, for goodness sakes." Rose glared at her. "You gave us both a fright. When Wilkens came for me so upset, all I could see in my mind was you shot like poor Ethan."

Pain ripped through Brianna at the mention of her twin. In spite of everything over the last month, she still hadn't accepted in her heart that her twin was dead.

"I'm sorry, dear." Rose laid a hand on Brianna's shoulder. "But Wilkens seemed sure you'd been shot."

"Not for lack of trying." Brianna's voice was sharper than she'd intended, and the butler flinched as if struck.

She sent him an apologetic smile. "Thank you for fetching help, Wilkens. I'm fine, only dirty."

"Let's get her inside," Rose interrupted. Once in the

kitchen, she faced Brianna. "Tell me what happened tonight."

Brianna reached up and yanked off the wig. She scratched her scalp and neck. "I'll have you to know, I spent an hour in a rotted, hollow log hiding from a Yankee patrol."

Rose blanched. "No, how could—"

"They knew I was coming. I overheard them. Rose, whoever betrayed Ethan is still here." Brianna blinked away the gathering moisture in her eyes. "Alive and well," she added with bitterness.

Rose pursed her lips and tapped her fingers together. "I will start checking at once." She looked Brianna up and down. "Child, you are filthy. Wilkens, see that a bath is readied immediately. And wake May."

"It'll take a night of scrubbing to get her ready for that party tomorrow night." Muttering, he ambled off in the direction of the maid's room.

As soon as Wilkens was out of sight, Brianna turned to Rose. "Who knew I was going out tonight?"

"I knew, and General Beauregard's messenger. And, of course, my staff."

"Do you think"—Brianna lowered her voice to a whisper—"it could be one of—"

"No. They've all been with me for years."

"Then, who?"

"The informant could even be at Richmond. I will talk with General Beauregard personally." Rose patted her arm. "Try not to worry. I'll get to the bottom of this. Remember, no one but you, the general, and I know that *you* are the Rebel Fox."

"Major Caldwell is heading up the search," Brianna said.

"I suspected as much."

"Then, why didn't you tell me?"

"I only learned of it tonight. From now on, you must do everything in your power to avoid him."

"But what of the party? He's sure to attend."

"A word dropped in the right ears and unwanted admirers will be kept away." Rose brushed the problem aside. "Ah, here comes May. Now to get you clean."

It took a total of three full tubs of water to remove all traces of her disguise. The dye had been more stubborn than usual. Wilkens's prophecy had been right.

Brianna tingled from head to toe when she stepped from the tub over half an hour later. As the night air touched her, she shivered. Accepting the towel from May, she began to gingerly pat her tender skin dry. She was convinced she'd still smell of the strong soap come tomorrow night's party. Wrinkling her nose, she rubbed at a leftover spot of dye on her wrist. Damnation—would she never be clean again?

From the doorway came Rose's laughter. "If you keep that up, there won't be any skin left."

Brianna sent her a dark glare.

"May, you can go on back to your bed now. I'll see to our guest."

The young maid smiled, wished them a good night, and hurried off. The door clicked shut behind her.

"Now, don't forget to use that scented lilac oil in your bath before the party. And be sure to rub some onto your arms and shoulders afterward," Rose recited the instructions.

"I know what to do." Brianna raised her chin. "You've taught me well."

"Of course I have." Rose preened. "Captain Lewis is still to escort you, isn't he?"

"Yes. Before I slipped out for our meeting, I heard him tell Aunt Harriet that he would be at the house early for the party." She rubbed at another spot on her elbow. "And he accepted my headache as reason not to receive any callers today."

The excuse had also saved her from meeting with Major Trevor Caldwell again. Or at least it had postponed his pursuit.

"The illness was a good ruse." Rose beamed her approval. "We couldn't take the chance of you being detained today."

"The gown was delivered, and it fits perfectly." Brianna changed the subject. Remembering how she'd hidden above the stairs to listen to what the major had to say made her feel foolish.

Rose clapped her hands. "Good. For a while I feared the dress would not be readied in time. A few extra coins soon changed that."

Brianna thought of the breathtaking white gown shot through with threads of gold. It had taken two seamstresses to prepare the almost twenty-five yards of silk muslin for tonight.

"You can concentrate on attracting the senator's new aide."

Brianna nodded, confident of success. They'd gone over the plan so many times that surely nothing could go wrong.

"We should get you home soon, so that you can be well rested for tomorrow. It's time to resurrect young Timmy," Rose said.

She smiled wickedly as she held out a set of grimy clothes to Brianna. Patched breeches, a mended shirt, and a too-large jacket dangled from her arm. In one hand she twirled a moth-eaten woolen cap.

Brianna wrinkled her nose in distaste. It appeared she wasn't to be clean for long. "Timmy" had served them well, Brianna mused as she slipped into the rough clothes. No lady of good breeding would be out at this time of night, but young Timmy could come and go without attracting undue attention. She shoved the shirt into the breeches and picked up the hat. She wound her hair into a coil, then tucked it up under the cap.

"Satisfied?" Brianna cocked her head.

Rose leaned over and pulled the woolen cap lower so that it hid the upper portion of Brianna's face. "It wouldn't do for you to be recognized."

Brianna agreed. Over the past month, she'd become a mistress of disguise with Rose's aid. Rumors abounded that the Rebel Fox was a Negro slave, a freeborn servant, a young boy, and an old lady. Anything to confuse the Yankees, she thought, slipping her feet into a tattered pair of boots and wiggling her toes into a comfortable spot. Her disguise complete, Brianna stood for Rose's inspection.

As she looked her up and down, Brianna slouched, shifting from one foot to the other. Next, she wiped her nose with her shirt sleeve. "Well, ma'am?"

Rose grinned. "Very good. But too clean for a young boy." She reached out, scraped a clump of mud off the shirt, and dabbed a streak of the wet dirt across Brianna's cheek. "Much better."

"Now are you satisfied?"

"You're ready. Off with you."

"Yessum, ma'am." Brianna gave Rose a cheeky grin and touched a finger to her cap in salute.

A quarter hour later, Brianna eased the door open to Aunt Harriet's two-story home. The house was in pitch darkness. She paused a few moments to let her senses become accustomed to the sudden shift from moonlight to nothingness.

On tiptoe she crept through the lower rooms to the stairs. Halfway up, she was brought to a halt at a rustle of sound above. A figure stepped out, extending a lit candlestick. Brianna jumped and grabbed for the railing to regain her footing on the stairs. Her heart raced for her toes, and she screamed.

"Who's there? I tell you I'm not alone," a voice called.

As Brianna recognized the figure, her earlier shriek turned into a gurgle of laughter. She could scarce believe her eyes.

Aunt Harriet stood before her in a ruffled lace nightgown and matching cap. Tufts of red hair stood out around her face. In one hand she held the candlestick and in the other, a fireplace poker. She shook the poker threateningly.

"Aunt Harriet." Brianna bit the inside of her cheek to keep from laughing. "It's me. Brianna."

"Oh, land's sakes, girl. You scared me. Where have

you been? And dressed like that?"

At the word "girl" Brianna flinched. Trevor had called her that earlier tonight when he'd clasped her with his strong hands.

"Off gallivanting around for the Widow Greenhow, I'd reckon. And you too sickly this very afternoon to receive callers," her aunt scolded.

"Shh. Aunt Harriet, you'll wake the house." Brianna took the stairs separating them two at a time. "You know what I do." She clasped the candlestick. "And why," she added.

"Girl, you're gonna be too ill for that party tonight. And your dress so pretty, too."

"Not on your life. I plan to be the belle of the ball. We need to talk. Let's go up to my room." Brianna led her inside the bedroom, eased the poker from her hand, and shut the door.

"Now, Brianna." Aunt Harriet sat stiffly on the bed. "I won't have any more of you running off around the countryside."

Brianna plunked the candlestick and poker down on the table with a thud. She whirled to face her aunt. No one would stop her from keeping her word to Ethan. She'd chosen this road, and she'd see it through to the end. No matter what.

"Girl, from now on you must tell me before you leave each time."

"You know I can't do that."

"When I found your room empty, I was sorely tempted to notify the soldiers."

"No, Aunt Harriet. You must *never* do that."

The old woman held up a hand. "I will only consent to you continuing this madness if you keep me informed."

Brianna met her aunt's sharp eyes. She was family. What harm could it cause? "Very well."

"Now, what were you up to this afternoon pretending to be ill?" Aunt Harriet demanded, a glimmer of excitement on her wrinkled face.

Brianna tensed. "I was avoiding a certain caller. And besides, I couldn't chance being delayed for my . . . meeting."

"Trying to avoid Grant Lewis didn't do any good. He said to tell you he was very disappointed. Said he'll be here promptly tomorrow to escort you to the senator's party." Aunt Harriet sniffed. "Such impertinence."

Laughter teased Brianna's lips. "Good. I had counted on Grant escorting me."

"Well, you also missed that handsome Major Trevor Caldwell," Harriet paused and stared off into space. "Now, that's a man. Why, if I were a few years younger."

Brianna threw her a disbelieving glance.

"Oh, well—quite a few years younger."

"Aunt Harriet."

"Come, girl. Don't tell me you don't find the major . . . inviting?"

Too much so for her own good. "He's positively insulting. And he's no gentleman," Brianna responded sharply.

"Land's sakes. Don't you have eyes? He's worth a passel of Grant Lewises." She leaned forward and lowered her voice. "And believe me, what a woman truly wants isn't a gentleman."

Brianna stared at her aunt open-mouthed. Prim and proper Harriet Devland couldn't have said that.

"Well, good night, dear." Aunt Harriet struggled to her feet. "It's time you got some sleep. Do think on what I said."

The door clicked shut behind her.

Every time Brianna closed her eyes she was back in the filthy hollow log. She could still feel the bugs, dampness and heaven knew what else that had been in the log with her. Her eyes snapped open, and instinctively she brushed at her arms, the memories too strong to ignore.

Streaks of color painted the early morning sky before Brianna drifted into a restless sleep. Yankee soldiers led by Trevor Caldwell filled her dreams.

Hours later, she awoke with a start. The pounding on her door wasn't a dream, but stark reality.

Soldiers? She'd been recognized last night. She'd been found out. The terrified thoughts chased each other across her mind.

Before she could move, the door swung open. Harriet Devland bustled in, Brianna's new gown draped over her arms and the ever-present cane in one hand.

"Land's sakes, look at you. Still abed."

Brianna stretched, a sigh of relief on her lips. The commotion had only been Aunt Harriet, not the soldiers from her dreams.

"Good morning to you, too."

"Humph. More like afternoon."

Brianna sat up. "Any news of last night?" She lowered her voice. "Anyone looking for me?"

"Of course not." She brushed off Brianna's fears. "No news that I've heard of, and you're the only one who's still abed. Not that you didn't need your rest for tonight."

"Everything must be perfect tonight." Brianna slipped out of bed and paced the room.

"I had Mary press your gown." Harriet carefully spread the gown across the patchwork quilt covering the bed. The sunlight shone on the white silk muslin. The golden threads caught and held the light, then sent it back in a shimmer of incandescence.

Brianna gasped in awe. "It's perfect."

"Come on." Harriet tapped her cane on the floor with impatience. "There's much to do before Captain Lewis arrives to take you to the senator's party."

The party. If Trevor attended, would he recognize her from last night once they were face-to-face again? She forced the question out of her mind. She had a job to do, a promise to keep.

"I must get that information the general needs." Brianna worried her bottom lip with her teeth. "The right bait—"

"Land's sakes, girl. We're talking about healthy men—you and this gown is all the bait you'll need." Aunt Harriet stamped her cane on the wood floor. "If that don't attract Major Caldwell, I'll eat my new bonnet."

Brianna giggled at the picture of her usually prim and proper aunt chewing with bonnet ribbons hanging from her mouth.

"There's much to do. Come on." Excitement tinged the old woman's voice.

The time passed in a whirl of activity: an overdue breakfast, followed by a bath with a generous amount of Rose Greenhow's lilac oil to ensure any lingering traces of last night's disguise were completely gone. As Brianna moved about the room in her thin chemise, the lightest scent of delicate flowers accompanied her.

She tried not to fidget while Aunt Harriet and her maid, Mary, pulled and laced her. She hated the corset, but this dress fairly begged for one.

Aunt Harriet oversaw every detail down to the layers of petticoats that enveloped Brianna. At last Mary flung the gown over Brianna's head and helped ease it down over the petticoats.

The gown fit perfectly. The low-cut bodice hugged her like a lover. The wide skirt shimmered with every move she made.

Brianna pulled at the bodice, trying to raise it with no success. She turned to her aunt. "Don't you think it's—"

"It's right as bean water. You won't catch the eye of a man like the major if you look like an insipid miss." Harriet bobbed her head up and down, her red curls bouncing with the vigorous gesture.

Brianna wasn't sure she wanted Trevor's eyes on her tonight. His gaze disrupted her very thoughts and threatened to scatter her senses. Tonight she needed all her faculties to sort the important information from the gossip.

"It's perfect," Aunt Harriet continued. "If nothing

else, the Widow Greenhow does know her gowns." She frowned at the grudging compliment.

Brianna held back a laugh at her aunt's words. She'd accepted that the two women would never be close friends; she only hoped that the animosity between Rose and her aunt didn't intensify with the summer heat.

Attempting to distract her aunt, she whirled around, her skirts swaying and rustling in a wide arc. "I'll be the belle of the ball."

A flutter of anticipation flitted like a butterfly turned loose in her stomach.

Suddenly a picture of Trevor Caldwell leaning over her, his uniform dark in the moonlight, arose like a specter before her. Brianna's stomach plunged, and her breath rushed out in a gasp. She swallowed the lump that formed in her throat.

"Surely there's some news of last night?" She turned to face her aunt and the maid.

Aunt Harriet shook her head, but Mary piped up, "Only that the Rebel Fox spy showed up the Yankees again." She smiled, proud at being the one to carry the news. "Heard he snuck through their trap and got clean away."

The young maid's words reassured Brianna, and she drew in a calming breath. Everything was fine, she told herself. There was no way that the major could have recognized her. None at all. Still a nagging worry stayed with her.

As the maid brushed and pinned Brianna's hair, Aunt Harriet fussed about, adjusting the shimmering gown. She tugged at the closely fitted bodice and fluffed a ruffle, then stepped back to survey her work. She leaned forward to tuck back a stray tendril of Brianna's hair.

"No, no." Harriet waved the maid back out of her way with a sweep of her cane. "I'll do it."

Clucking like a mother hen, she repinned a curl, not content until Brianna's hair lay in long ringlets that cascaded over her shoulder. Her hair glimmered in red-gold splendor, the perfect offset for the golden threads in the gown.

"Finished," Aunt Harriet proclaimed, at last satisfied. "You'll capture the attentions of many a gentleman tonight." She patted Brianna's shoulder. "And of a few true men, I dare say." She sent her a knowing wink.

Captain Grant Lewis arrived as promptly as Aunt Harriet had predicted. When Brianna walked down the stairs to meet him, his awed expression assured her of the gown's success.

"You are a vision." Grant came forward. "An angel."

Brianna smiled. He'd voiced just what Rose had wanted her to be seen as this night. Everyone trusted an angel.

"I hope you're feeling better?"

"Yes, I am. Thank you." Brianna took his arm.

"I was concerned yesterday when you were too ill to receive me."

"Ah, but I'm quite recovered. And I plan to make it up to you." Brianna squeezed his arm. "I'm glad you're back."

"Miss me?"

"We all did." She delicately sidestepped his real question.

She'd scarcely thought of him this last month after his regiment had been posted away from the city.

Ethan and Grant had been constant companions before the war—losing money at cards and chasing the same skirts. Their friendly competition had provided many laughs. The friendship had remained steadfast even when Grant joined Lincoln's army. Brianna's smile wavered at the memories of Ethan. She forced her attention back to Grant.

Brown, wavy hair covered the tips of his ears. A twinkle of laughter shone in his sherry brown eyes. He stood tall and handsome in a reckless sort of way. Brianna found herself comparing him to Major Trevor Caldwell. Grant lost by a full length.

She shook herself mentally. She must learn to curb her thoughts where that man was concerned. It was all the fault of Aunt Harriet and her silly notions of last night.

As if she'd conjured her up, her aunt piped up from the doorway, "Enjoy yourselves."

"Thank you, ma'am." Grant bowed over the elderly woman's hand.

"Such a gentleman." She winked at Brianna over his head.

Brianna choked back her answer.

Grant led her to the hired carriage and assisted her inside. As the coach travelled down the street, Aunt Harriet's words of last night played over in her mind. A picture of Trevor bent over her in the street accompanied them. Would he be there tonight? And would he recognize her from last night? She didn't know if the slight tremor of her hands was from fear or anticipation.

Brianna knew the moment that Trevor walked into the ballroom. She felt his presence even before she saw him. The music faded away, and the conversation around her turned into an annoying buzz. Instinctively, she glanced to the door. And there he stood.

The dancers separating them turned into a sea of rainbow colors, then ceased to exist. All she saw was one blue-uniformed officer. Dark hair curled over his forehead. He smiled at something the man beside him said, and his mustache curved in an alluring tilt. As Trevor spotted her, he surged forward with firm, decisive steps. She watched him approach, her eyes widening as he drew closer. What if he recognized her?

Brianna gripped Grant's arm. "Aren't you going to ask me to dance?" She tore her gaze from Trevor.

Even though she was no longer watching him, she could feel him. It was as if he'd stroked her with a touch of his hand. An age-old sense warned her to flee. Without pausing for an answer, she caught Grant's hand and led him to the crowded dance floor.

Brianna made sure over the next two hours to always know where Trevor was amid the crush of people, and to be sure that she was someplace else. She danced with Grant so many times she lost count. The evening dragged on, and she wished she were anyplace else. A quadrille, a german, too many waltzes to count—with so many different partners. And still she hadn't encountered the new aide. When Grant offered to go for refreshment, she gratefully accepted.

Brianna stood alone for the first time that evening. Trevor's lips turned up in a slow grin of anticipation. The dutiful puppy had left her side at last. He winced at the adulation in Captain Lewis's eyes. It seemed they were in competition for the Rebel Fox and Brianna Devland.

Her efforts to ignore him had intrigued him. She was working so hard at it. Each time their gazes had met, hers had skittered off. However, he'd felt her attention following him repeatedly this night. Even now, she was searching the room. For him, he was sure. It was time to put an end to her game—they both knew the ultimate result. He strode forward.

Besides, the opportunity to usurp Grant Lewis was too strong to resist, especially when it carried with it the feel of Brianna in his arms again. The delicate scent of her had stayed in his mind—too faint to intruded, too strong to dislodge. He was eager to see if she wore the same scent that had haunted his dreams.

The strains of another waltz began as he reached her. "May I have this dance?" Without giving her a chance to respond, he pulled her into his arms.

Brianna stared up at him, and her heart leapt for her throat and lodged there. She should have known he'd take her evasion as a challenge, she told herself. And he was a man who was used to winning. Had she secretly been hoping for this? She shook her head in denial as Trevor whirled her around.

"It's a little late to refuse, isn't it?" Trevor bent closer and whispered in her ear. The scent of lilacs wafted up to him. Ah, it was the same. He drew it in deeply.

His mustache brushed her ear, and Brianna shivered with a sense of delight. "Cold?" he whispered. His breath trailed along her neck.

When he drew her closer, Brianna forgot to protest. Somehow it felt right. Her hand fit his perfectly, held firmly but not too tightly. His other hand rested on her back, and warmth stole through her gown at the touch. As he whirled her around the room, the crowd ceased to exist, and there were only the two of them surrounded by a sea of blended color. She swore she could feel the warmth of his flesh against her hand, in spite of the jacket he wore.

As if of their own accord, her eyes closed. The waltz ended, and a second one started up almost immediately. Trevor never released her. He smelled warm and clean and male. She drew in a deep breath and savored it.

The music drifted to a close, and this time Brianna reluctantly opened her eyes. She wanted this to never end.

"As much as I hate to release you, I must. Your young admirer has a murderous look in his eyes," Trevor chuckled.

When they reached the edge of the dance floor, Grant stood waiting.

"See," Trevor whispered. In a louder voice, he spoke to Grant. "Captain, I will turn the lady back to you. For now." There was a decided smirk to his smile as he left.

Grant met this with a glare of near hatred. He turned to Brianna. "I apologize, dear Brianna. I fear the major and I are both fighting for a promotion. And he does enjoy flinging it in my face. Shall we dance?"

Halfway through her second dance with Grant, Brianna backed into a solid wall of flesh. Trevor. She knew it was him—without turning around.

"Excuse us," Grant apologized in a terse voice, turning Brianna away from the man who'd molded himself to her back.

Trevor tapped Grant's shoulder. "May I?"

"The lady is with me, Major." Grant's voice rose in anger.

Ignoring him, Trevor laid his hand on Brianna's bare shoulder in a feather-light touch. She gasped as heat seared her skin from her nape to the small of her back.

"Did you think I could stay away, Brianna?" Trevor fought to keep the jealousy at bay and won. Each time he'd watched Grant touch Brianna, his temperature had inched upward, until he had to act.

"Sir, you are annoying the lady."

"Brianna?" Trevor asked. "Tell him to leave us. You know it is what you want."

His voice wrapped around her like a bolt of unfolding silk. Unable to refuse, she looked up at him. The burning desire she saw there made her knees weak.

Grant knocked Trevor's hand from her shoulder. "Major, leave the lady alone. You have bothered her enough for tonight."

Around them, conversation ceased. The music crashed to a halt. Everyone turned to the trio in the center of the ballroom.

Trevor placed his hand on Brianna's shoulder again. His very stance offered a challenge. "Let Brianna speak for herself."

"Unhand her." Grant stepped forward. "I demand satisfaction for this outrage. Sir, I challenge you."

Brianna gasped in shock.

Grant caught her hand. "I learned some things from my Southern friends. Like how to take care of his kind."

A duel? It was madness. "No, listen—"

The men brushed her protests aside. Trevor stepped back, releasing her. Brianna knew no amount of reasoning would stop them now. But she could.

"Oh, my." She moaned, drawing both men's attention. She raised her hand to her brow and fluttered her lashes. "I . . ." she trailed off.

Aiming her body toward Trevor, she closed her eyes and went limp. Before she reached the floor, strong arms caught her. Trevor scooped her up, holding her close. So close his chest threatened to crush her breasts.

The pinpricks of heat from his touch almost caused her to open her eyes. It wasn't supposed to feel like this.

Trevor lowered his head, and his mustache tickled her ear as he whispered, "I know you're pretending."

Brianna forced herself to lie still.

"Shall I carry you out to the gardens to revive you or wait until after the duel?"

Chapter Four

Brianna's eyes snapped open. Then just as quickly closed again. If she let anyone know she was awake, the duel would go on. Damnation.

She forced herself to lie still in Trevor's arms as he turned and carried her from the ballroom. What she ached to do was slap the knowing smirk from his face. What she had to do was remain limp. For now.

Trevor watched her eyelashes flutter against her fair cheeks. He bit the corner of his mouth to keep back the full grin that wanted to break forth. Brianna Devland was one hell of a lady. And, secretly, he questioned just how deep her ladylike demeanor went.

Oh, how he'd like to find out. In bed preferably. As he gazed down at the beauty in his arms, his footsteps slowed. Unexpectedly, a surge of protectiveness swept over him. In that instant, he knew he never wanted to release the beauty who fit so perfectly in his arms. Silently, in a wordless vow, he swore to make her his.

As if to taunt him, her eyelashes fluttered again, and he glimpsed a touch of blue as she sneaked a peek.

"My lady awakes."

"Damn you," she whispered.

Trevor's deep chuckle vibrated against her side. "Tsk, such language from a lady."

"You low down son of a—"

His chuckle rumbled again.

"You bas—"

"Surely you can get more creative than that."

Brianna raised her hand, intending to slap his smug face.

"Do that and I'll drop you," he threatened softly.

"You wouldn't dare—"

As he started to release her, Brianna grabbed his shoulders with both hands.

"That's more like it, my sweet. I do have to protect myself . . . somehow."

Brianna opened her mouth, but whatever words she'd been about to speak froze on her lips as Trevor lowered his face to within a breath of hers. His warm breath mingled with hers, and she could smell the punch blended with whiskey that he'd drunk earlier. It was sweet and tangy and intoxicating. Gooseflesh spread up her arms, but for an entirely different reason than ever before. He was going to kiss her, wasn't he? And she was going to stop him, wasn't she?

Before her mind could form an answer, he straightened. Glancing around, he seemed to find what he wanted.

He strode toward a bench tucked under a tree at the edge of the garden. Rose bushes enclosed one side, and he angled his course for it with no-nonsense steps, never faltering.

His chest rose and fell rhythmically beneath Brianna's ear. She could feel the steady beat of his heart echo through her. In his arms, she felt as a feather. But a well-protected feather.

Trevor sank down onto the bench with Brianna still in his arms. Gently he eased her beside him. The sweet smell of roses in bloom filled the air. She stared up at him—silent for once. What now? her mind asked.

Moonlight darkened his hair to a velvet sheen. Brianna ached to touch it. It looked as soft as an animal's pelt. She detected a bit of the wild animal in him just then. He was too tempting by a long way.

She knew he was going to kiss her for sure this time even before he lowered his head. Then the moonlight was blotted out. In the ensuing darkness she felt powerless to resist. Even more, she wasn't sure she wanted to resist. All reason fled with the hiss of his let-out breath.

His lips brushed hers ever so softly, licking the peak of her upper lip; then descended a second time to steal her breath away. She could have fought the man, but not the sensations rippling through her. Never had a man dared kiss her like that. Never had a kiss invoked the feelings she was experiencing now. One thought slipped into her mind. Aunt Harriet was right about gentlemen.

She should stop him, shouldn't she? And she would. Yes, she really would. In another minute.

As if of their own accord, her arms wrapped around him. Her fingers curled into the thick hair covering his neck. It was as soft as she'd imagined it would be. A sigh escaped her lips to be caught by Trevor's mouth.

Trevor held her close with one arm, stroking his free hand along the length of her back. Down and up, then down again. Feather-light touches interspersed with more fervent caresses before his hand slid around to her ribs and upward to the underside of her breasts. Wherever he rested his hand, it seemed to burn through to her skin. It seemed he knew where to touch, where to pause, where to stroke.

As Brianna emitted another sigh, he drew her more fully into his arms and partway across his lap. Her breasts tingled where his chest pressed against them. She felt the cool metal of one uniform button against her heated skin exposed above her daring décolletage.

She ran one hand down his neck, over his shoulder, and onto his chest. Her fingertips encountered the cool metal of another button. She traced the outline of the eagle, and reality returned with a vengeance. That symbol belonged to a *Yankee* uniform. She snatched her fingers away as if they'd been burned.

No, her mind shouted in denial. What was she doing kissing a Yankee? Hadn't the Yankees killed her beloved Ethan?

Brianna shivered from the sudden chill she felt in Trevor's arms. She pushed against his chest with her one hand. When he didn't move, she brought down her other hand and pushed harder. She wrenched her mouth away from his.

Trevor pulled her back against him, ignoring her hands spread against his chest. He took her lips once more.

Brianna struggled in his arms, desperate to break away. Why did he have to be so large? Her hands seemed lost against his broad chest, and quite useless. She pushed harder, leaning away as far as she could. It was rather like trying to move a mountain with a plow.

Reckless now, she bit down on his lip.

"Yeow." His yelp rent the night air. "What was that for?"

"Let me go," Brianna spat between clenched teeth.

"I didn't feel you resisting a minute ago."

"A gentleman would never remind a lady of an indiscretion."

"Hell, I'm no gentleman. And you're no lady."

Trevor released her and wiped his hand across his mouth. A spot of blood glistened on his finger.

Brianna stared at it transfixed. She hadn't meant to draw blood. Only to gain her release.

She reached out and gently touched his lip. "I'm sorry."

Trevor raised his arms, then dropped them to his sides.

"You'd better return inside. I'll call on you tomorrow, Brianna."

"No."

"We'll talk tomorrow," he insisted.

"Trevor—"

"Dammit, Brianna. Go inside. Right now I'm not in the best of moods to talk."

What he wanted was to have her back in his arms. It didn't matter that she could be a spitting wildcat when it suited her. He still wanted to draw her close, wrap his arms around her, and kiss her for a very long time. He wanted her.

Brianna stared at him, reading the desire in his eyes.

"No. Never again." Her words were soft, barely discernable.

"Tomorrow." His assured voice was loud in the surrounding quiet.

"Never." She had to get away from him if she was to keep her promise to Ethan.

Brianna surged to her feet. Without sparing Trevor another glance, she raced away.

His soft laughter followed her across the garden.

Brianna burst through the side door, paused a moment to assure her hair was in place, then fixed a smile on her face for anyone who might dare glance her way. Would anyone be able to tell what she'd been doing? She felt her cheeks redden with heat at the thought.

She glanced down at her dress. Surprisingly it was still in order. Gathering what calm she could, she wrapped it around her like a full cloak. She searched the room for Grant. It was past time to call it an evening.

Grant spotted her before she reached him. He immediately left the two men he was talking with. Anger radiated from him with every step.

Oh, no. She'd forgotten all about him while she was in the garden. She braced herself for his wrath, and prepared an innocent smile for him.

"Where have you been?" Grant didn't give her a chance to answer before he continued. "How could you let that oaf carry you out of here, and in front of everyone?"

"I didn't exactly have a say. I fainted, remember?" Brianna faced him, giving back as good as she got.

"What did he do to you?"

Her eyes widened at the question. Could Grant tell? Was it that obvious?

"He didn't do anything. I merely fainted." She tried to get Grant's mind off the garden.

"How are you feeling now?" he asked grudgingly.

She swallowed down the response that sprang to her lips. *No, she was not fine.* She wanted to get out of here as soon as possible. She offered a wan smile and raised a hand to her forehead.

"It seems my headache has returned. Would you please see me home?"

Stiffly, Grant offered her his arm, and she latched on to it like a drowning man would a rope. She smiled up at him. "Thank you, Grant."

As soon as they were outside, he left to find a coach.

Brianna waited impatiently for the hired coach. Would it never come? She glanced back at the lit ballroom. Was Trevor inside? Was he even now watching her? Or approaching?

The coach arrived, and she breathed a sigh of relief. She'd made her escape. She smiled her thanks to Grant as he helped her into the coach, but he ignored her.

The hired conveyance seemed stuffy inside after the rose-scented garden. No matter what she thought on, Brianna couldn't erase the garden incident from her mind. She fanned herself and allowed Grant's cool anger and stilted conversation to wash over her. He never stayed angry for long. She responded "yes" and "oh" at the appropriate times, not really paying any more attention than was absolutely necessary.

Brianna drew in a relaxed breath when the coach drew to a halt in front of Aunt Harriet's house. She'd been half-expecting to be waylaid by Trevor.

The next morning was filled with shopping. Aunt Harriet had insisted she have a new bonnet and had not been content until she and Brianna had visited every shop. At last her aunt had found the perfect one.

Brianna listened to her extol the virtues of the new hat all the way home. The instant they crossed the threshold, Aunt Harriet toddled up the stairs, eager to try on her find and see for herself in her own mirror.

Scarcely had Brianna had time to remove her own hat when a knock at the door sounded. She spun around and flung open the door. A Yankee soldier stood on the porch.

"Miss Brianna Devland?" he asked in a voice steady with authority.

Brianna's heart leapt for her throat, then reversed direction to plummet to her stomach. She'd been found out. Eyes round with fear, she stared at the man.

"Yes." She forced the word out between dry lips.

"Beggin' your pardon, ma'am." The soldier yanked

off his hat and held it with both hands. "I didn't mean to startle you."

What had he expected her reaction to be? She looked past him to the street. Only a lone horse was in sight. Where were the men he'd brought with him? Or had the Union felt it only needed one soldier to bring in a woman spy? Brianna stiffened and raised her chin in pride. Let him try, just let him try. Ethan had taught her well how to defend herself.

"Ah, ma'am." The soldier cleared his throat. "The name's Private Gordon." He shifted from one foot to the other, gripping his hat tightly between his hands. He ran his fingers around the brim of his cap.

Goodness gracious, was he nervous? Brianna tilted her head and studied him. Young was her first impression. Too young and jittery for the job she'd supposed he'd been sent on. She was sure of it now.

"How may I help you, Private Gordon?" She flashed him her best disarming smile, just in case.

"Ah, no, ma'am. That is, I've been sent by Major Caldwell—"

A gasp escaped Brianna's lips at the name.

"He asked me to deliver this to you." He shifted his cap into one hand, fished in his shirt pocket, and held out a folded piece of paper.

Brianna swallowed down her own trepidation and accepted the note. Opening it, she scanned the message. As relief rushed over her in waves, a smile tipped the corners of her mouth. An invitation—it was an invitation to a dinner party. For tomorrow evening. She almost laughed aloud. Only a silly invitation. That's all it had been.

She offered the soldier a sincere smile. "Thank you, Private. Would you please relay my regrets to the major?"

"But, ma'am—"

"I'm sorry, but it is impossible for me to attend the party with him. Please tell the major that." She refolded the note into a square.

She had to avoid Trevor no matter what. Too much danger lay in his search—not to think of what his touch did to her senses. Brianna shivered in memory. She'd behaved wantonly in his arms. Whatever had she been thinking of? And with a Yankee?

"Oh, also please tell Major Caldwell that I request he recall my parting words last night."

A look of puzzlement came over the young soldier's face. "Ma'am?"

"The major will know what I'm speaking about."

"Yes, ma'am. Good day."

The soldier tugged his hat on, turned on his heels and almost ran to his horse.

Brianna watched him ride off before she closed the door. Holding her hand to her throat, she leaned against the door. Fear still coiled in the pit of her stomach. The fear rose upward, and she swallowed it down with determination. She wouldn't quit. She would keep her promise to Ethan. There was nothing more to think over.

Crossing to the parlor, she tossed the note onto the table. She hoped her return message would discourage Trevor. *Don't count on it,* a little voice muttered.

"Dear? Brianna?" Aunt Harriet called out.

"Down here, Aunt."

Brianna rushed across to the stairs. As her aunt descended the steps, Brianna caught her arm and helped her down.

"That's a good girl. Thank you." Aunt Harriet patted Brianna's hand where it lay on her arm. "Why don't we go sit in the parlor by the window. I do love to watch the people pass by." She winked.

"Of course." Brianna smiled at her aunt.

She'd be willing to bet that new bonnet that Harriet Devland had more on her mind than looking out the window. Trying to show patience, she drew up the petit point footstool for her aunt, then seated herself in the chair opposite her.

"Did I hear someone at the door?"

"Yes, it—"

Aunt Harriet spied the note on the table and snatched it up. Holding it away from Brianna at arm's length, she read the neatly penned words.

"Oh, my. I missed the handsome major." Dismay etched her words.

"No, Aunt Harriet, he sent the note with a young soldier." Brianna reached for the paper.

Aunt Harriet shifted it to her other hand, reading the words again. A broad smile spread across her wrinkled face, and her eyes twinkled with satisfaction.

"You're going, aren't you?"

"No." Brianna grabbed the note and refolded it.

"What? Why ever not?"

"I've already sent my refusal," Brianna answered firmly.

"Whatever for?"

"Aunt Harriet, he's a Yankee."

"So's Captain Lewis, but I don't see that stopping you."

"Grant was Ethan's best friend."

"Humph. All those boys ever did together was get into trouble."

"Aunt Harriet."

"It's true." She crossed her arms over her chest as a deep sigh shook her. "I am sorry that the major didn't stop by."

Brianna opened her mouth, but was cut off by her aunt.

"Now, don't you go giving me that tale of yours about him being a Yankee." She wagged her finger at Brianna. "The heart don't notice what color the clothes are. Especially when the person isn't wearing any." She smiled a satisfied smile.

At Brianna's startled look she added, "I wasn't always this old you know." Aunt Harriet stamped her cane on the floor. "You could do a lot worse than set your cap for the major."

Set her cap indeed. She was trying her darndest to outrun him. In the opposite direction.

"Aunt Harriet"—Brianna's voice lowered—"it was the Yankees who killed Ethan. I can't up and forget that."

"Humph. It was the war that did it. That and his spying. Mark my words, dear, nothing good will come of this here spying." Aunt Harriet slipped out her handkerchief and dabbed at her eyes.

Brianna choked back her own tears.

"Girl? I want you to quit. Right now." The words

were more a plea than an order.

"I can't." Brianna faced her aunt. "You know I can't. Not until I find the person who betrayed Ethan. That person might as well have pulled the trigger himself. And I swear I'll find him."

"But what of the danger to you?"

Brianna forced a cocky smile. "Aunt Harriet, you know the North doesn't hang spies. They merely put them across the line." She flung out her arm. "And I know how to cross that line again." For her aunt's sake, Brianna sent her a confident wink.

"But—"

"Don't worry, Aunt Harriet. I'll be fine."

"Girl, you never know when Northern sentiments might change. Be careful."

At a knock on the door, both women started. Aunt Harriet put her hands to her breast.

"I'll go." Brianna jumped to her feet.

"You'll do no such thing." Aunt Harriet raised her chin. "Let one of the servants answer it. Where are your manners? A lady doesn't answer the door."

Brianna hid her smile behind her hand and coughed. There was no way anything would keep Harriet Devland cowering for long. Determination and a faint light of battle shined in her eyes, bringing a flush of color to her wrinkled face. Looking at her, Brianna lowered her hand. She hoped she would be the same when she was her aunt's age. Had her aunt been younger, Brianna had no doubt it would be Harriet who would be carrying the messages back and forth across the lines.

"Ma'am?"

Brianna started at the question. She'd been so lost in thought that she'd missed the servant's announcement of the caller. She turned to their visitor.

"Wilkens. What on earth are you doing here?" Brianna glanced around. "Has something happened to Rose?"

"No, ma'am," he assured her. "The cook baked one of her special chocolate cakes, and knowing how Miss Harriet has a fondness for them, she had me bring some right over."

Wilkens held out the chocolate cake.

"Please tell Mrs. Greenhow thank you for me." Harriet reached for her cane. "I'll have it taken to the kitchen."

As she started to pound the floor, Wilkens caught the cane, stilling it.

"It's best if you eat the cake now, ma'am." He turned to Brianna. "There be some things in there that won't keep."

Brianna took the plate from his hands and set it on the small table. Moving so that she stood between the window and the table, she unwrapped the cake. It appeared to be only a thick slice of rich dessert. She licked a cluster of crumbs from her thumb.

She eased her finger into the center of the cake. It crumbled apart to reveal a darker color inside. Her eyes widened. Carefully she dislodged the thin packet wrapped in dark paper. Brushing aside the crumbs, she drew out a folded paper.

"General Beauregard needs that map by noon tomorrow."

That would mean she'd have to leave well before

dark. "She rarely sends me out during the day."

"I know, Miss Brianna. But this is important."

"If I'm to go in daylight, I'll need a pass."

"It's under the bottom layer of cake."

Brianna grinned. "Very good."

"Thank you, Miss Brianna. I thought of this one myself."

She smiled at the butler's obvious pride. Surely Rose was right about Wilkens's loyalties. She hoped so.

"Now, you be careful, Miss Brianna." He patted her hand clumsily. "You just take as much time as you need getting back."

His concern touched her. "Thank you, Wilkens."

"I'd best be getting back. She said to tell you not to worry none; she's personally saw to it that General Beauregard knows about the trouble we been having. He's checking, too." Wilkens patted her hand again. "You be careful."

"I will."

Brianna scarcely noticed when he left. Would Rose or the general uncover the traitor who was responsible for Ethan's death? She bit her lip.

"Aunt Harriet, I'm going up to my room for a while."

She still had a couple of hours before it would be time to leave for Fairfax Court House.

"You go on and get some rest. It's sure you won't be getting very much tonight."

Brianna was lost in thought as she climbed the steps. At Ethan's door she paused. He'd warned her of another spy. If only he hadn't found out too late.

What was it he'd said?

"Beware spy." His warning drifted back to her.

Brianna reached out and ran her fingertips over the doorknob. She still couldn't believe it had really happened. Tears filled her eyes, and she brushed them away with the back of her hand. She'd tried so hard to forget that day.

Letter. Ethan's last words had also been of a letter. Perhaps it held the answer. Oh, how could she have forgotten about it?

He'd said the letter was in the third, and that was all. The third what?

Brianna turned the knob under her hand. Slowly, she eased the door open. The room looked as he'd left it. It looked as if it were waiting for Ethan to walk back in. They'd kept it that way to allay suspicion.

It was harder to step into the room than she'd imagined it would be. Memories almost overwhelmed her: the evening he'd teased her and she'd tossed his discarded shirt at him. It had hit him right in the back. The laughter in his eyes when he'd chased her and caught her, then tickled her unmercifully.

Tears threatened again, but she brushed them away. This room held so many loving memories, it was not the place for tears. There was the framed miniature of Ethan and her together. Papa had commissioned it for their sixteenth birthday.

Brianna crossed to the table and picked up the miniature. It was of the two of them, holding hands and smiling. Gently she brushed a finger over the image of her twin.

Ethan. Dear, dear Ethan. How could you have died

and left me behind to do this alone? She wanted to shout the question, but knew there was no one to answer her. Ethan was gone. And she must honor her promise to him.

"I swear to you I'll find the one who did this to us," Brianna whispered to the miniature. "As sure as I breathe."

She placed the miniature back on the table. Drawing in a deep breath, she took a long, measured look around the room.

"Where? Where did you hide it, Ethan?"

Only silence answered her.

"Third what?"

Brianna crossed to the dresser and drew open the third drawer. Carefully, she checked each item. Nothing.

Next, she searched the armoire. Counting to three, she pulled out every third piece of clothing. She checked pocket after pocket, but to no avail.

Reckless now, she tossed aside garment after garment, examining each. Nothing but two handkerchiefs and a Yankee greenback. Damnation.

She kicked a discarded pair of shoes aside. Crossing back to the dresser, she went through every drawer. They yielded nothing—not a single scrap of paper.

Brianna pushed the last drawer closed. The wood blurred before her eyes. She blinked, but it remained obscure as if a veil were drawn over it. Outlying objects shone crystal clear in her side vision. *It was happening again.*

In the past, these sensations had always warned her

of a coming connection with Ethan. She'd felt them when they were separated and he was hurt or in trouble. *It couldn't be happening now,* sanity argued. *But it was.* She knew it with absolute certainty, and she waited for what was to come.

Suddenly the room swayed around her. She experienced a sense of movement, of rocking, and noise. Voices surrounded her. Shouts, cries and the crash of waves.

If she didn't know better, she'd swear Ethan was in trouble. All her life she'd experienced her twin's pains and fears. No one could explain it, and through the years, she'd come to accept it.

Unexpectedly her stomach roiled, and nausea overwhelmed her. Brianna staggered to the bed and grabbed the post. She clung to it while the room spun around her.

Chapter Five

Gradually the room stopped spinning.

Brianna leaned against the bedpost. The odd feeling vanished as quickly as it had come on, leaving her shaken and confused. What had happened to her?

Dazed, Brianna stood, and when the room didn't lurch, she walked to the door. Giving the ransacked room a last glance, she slipped out into the hall, closing the door behind her.

Had she imagined it? What had happened to her in Ethan's room? Maybe Aunt Harriet had been right—she needed rest. She'd barely slept last night. It seemed all night that Trevor had never left her thoughts in peace for a moment. The faint rays of dawn had finally lulled her to sleep. That was it—she was tired. A good nap and everything would be all right.

"Brianna? Girl?"

The words sounded far off, and Brianna tried to shut them out. Rolling over, she pulled the pillow over her head.

The voice persisted. Suddenly the pillow was yanked from her hands.

"Brianna. Look. I had a wonderful idea."

Aunt Harriet's voice penetrated through the haze of sleep, and Brianna sat up, rubbing her eyes. As her aunt drew open the drapes to let the bright sunlight in, Brianna blinked.

"Aunt Harriet."

"We need the light for you to look at this. What do you think of it?" She held out a little yellow square.

Brianna stared at it. The square was about the size of a large coin and made of silk. She hadn't the slightest idea what it could be.

"Well?" Her aunt stood smiling proudly, waiting for an answer.

"What is it?"

"Oh, good. Even you didn't recognize it."

"Aunt Harriet—"

"It's the map," she whispered.

"What?"

"I folded it up and sewed it inside the silk square. With a tucking comb and your hair up on your head, no one will ever find it."

Brianna smiled in amazement. "That's a wonderful idea."

She couldn't believe her aunt had thought of it. Now that Aunt Harriet knew of her missions, her aunt couldn't wait to help.

"Well, let's get going, girl. I want to try your hair up with this map." She bustled over to the dressing table. "All the arrangements are readied, and a farmer's wagon is waiting down the street for you."

Brianna tossed off the cover. She drew in a deep, calming breath. Everything was in readiness—except for her.

Across the back of a chair lay a familiar gray gown. She crossed to it, fingering the skirt. The material was coarse and rough to the touch. The gown had been hidden away in a trunk since the last time she'd worn the disguise, almost a month ago.

This time she was to go as a farmer's or merchant's daughter, probably with an almost empty wagon load of near-rotten produce. She wrinkled her nose at the thought.

"What are you wrinkling that nose at?" Aunt Harriet wagged the semicircular tucking comb at her.

"The last time I used this disguise the vegetables I had were as old as you."

"None of your cheek. We must hurry if we're to get you gone on your mission." She dropped her voice to a conspiratorial whisper.

"Aunt Harriet, I think you're enjoying this," Brianna accused.

Her aunt covered her smile with a hand, but her twinkling eyes gave her away.

"You are enjoying it."

"Shh. Let's get you ready."

Fifteen minutes later, Brianna stared at the girl in

the mirror. The gray, coarse gown fit her differently than her usual ones. She felt a sense of freedom without the usual hoops or petticoats she was accustomed to wearing.

She turned this way and that, checking from different angles. Her hair was pulled up into a knot. She shook her head, testing the comb, but not a curl came loose. It appeared secure enough.

"My, my. Didn't we do a fine job?" Aunt Harriet beamed.

Brianna tilted her head. No trace of the silken square with the secret map could be seen. Hopefully she wouldn't be searched.

"Yes, Aunt Harriet. We did."

Unexpectedly, her aunt caught Brianna's hand. "You will be careful, won't you?"

Brianna swallowed down her own trepidation. For the hundredth time she reminded herself of her promise to Ethan.

"I'll be careful. If anyone calls—"

"I'll chat away with them in the parlor, and tell them how bad you are feeling."

Brianna clasped her aunt's hands. "That's fine for this afternoon, but tell anyone who asks that I have gone to a party tonight. With all the dinners and parties in town, no one will figure out which one I'm at."

"Good, good, and in the morning?"

"I'm out riding. Yes, that sounds fine, doesn't it?" Brianna bit her lip. "Well, I had best be off. It will be a long trip."

Aunt Harriet pulled her close for a hug. Sniffling, she pushed her toward the door. "See you tomorrow."

As Brianna slipped out the back door and down the street to where the wagon waited, the word tomorrow kept running over and over in her head. She hated these long trips. There was so much more chance of a mistake. A deadly one.

She climbed up into the wagon, thankful not to have the added bulk of her petticoats or hoops to handle. Gathering up the reins, she urged the old horse on his way. She tried to appear calm as she drove the wagon out of the city, but a vague sense of unease nagged at her. She brushed her fingers across the rifle lying on the seat beside her. She hoped she wouldn't need to use it.

She knew how to shoot, thanks to Papa and Ethan. Once again, the pain of losing her twin struck her. Brianna had to blink back the tears that threatened to obscure her vision.

She tried instead to think of the happy times back home in Tennessee. At Papa's insistence Ethan had taught her how to shoot, but she'd refused to shoot at anything living. Granted, she'd been plenty accurate with the bottles, but she'd never aimed her rifle at a helpless rabbit or a human before.

If it came down to it, could she pull the trigger when she had a man in her sights? She honestly didn't know. She hoped she'd never need to find out.

In spite of her nervousness, the trip to the outskirts of town was uneventful. She encountered nothing more dangerous than a few admiring glances from some soldiers—although her heart almost stopped when the uniformed men pulled in their mounts and shouted a greeting.

It took everything Brianna had to wave to the Yankee soldiers instead of sending the horse and wagon charging across the bridge at breakneck speed. Her smile was frozen on her face, and she barely breathed while the wagon wheels clattered on the Chain Bridge.

She released a sigh of relief when she was across. Maybe her fears had been unfounded. She raised her face to the sun and soaked in the warmth.

It seemed she'd no sooner taken a breath when the wagon hit a rock with an earth-shattering jolt. Brianna grabbed the side to stay seated and was nearly thrown out when the wagon quivered violently. As the axle struck the ground, the horse reared, and Brianna soared into the air.

She hit the ground with a thud, the breath knocked out of her. The next instant an object came toward her, and she barely had time to duck before her rifle sailed over her head. She let loose a scream. She only hoped the horse and wagon weren't next.

Brianna kept her eyes tightly closed for the space of a few seconds. Nothing else came flying her way. Tentatively she opened her eyes.

A few feet away, the horse and wagon lumbered to a halt. The wagon sat at a crazy angle, one axle imbedded in the dirt. She glanced around. Several yards in the other direction lay the wagon wheel.

Damnation. Now what? She'd known something was going to go wrong this trip.

She flexed her arms and legs. Nothing broken. Thank goodness. She stood to her feet and brushed the dust off her skirt and hands. Surveying the tilted wagon, she felt a rush of despair. Now how was she going to get to Virginia and Captain Vincent's safe home, much less to Fairfax Court House?

The wagon was a complete loss now. There was no way that she could put the wheel back on by herself. She eyed the horse with disgust. He was obviously made to pull a wagon. His bony back would make for a horrible ride. Added to that—no saddle and no bridle. She could fashion a makeshift halter out of the harness, but it would take time. And there was no guarantee that this horse would even let a rider on his back. Damnation.

Brianna hung her head and felt the tears building. Oh, no, she wouldn't cry over something like this. The only thing to do was get started on making that halter. She took a step forward, remembered her rifle, and turned around and scooped it up.

She spun back around, and her breath stopped in her throat. She stared into the barrel of a pistol. Her eyes flickered, and now there was also a rifle pointed dead center at her chest.

Refusing to give in to the terror, she forced her gaze upward to the three riders. They were clothed in Yankee uniforms. She fought down the rising panic that threatened to consume her and send her running for her life. If she allowed that, they'd surely shoot her down.

Her voice felt paralyzed, locked in combat with her fear. She licked her lips, but no words would come out of her parched throat.

Was her hair still held in place? She resisted the overwhelming impulse to check the tucking comb and curls. Was the secret map peeping out to condemn her?

Somehow she feared these men might not take into consideration that the North wasn't killing Confederate spies—yet. The Yankee soldier who'd killed Ethan hadn't stopped to arrest him, an inner voice reminded her. Staring back into the gun barrel, she realized she might be facing the same fate.

Say something, her mind prodded. Although she opened her mouth, nothing came out.

"What's the matter, miss? Can't you talk?" one soldier asked, then laughed.

His rough voice and laughter sent shivers down Brianna's spine.

"I think we just caught ourselves a damn Rebel." The soldier with the rifle spoke up.

Brianna's eyes widened. She looked from soldier to soldier, searching for a way of escape without letting the men catch on. They stood between her and the horse and wagon. Even if the soldiers weren't in the way, the horse wouldn't do her any good still harnessed to the broken wagon. For the first time since she'd faced the center soldier's pistol, she felt the wooden stock of her rifle between her hands. She gripped it tighter and swallowed.

"You planning on using that on us?" The soldier cocked his pistol, never wavering in his aim.

Brianna shut her mind against the growing terror. She tossed her head, only one loose curl brushed her neck. At least the map was safe. It couldn't condemn her.

She forced a crooked smile. "Actually, I was deciding on whether to shoot that nag or the wagon." She'd tried to pitch her voice differently, imitating the Northern women. If she spoke carefully, she could keep the trace of Tennessee out of her voice.

Her comment was met with silence and distrust.

"Well, which do you think?" she asked, trying to sound confused. "That wagon would be easier to hit, I'm sure. But Pa always said I couldn't hit the side of a barn on a good, windless day."

Taking a chance, she raised one hand to her hip and let the rifle hang limply. Maybe, just maybe, if she gave them a reason to believe she didn't know how to hold a rifle. . . .

"My pa's likely gonna beat me either way. If I don't make it to that farm and get a load of fresh greens and potatoes back to his store this afternoon . . ." She let the sentence trail off.

Tears threatened again, only this time Brianna welcomed them. Sniffling, she let the tears spill onto her cheeks. She pulled her lower lip between her teeth.

"Pa promised me a new bonnet if I'd do this one job. Now I just know he's gonna beat me real bad. And I'm not ever gonna get that pretty bonnet with the pink ribbons."

Brianna tilted her head and looked up at the soldiers. She hoped the tears showed. For added effect, she gave a little hiccup.

"Pa's gonna be real mad." She paused, trying to determine what regiment the men might be with. From the voices, she thought she remembered a hint of the broad Massachusetts accent in at least one of them. "Most all his vegetables go to one of the Massachusetts regiments," she stated proudly.

"Well, ma'am, that just might be our regiment."

"Really?"

She let the rifle drop to the ground and gave the men a bright smile. Against three armed men, a smile would probably do her more good than her rifle. She didn't have a hope of getting all three before one of them shot her. "I hear they're the bravest men in our whole Union Army. Is that true?"

"Yes, ma'am."

"It sure is."

"Absolutely."

The three men all spoke at once to assure her of the fact.

"Oh, my." Brianna raised her hands to her chest. "And here I stand with three soldiers from that fine regiment. Oh, my." She cautiously examined the men. They now appeared relaxed and less distrustful of her. It appeared she'd been successful in convincing them she was a Unionist.

"I apologize for scaring you, ma'am. I'm Sergeant Malvern." He holstered his pistol and nodded to the man on his right, who immediately slid his rifle into its scabbard. "This here's Privates Seaver and Price."

Both men doffed their caps to her.

"We heard a scream, and when we came to check it out, we found you pointing that rifle of yours at us."

"I was not," Brianna declared in a huff. "The thing tumbled out the wagon after me. I could have been hurt by it. I was only picking it up to put it back in Pa's wagon."

"Ma'am, maybe next time you should watch how you pick up a rifle and where you point it."

"I don't even want to touch it ever again." She wrinkled her nose at where the gun lay in the dust.

"I'll put it back in the wagon for you, ma'am," one of the privates offered.

"Oh, thank you." She sent him a shy smile, then frowned deeply. "How am I ever gonna get those fresh vegetables at the farm now?"

Suddenly, Brianna opened her mouth and looked at the sergeant as if she'd just now had an idea. "Do you think three strong men like you could fix my pa's wagon?" She paused, then rushed on, "Oh, my, I am sorry. That's just asking too much from you nice soldiers. After all, you are fighting those dreadful Rebels and all."

She held her breath, hoping her plan worked. She didn't have long to wait. The men looked at each other, then dismounted.

"We'd be happy to help you, ma'am," the sergeant offered. "We'll just take a look-see at your wagon."

After a few minutes of discussion, the men returned to where Brianna waited. She hid her crossed fingers in the skirt of her dress.

"We'll have you ready in no time, ma'am."

"Oh, thank you all so much. Maybe Pa'll buy me that new bonnet after all. When is your next dance? I'll be sure and save a dance for each of you."

"It's next Saturday night. If you think you could maybe steady the horse, ma'am, we could fix that wheel in no time."

"Oh, sure." Brianna started toward the horse.

The sergeant smiled at her eagerness and went back to the wagon.

Brianna talked to the horse in low tones, all the time keeping her attention on the soldiers. Between the three of them, the soldiers had the wheel back on the wagon in less than half an hour.

She thanked the men prettily, trying not to let her nervousness or impatience show. It was going to be very late when she reached her night's lodging. When at last she waved goodbye to the soldiers, she whispered a prayer of thanks. This one had been much too close for comfort. She didn't know how much longer she could continue as a spy. Her words of promise to Ethan rang through her mind, and she renewed her determination. She had to keep on.

Brianna took up the reins, wrapping her hands tightly to hide their shaking, and urged the horse on. The trip would have to be made at a slower pace now with the hastily repaired wagon wheel. She had a long way to go yet.

It was well past dark, and Brianna was completely worn out by the time she reached the Virginia home of Captain Vincent. He was absent on duty with the Confederate Navy, but his family gave her a warm welcome. After a meal, she tumbled into bed, exhausted and drained from the tense ride.

The next morning Brianna's feeling of unease returned full force. She tidied her hair, making sure not a strand was out of place. Clad in a smart riding habit from the Vincents, she set off for Fairfax Court House. One of the Vincent girls accompanied her as her "cousin."

The sun shone, making the dew on the grass sparkle like freshly dropped jewels. The air was fresh and clear, with none of the odor Brianna had come to associate with Washington and the ever-increasing troops. She tried to enjoy the calm scenery and her "cousin Jane's" nonstop chatter. Surely nothing else could go wrong.

They crossed the river at Dumfries and sped toward the Fairfax Court House. Almost at their destination, a Confederate picket stopped them and ordered they turn around. He insisted that the general had given orders that no more women were to pass the lines, as he suspected female Yankee spies were slipping through.

Brianna didn't know whether to laugh, or to scream in frustration. After all she'd gone through to get here, she wasn't about to turn back around until she'd finished her mission. Several minutes of arguing followed. She gave away no information, but kept insisting that she had to see General

Bonham at once. Finally, she persuaded the soldier to allow her through. She didn't know if the soldier had believed her or had simply gotten tired of their shouting match. She didn't really care which.

Brianna hugged her pretend cousin goodbye and faced the soldier. With exasperation, he passed her through to the provost marshal, who escorted her to General Bonham's office.

The general crossed to her immediately. "Can it be? Is it really you, Miss Devland?"

Brianna gave him a sincere smile. Her father and Senator Bonham—General now she corrected herself—had been close friends in Washington.

"Yes, it's me. Oh, it is so good to see you again." Brianna gave him a hug, which the general returned gruffly.

"Shame on you. Telling my men you had a message. Here, let me look at you." He held her hands. "Prettier than even I remembered. What's the news of your father?"

"Papa's home in Tennessee now. And I do have a message for you." She stepped back. When she spoke again, the earlier softness was gone from her voice. "Will you promise to forward it to General Beauregard immediately?"

At his disbelieving look, she rushed on, "If you don't promise, I swear I'll ride on myself."

The general's smile faded. "You have my word. I'll have it forwarded at once."

Assured of his pledge, Brianna reached up and removed the tucking comb. As her hair tumbled down her back, she freed the silk square from its pins. She held it out to the general.

"Please deliver it to General Beauregard only."

In awe, her old friend took the small package. "I'll never forget that sight."

"Just be sure you don't speak of it to anyone else." She chuckled, removing a ribbon from her pocket and tying her hair back.

She turned to leave, but he stopped her.

"Wait. I have a paper for the messenger. That must be you."

"It is today." Brianna tried to make her voice light.

Where on earth would she safely hide a message? She couldn't very well put her hair back up in that special way without help, and she couldn't picture the former South Carolina congressman acting as ladies' maid. Besides, the fewer people who knew about her secret hiding place the better.

General Bonham returned with a folded piece of paper. "It's a list of information that General Beauregard needs desperately. And as rapidly as possible."

"I'll see it's delivered," Brianna promised.

She sat down in the chair and slipped off one of her riding boots.

"Miss Devland?"

"Do you have a knife?"

He blinked, but handed her a knife right away.

Brianna pried up the inner sole of her boot, slid the paper underneath, and pressed the lining back down. It would have to do. She pulled the boot back on. Standing, she walked around the room.

Satisfied that no crackle of paper could be heard, she turned and hugged her old friend goodbye.

Her horse was waiting, still saddled outside. A soldier helped her mount, and Brianna was escorted back across the lines. Now all she had to do was make the ride back to Washington. It was still several hours before noon, and she hoped to reach the town that afternoon. She would have to ride hard. She flicked the reins, and the horse burst into a gallop.

Brianna was tired, sticky, and irritable when Washington came into sight. Eager to reach home, she took the most direct route through the streets, although she kept her mount to a sedate pace. The last thing she needed was to attract undue attention.

The pounding echo of hoofbeats alerted her, and she glanced up. At the opposite end of the street a rider was approaching. She drew her horse to the side to give plenty of room to the other rider. He was obviously in a hurry.

As the rider drew nearer, Brianna blinked, then groaned. It couldn't be. She only had time to wonder how many more things could go wrong before Major Trevor Caldwell was upon her.

She forced her lips into a smile of greeting.

"Where have you been?" He practically shouted the question at her as he grabbed her reins.

"I don't need to account to you," Brianna snapped, before she could stop herself. The last thing she needed was to make him suspicious.

The trip must have made her not only tired, but careless with her tongue. She had to say something to soften her remark. For the life of her, she couldn't think of a thing.

"I'm sorry, Brianna." Trevor nudged his horse closer, until his leg brushed against Brianna's. "I called at your aunt's, and she said you'd gone riding. But that was hours ago."

The heat from Trevor's leg seemed to transfer to hers. Brianna wanted to move away, but didn't seem to be able to muster the strength. Why was it when she was around this man her strength deserted her? Her leg warmed, and she could feel the muscles in Trevor's leg move against hers. Damnation, it felt good.

"I . . ." She paused and licked her lips. Funny, the sun didn't seem so hot a few minutes ago.

"I didn't mean to yell at you." Trevor dropped his hand onto her arm. "I was worried," he admitted.

Her arm began to warm to his touch as well as her leg. Brianna gulped and pulled on the reins, trying to put even a small amount of distance between her and Trevor. He must have a fever to be giving off that much heat, she thought. She glanced at his face, but it didn't appear feverish. He looked perfectly healthy. His eyes weren't bright with fever; instead they practically devoured her.

She licked her lips which had suddenly become parched. She watched as his eyes followed her tongue. "I . . ."

"Yes, Brianna." His voice was a low, throaty murmur.

She leaned toward him and almost fell off her horse. Grabbing the saddle, she steadied herself.

Trevor's chuckle stroked her, warming her blood as his touch had warmed her skin. What was he doing to her? What power did he have over her? None, she ordered her mind.

"Maybe we'd better get you home and out of the sun." His voice still held a deep resonance.

"Yes," Brianna answered, finding her voice. "I was riding home when you stopped me."

"I'll see you home." Trevor turned his horse and came alongside hers. The soft clop-clop of hooves accompanied them, filling the silence.

Brianna breathed a sigh of relief. If nothing else, her near tumble from her mount had sidetracked Trevor.

"Brianna?"

She turned and smiled at him.

"Where have you been?"

Her voice froze at his question.

Chapter Six

Brianna frantically searched her mind for an answer to Trevor's question. One he would accept.

She didn't think she could utter a word right now—any more than when those three soldiers had come upon her unexpectedly. However, she wasn't facing the barrel of a gun this time, she reassured herself. But she well could be if Trevor suspected the truth.

What had Aunt Harriet told him? She could only hope their stories would match.

Brianna tossed her windblown hair back over her shoulder and faced him.

"Riding. For way too long. And I fear I'm going to pay the price tomorrow." She rubbed one hand over her backside, which really did ache from too many hours in the saddle.

A smile turned up the corners of her lips as she watched Trevor's attention shift to follow the rubbing motion of her hand. Distracting him had been easier than she'd dared hope.

"And where did you find to ride to for so long?"

His voice was as firm with steely determination as when he'd asked the first question. So much for distracting him.

Brianna feared nothing distracted Trevor Caldwell when he wanted something. And right now he wanted answers.

"A cool, shady clearing. Where I sneaked a delightful nap."

She blinked her eyes and smiled up at him. She hoped her tiredness could be mistaken for sleepiness.

The clearing really existed, only she hadn't visited it today. She remembered the shady clearing well. It was a secret place she and Ethan used to go and hide.

"It was completely deserted."

"Care to take me there?" Trevor asked softly.

Brianna raised her eyebrows at his question. He had to be joking. "After what happened that night in the garden, you dare to ask?"

"Brianna." The word was a mere whisper, bringing with it a host of memories.

"Only with a whole passel of chaperons, Major Caldwell. If you think different, you must be three bricks shy of a load."

Trevor's laughter rang out strong and clear. "Are you scared, Brianna?"

"I would be if I had a lick of sense."

He laughed again. "Tell me about your secret clearing."

Brianna smiled. This was much safer than his earlier question. She'd indulge him.

"My brother and I discovered it a couple of years

ago. We used to—"

"Have you heard from him lately?" Trevor pulled his horse to a halt and faced her.

"Why, Major, you know all mail service has been stopped between Washington and the South."

"Would that stop you, Brianna?"

"I haven't heard from Ethan." A hint of bitterness tinged her answer. "Satisfied?"

"Never." Trevor made the word sound like a vow.

Her earlier assurance deserted her. Brianna licked her lips nervously.

Trevor watched the movement with an intensity that almost frightened her. "I don't think I'll ever have my fill of you." The words were so softly spoken that she had to strain to hear them.

He leaned across his horse, caught the back of her head in his hand, and drew her closer. The next instant his lips crushed hers.

Brianna felt as if the horse beneath her had just bucked. Trevor's kiss was every bit as unsettling as being thrown from a horse.

"I . . . I thought you were seeing me home."

A slow smile began at the center of Trevor's lips and spread out to a wide grin. "Whatever you say, my sweet."

He dropped a quick kiss on her parted lips and drew away.

Once again, Brianna slipped in the saddle. *Damnation,* she thought, *the man kisses me and I nearly fall off my horse.* She, who'd been riding practically before she could walk, unable to stay seated on an unmoving horse.

"Careful." Trevor steadied her a moment.

Careful is right, she thought. This man posed more danger to her than the entire Union Army put together.

A frown creased Trevor's face, and he stared at her a moment. His mustache was drawn into a straight line above his lip.

Brianna stared back. What now? In agitation she wiggled her toes in her boots before she caught herself. The last thing she needed was for the general's message to crackle within her boot. She stilled her toes.

"What's the matter?" she asked.

"Your clothes."

She tensed in spite of herself. What was wrong with her clothes? What had his trained eyes picked up that she had missed this morning when she'd dressed in the borrowed riding habit?

She hoped the few quick stitches Mrs. Vincent had taken in the jacket this morning didn't show. Had she somehow pulled them loose in the long ride? Trevor was staring at her so intently Brianna felt as if he could see every extra thread. And what lay beneath.

"I'd picture you in a deep blue velvet to match your eyes." Trevor's gaze ran the length of her. "Somehow this green doesn't seem like you."

"Oh," Brianna sighed in relief. As he continued to stare, her stomach churned. "I have a blue one at home," she volunteered.

Now she sounded like an insipid miss trying too hard to please. She'd never in her life been accused of that before by anyone. And she wasn't about to give her conscience the right to accuse her of that now.

"Speaking of home, I did promise to escort you there, didn't I?"

"Yes, I do believe I heard that." She raised her eyes at him in accusation. "Earlier."

"Don't blame me," Trevor challenged. "You started it."

"Me?"

"By rubbing that oh-so-tempting backside of yours."

Brianna opened her mouth to retort, thought better of it, and shut her mouth again.

Trevor's rich laughter rang out, stroking her like a hand petting a favorite cat.

Brianna flicked the reins and sent her horse trotting ahead. In a matter of seconds Trevor caught up with her. They rode in silence, the soft clopping of horse hooves echoing with a dull thud on the hard-packed dirt street.

As they reached Aunt Harriet's house, they drew their mounts to a halt. Trevor reached across and held on to Brianna's reins, tugging her horse alongside his, until the two horses were almost touching. His leg brushed hers again, and she pulled her knee up away from the intimate contact.

"Brianna."

She refused to meet the question she knew would be in his eyes. Instead she concentrated on the space between her horse's ears.

"What?" she asked.

"Come with me to the dinner party tonight." It was an order, not a question.

When she turned to refuse his command, she saw the entreaty in his eyes, and she almost answered yes. She snapped her mouth closed before the word could slip out.

It would be insanity to go with him. It would be inviting trouble. It would be a piece of heaven. He was a Yankee officer, sanity warned, the officer in charge of capturing the Rebel Fox.

"I can't," she answered. She couldn't trust him or herself.

"Can't?" Trevor's voice hardened. "Or won't?"

Brianna met the anger in his gaze. "Both," she said in honesty.

Trevor's budding anger melted. "I'm not giving up, Brianna. You will be mine." He nodded and turned his horse away.

"Where are you going?" she asked without thinking.

"I think I'll go hunting."

Her heart leapt for her mouth. She just bet he would. For the Rebel Fox. Was that what he'd been doing earlier with her? Hunting?

Her horse stepped back, and Brianna realized that she'd been gripping the reins tightly. She loosened her hold and wiggled her cramped fingers.

"Happy hunting," she called out with false cheer.

"It will be. I always get what I go after."

A shiver ran along her back. She knew one fox who was going to be safely out of his reach tonight.

Brianna turned in the saddle and watched Trevor

until she could barely make out the shape of man and horse in the distance. Sighing, she dismounted and tied her horse's reins to the post in front of the house. She would send one of her aunt's servants out to take care of the tired animal. The poor thing must be even more tired than she felt, and right now she could barely stand. But the day wasn't over yet.

The Vincents' horse would be rewarded with a well-deserved rest in a shady barn. Tonight he would disappear like magic and be safely back in his own Virginia barn by tomorrow night, along with the borrowed green riding habit. She envied the horse. She still had a full day's work ahead of her.

Brianna trudged up the steps to the house. She needed to let Aunt Harriet know that she had returned safely and none the worse for wear. However, before she reached the door, it was thrown open.

"Well? How did everything go?" Harriet Devland peered out the open door. She looked up and down the street. "He's gone, isn't he?" Her voice was colored with disappointment.

Brianna didn't need to ask who. She was sure Aunt Harriet had watched every move she and Trevor had made, from the vantage point of her parlor window. She wished little Billy Warnton would throw a rock through that window. Yet even that probably wouldn't stop Aunt Harriet.

"Yes, he's gone," Brianna admitted.

"I wanted another look at him. When are you going to remember your manners and bring a nice-looking man like the major inside?"

"Aunt Harriet."

"Well. He called earlier, and I did like you said. Told him you went off riding. I tried to get him to stay a while, but he wouldn't."

"You asked him to stay?" Brianna was horrified at the thought of running into Trevor unexpectedly in her aunt's parlor, and her on her way back from a mission, too.

"Of course. No woman in her right mind would let a man like that go without asking him in for a spell. But look at you."

"What about me?" Brianna was having trouble keeping up with her aunt's active mind.

"You are a sight. I don't know when I've seen so much dust outside of a duststorm. Girl, you won't catch a man looking like that. Let's get you cleaned up."

Brianna gave in without an argument. Right now nothing sounded better to her than a hot bath.

"That sounds too good to be true. But afterward I must ride over to Rose's house. We'll have to save most of our talk for later."

"Oh, yes, later. Seeing the major made me forget."

"Forget what?"

"That Lewis boy stopped by."

"Grant?" When had her aunt started thinking of him as a boy? The answer to that was easy: when she'd set her eyes on Trevor Caldwell.

"Yes. Said he'd be back later." Her aunt brushed him off as she would a pesky fly. "Now, your bath first. A lady never goes calling in a dusty riding habit."

"Yes, Aunt Harriet."

* * *

An hour later, suitably attired in a lavender muslin gown and feeling refreshed, Brianna descended the stairs. Her right shoe was a bit uncomfortable, and she stomped her foot on the last step. The general's message had fit much better in the riding boot than in her thin slipper.

"Brianna, dear," Aunt Harriet called in warning. "Look who's here. Captain Lewis." Her voice lacked the warmth reserved for Major Caldwell.

Brianna immediately stopped adjusting her slipper, and crossed into the parlor. At her entrance, Grant stood.

"Brianna. I am so glad I caught you at home." He clasped her hands in his.

"Grant." She returned his smile.

She was happy to see that his anger at her from the other night was now forgotten. Some things never changed, even with a war. Grant's anger was as hot and short-lived as ever.

"Aunt Harriet said you called while I was out riding."

"Yes. I wanted to talk with you." He continued to hold her hands in his.

Aunt Harriet coughed and snapped her cane on the floor. Grant started and dropped Brianna's hands. He turned to her aunt with a charming smile.

"Miss Devland, could you forgive me if I asked for a few minutes alone with your beautiful niece?"

"Very well." She allowed him to help her to her feet and accepted his kiss on her hand.

However, Aunt Harriet left the room muttering something about gentlemen.

As soon as her aunt was well past the door, Grant caught Brianna's hands and drew her to the chair.

"Please sit down, Brianna. I want to talk to you."

A puzzled frown creased her forehead. This wasn't like Grant at all.

"Brianna?" Grant sat on the edge of the chair facing her. "You know that since Ethan left I feel responsible for you."

"There's no need—"

"You and your aunt are all alone. I want you to know if you need anything, I'll be here for you."

"Thank you, Grant."

"Brianna, General McDowell is giving a dinner party tonight. Will you come with me?"

Brianna bit back her groan. She'd so wanted to stay home tonight. She wiggled her toes, and the paper pricked the bottom of her foot. There would likely be many important people at the party. More important—people with information that General Beauregard needed.

"I'd love to go, Grant," she answered.

"Then, I'll have the prettiest girl there," he said with satisfaction.

And the one with the best ears, she thought with a smile. She intended to gather plenty of useful information this night.

"Thank you, Brianna. I really must get back to headquarters. I'll see you tonight." He kissed her hand and strode to the door.

Funny, she hadn't felt any more emotion from the

feel of his lips on her skin than she imagined Aunt Harriet had when Grant had kissed her hand. If it had been Trevor's warm lips on her hand. . . .

Brianna stopped the thought before it could complete itself. She would not think about him.

The moment Brianna was sure that Grant was well out of sight of the house, she called for a carriage. If she didn't get to Rose Greenhow's soon, the widow was likely to send out a searching party for her. The way that fortune had been shining on her lately, Major Trevor Caldwell would likely be leading that searching party.

It seemed that thoughts of that same Major Caldwell rode along with Brianna in the carriage. The deep, throaty caress of his voice, the feel of his leg against hers today—the disturbing memories stayed with her no matter which way she turned on the seat.

The sight of Rose Greenhow's brownstone brought a sigh of relief from Brianna. Now maybe she could chase thoughts of Trevor from her mind, at least for the duration of her visit with Rose.

At her knock, the door was opened by Wilkens. He smiled broadly at her.

"Welcome back, Miss Brianna," he greeted her. "I see you had a safe trip."

"Yes, thank you. Is Rose in?"

He chuckled at her question, then sobered. "She's been waiting by the window for nearly an hour or more. And I reckon she's about worn a path in that braided rug of hers that she's so proud of. You'd best go right on in to her."

"I reckon so." She laughed.

"Miss Brianna?"

She turned back to Wilkens.

"She also has a surprise for you."

"What?" Brianna asked with a combination of excitement and trepidation.

Wilkens firmed his lips into a line and shook his head. "You won't get an answer out of me. It's her surprise. You won't catch me spoiling it." With this, he strode off in the direction of the kitchen.

Now what, Brianna thought. Wilkens could be so mysterious when he wanted to be. He seemed to know everything that went on in this house. She couldn't help but wonder if he was the traitor. No, she brushed the possibility off. He was always genuinely concerned about her. He watched out for her. Yet the niggling thought remained with her: maybe he watched too closely.

"Wilkens," Rose called out. "Wilkens? Send Brianna in."

"Here I am." Brianna walked into the parlor. "Wilkens said you had a surprise for me."

"Where have you been? Do you have any idea how late you are getting back?"

"I appreciate your concern—"

"I didn't say I was concerned."

Brianna wrinkled her nose and gave Rose a hug. "But you were."

"Impertinent."

Brianna laughed, crossed to a chair, and kicked off her right slipper. She wiggled her cramped toes.

"What do you think you're doing?"

"Giving you the general's message. It's been sticking me in the foot since I first put this slipper on." Brianna scooped up the shoe and pulled the offending paper from it.

Rose read over the questions, and her eyes widened. "Oh, my stars. It will take nearly a week to gather all this. If we're lucky."

"I suppose that includes me?" A pretty, dark-haired girl with sparkling dark eyes entered the room.

"Selina." Brianna launched herself at the young woman. "When did you get back?"

"This morning." Selina James pulled back and grinned. "Mother finally tired of Boston and her relatives, so here we are. Back home in Washington. Although I do say it took longer than I had hoped. We've been gone almost two months," she wailed. "Did you miss me?"

"Terribly." Brianna's voice cracked on the one word. She had missed her best friend. There'd been no one to share the pain of losing Ethan, no one to talk with for hours.

As if sensing her friend's thoughts, Selina added softly, "I'm sorry about Ethan going back to Tennessee. You must miss him so."

Brianna flinched. She'd forgotten that not even her best friend knew the truth. And couldn't know. "Thank you," she murmured. Once Brianna had hoped that Ethan and Selina would eventually marry; they'd seemed attracted to each other. Several times she'd caught Ethan stealing a kiss from her friend.

"Well, are you pleased with my surprise?" Rose distracted Brianna's thoughts.

"Yes." Brianna smiled.

Rose sauntered over to the two younger women and linked an arm with each of them. "Come sit over here. I have one more little surprise."

She refused to say more until they were all three seated close together on the sofa. "Selina will be helping you at the parties from now on."

Brianna stared at Rose blankly for a moment. She had always known that Selina supported the Cause, but a spy?

"She's been helping me while she was in Boston." Rose spoke softly for only their ears. "I thought that since you two were such good friends it would appear natural if you attended the same parties. Together you can provide invaluable information."

Brianna's and Selina's eyes met, and they both grinned. It would be good to have a confidante in this, Brianna mused, one she trusted completely.

"I want both of you to attend General McDowell's party tonight," Rose decreed. "I'll arrange for escorts—"

"I've already accepted an invitation from Grant Lewis," Brianna confessed. "I planned on getting some answers for the general tonight."

"Good."

"But Trevor—Major Caldwell will be there."

"That's even better." Rose clapped her hands. "Then, we can put our plan into action tonight."

"What plan?" Brianna asked warily.

"I want you to start encouraging the major every chance you have."

"I don't think that's such a good idea—"

"My stars, Brianna. The man definitely is interested. Take advantage of it. We need to know how close he is. And what his plans are."

"I know what his plans are," Brianna muttered. Remembering their earlier meeting, she felt her cheeks reddening.

Selina had sat by in silence, listening to the conversation. At her friend's giveaway face, she grinned. "I agree with Brianna. I've seen the major." She sent her a sideways glance. "Why don't you turn him over to me, Rose?"

Brianna's head snapped up. She opened her mouth to protest. She didn't want any other women trying their charms on Trevor, not even Selina. "I . . ." She closed her mouth on the argument.

She couldn't trust him, and she trusted herself even less. Trevor posed too much of a threat—to her missions and to her heart.

"I think Selina has a good idea." Brianna's voice was tight.

"In a pig's eye." Rose crossed her arms. "Oh, no, Brianna. Major Caldwell is your assignment. I need Selina for something else. And besides, the major is already clearly interested in you."

Secretly, Brianna hoped that when Trevor saw her with Grant Lewis tonight, it would discourage him.

"Brianna?" Rose tapped her arm, waiting for an answer.

With a sudden rush of memory, Trevor's vow of

that afternoon came back to her. *I'm not giving up, Brianna. You will be mine.* Her hands shook with a betraying tremble, and she worried the soft inner skin of her bottom lip. Rose had no idea of what she was asking her to do.

Brianna turned to Rose and saw the question in her eyes. She'd given her word to Ethan; she had no other choice.

"Very well, Rose. After tonight I will accept Major Caldwell's invitations."

A distinct sense of impending doom followed her words.

Chapter Seven

The air was still heavy with humidity in spite of the gathering evening. Brianna waved her fan back and forth with a sense of lethargy.

She was too warm beneath the layers of petticoats and silk, tired to the bone, and fast running out of patience. Grant had left her within minutes of their arrival at the brightly lit house of General McDowell. An urgent call, he'd said.

She glanced around the room. Dinner would be served shortly. She was ravenous and hated the thought of eating only a ladylike amount of the sure-to-be-delicious food. The aromas of terrapin, Virginia ham, candied yams, and walnut-maple pie had been tantalizing her since she'd walked in the door.

A servant entered the room and announced that dinner was ready. General McDowell led the parade into the dining room. Brianna stood to one side, tapping her foot with impatience. The lace-trimmed flounce of her gown brushed back and forth across her matching slipper. Where was Grant?

"May I?"

Brianna's head snapped up, and she looked into

Trevor's smiling face. Crinkles of laughter edged his eyes.

"No, thank you. Grant should return shortly."

"Captain Lewis? I doubt it. You see, I placed the call that pulled him away from you. By the time he realizes it was a ruse and returns from headquarters, the evening will be over."

Brianna opened her mouth and closed it. Grant would be furious this time.

Trevor took advantage of her silence to extend his arm. He looked at her hands pointedly. Her knuckles were practically white with the pressure she was exerting on her fan. She released her grip and smoothed the edges of the fan.

Looking around for a way out, she spotted Selina beside a prominent senator. Brianna flashed her a help-me look, but Selina merely smiled and sent her a wink.

Brianna thought of Rose's instructions and wanted to stick out her tongue at the both of them. Instead she smiled prettily at Trevor and placed her hand on his arm. The muscles flexed beneath her fingertips, and she was sure he heard the resulting catch in her breath.

"Shall we, my sweet?" he taunted.

"Of course." Brianna sighed. So much for her private plan of discouraging Major Caldwell. She let him lead her into the room.

On the other hand, perhaps she could use his interest and dogged persistence to her own benefit. She glanced at his profile. Being aware of his hunt for the Rebel Fox provided her with a measure of safety. *A very small one,* an inner voice whispered in warning. She shrugged it off.

Perhaps she could even aid him in his search—in the opposite direction. Since she knew exactly what he was after, and he didn't, she would stay a step ahead. It could prove an entertaining game.

As if he sensed her thoughts, Trevor looked down at her. Brianna flashed him a disarming smile. Yes, if approached right, this could be fun. Trevor provided challenging company, never bored her, and couldn't be trusted one inch of a Tennessee mile. Her smile broadened.

Trevor pulled out her chair, and after Brianna was seated, he claimed the chair to her right. She spoke to the senator on her left and glanced down the length of the table until she found Selina seated between a lieutenant and a government clerk. She sent her a wink.

The low rank of her friend's escort had them seated toward the end of the table, far away from Brianna and Trevor. Trevor's long-time friendship with the general earned him a closer seat. Brianna fumed inwardly at the ranking of the Yankee society.

However, it did award Selina and her with the chance to eavesdrop on two different conversations at the same time. Together they just might be able to acquire the answers to several of General Beauregard's questions. Brianna peeked at her friend again. Selina had her head cocked to one side, listening intently to the pompous Lieutenant Roberts. On her opposite side, the young government clerk was trying to gain her attention. Brianna covered her smile with her napkin. Selina drew men like the magnolia blossoms drew bees.

"What do you find so amusing?" Trevor whispered.

Brianna jumped guiltily and faced him. He was practically on top of her. She tried to edge her chair away.

"If you do that, you could start a terrible argument between the senator and his wife."

"What?" Her movements stopped.

"I don't imagine his wife would like finding you in her husband's lap. No matter how delectable you look tonight."

Brianna scooted her chair back toward Trevor's.

She could swear she heard him murmur, "Much better."

"Doesn't everything look delicious?" She changed to the safe topic of food.

"Absolutely." His husky whisper stirred the hair at her neck.

Brianna looked up at him. He was staring intently at her.

"Absolutely delicious," he repeated.

She could have sworn her heart stopped beating for an instant.

"So, Major," the senator leaned forward and looked past Brianna, "how is the search for those Confederate spies going?"

Brianna's heart tripped. Its beating sped up, and

she was sure one of the two men beside her would hear it. She struggled to breathe naturally.

This is why I'm here, she reminded herself. She forced herself to glance up at Trevor and appear only slightly interested. *Please, don't let me give myself away.*

"About as well as can be expected," Trevor answered noncommittally.

"Hope you get them soon."

Trevor only murmured his agreement.

Brianna looked back at her plate. He was not a careless man who would let anything slip unwittingly. Her job was going to be harder than she'd first thought. She should have let Selina take him. A pain cut through her, and Brianna admitted she couldn't give him up.

"Had you heard Winston is moving his men out?" The senator paused and took a drink. "Colonel Leland will likely do the same. Hate to see them go. They're good units—no trouble. Rather we got the Zouaves out of the capital."

Those who'd been listening laughed in agreement. The rowdy antics of the Zouave troops had ceased to be amusing after their first week.

The senator shook his head. "Never thought it would come to this. The city's overrun with soldiers. Everybody said this war wouldn't last three months."

That's what both Papa and Ethan had thought, Brianna remembered. *They'd been so wrong.*

"No, Senator," Trevor corrected. "Only the fools did."

"Well, it's got to end soon. The South isn't equipped for a long war."

"You're right, but they'll keep fighting." Admiration tinged Trevor's voice. "I fear we're in for a long war. And the damned spies will make it last longer."

He was wrong. Brianna almost had to bite her tongue to keep from speaking out. What she was doing, what Ethan had been doing, would help the war end quicker. And set the South free to determine its own fate.

The talk of the South and their assured loss of the war brought back so many memories of Ethan and his belief in the Cause. It all seemed so worthless. Not one of the senator's comments had been worth Ethan's life, and yet he'd died for his beliefs. She blinked back the sudden sting of tears.

The delicious food lost its appeal for her, and she pushed the morsels back and forth across her plate. Colors and textures blended together in a heap.

She shifted when she felt an arm brush hers. It happened again—the lightest brush against her elbow. She swore the room could hear the rasp of material against her skin. But only she could feel the strong tendons flexed beneath the jacket.

Brianna didn't need the sideways glance to know it was Trevor. She knew instinctively that she'd recognize his touch in total darkness or bright sunlight. Her breath quickened. She toyed with a piece of pie.

"If you're through massacring the cook's efforts"—Trevor's whisper tickled her ear—"I think it's time to join the other guests."

Brianna looked around her to see people leaving the room. Damnation. How could Trevor's touch have distracted her so? She jumped to her feet and started for the door. Trevor's soft chuckle followed her.

The remainder of the evening passed in a whirl of pieces of overheard information and tidbits of gossip. By the time people began drifting to the door and calling for their carriages, Brianna knew the number of gun placements in Washington, Colonel Winston's proposed route, and Colonel Leland's departure date. Tiredness tugged at her like a persistent puppy.

When the general wished her a pleasant evening, she swallowed down her yawn, smiled, and thanked him. Once outside, she welcomed the chill night air. She needed something to revive her.

As she stood by Trevor, she felt another yawn building. She raised her fan to hide it.

"Come on, sleepyhead." Trevor caught her hand in his. "I'll see you safely home to your bed."

Brianna felt the warmth from his hand clear to her elbow. She smiled weakly. Had she sensed an undertone to his statement? Her breath caught in her throat at the thought. With clarity she remembered the feel of his leg against hers today, and his arm against hers tonight. How would it feel without the clothing separating them? As a rush of heat suffused her, she waved her fan back and forth with renewed vigor. The cool evening air did nothing to stem the heat in her cheeks.

Almost as if he'd known her thoughts, Trevor clasped her free hand in his. He laced his fingers between hers, stilling their nervous movements. Brianna turned and stared up at him. Something special passed between them; she knew it as sure as she breathed.

Tonight. The word was whispered on the breeze that caressed her heated cheeks.

Had she heard the word or only imagined it? The clatter of wheels signalled the approach of their carriage.

Before she could voice the question nagging at her, Trevor caught her up and swung her into the carriage. In one quick move, he joined her.

Brianna was unprepared for the first jolt of the carriage as their driver flicked the whip. She rocked back in the seat. Struggling to right herself, she succeeded barely before the next jerk shuddered the coach. Trevor pulled her into the protective cushioning of his arms.

He turned toward her, and she knew he was going to kiss her. *It's what you want,* her mind whispered in the near dark of the carriage. Was it?

The second Trevor's lips touched hers, she had her answer. Yes.

He enveloped her in his arms, with a hold that was half-tough, half-tender. The rough material of his jacket scratched her shoulders, but she didn't care. It made the velvet of his lips seem even smoother against her own. They were cool from the evening air, but held the promise of warmth to come.

She gave herself up to that promise, her own lips melting under his. He touched, tasted, savored. She gave.

Much too soon it ended. Trevor pulled away, straightened his jacket and gazed down at her.

"Ah, my sweet. I've been wanting to do that since you walked in tonight." He touched his lips to her chin and murmured against her skin, "Don't expect an apology, my little Rebel."

She stared up at him and said the only thing she could say—the truth. "I didn't ask for one."

The low growl deep in his throat was her only warning before he drew her back into his embrace. The jolting of the carriage wheels, the hard seat, the brisk air all ceased to exist for her. The only thing of importance was the feel of his strong arms around her, the beat of his heart under her palm. The sweetness of brandy, his crisp scent, the tangy taste of him all blended together.

She raised her head to meet his next kiss. This time he was neither gentle nor searching. His lips plundered hers, demanding all she could give. North and South no longer remained—only the sensations that swept through her body in waves. Enveloping fire. Breathlessness. Desire.

He teased her lips apart, licking and kissing. Dipping the tip of his tongue into her mouth, he touched her tongue and withdrew only to start the teasing over again.

When she'd first felt his tongue against hers, she'd been startled. But he'd been elusive, his tongue dipping in, then retreating, then returning to touch lightly again. The game excited and enticed her at the same time. She strained against him, silently cursing the full skirts and small carriage.

It was as if she was searching for something, but she didn't know what. Right now, she didn't particularly care.

"Easy, my sweet," Trevor whispered into her open mouth.

His breath teased her, making her want more. Her hands clenched his shoulders, searching, seeking. She spread her hands open, feeling the rough material against her palms. His heartbeat quickened beneath her hand. She kneaded his chest like a satisfied cat.

He stroked her temple, the side of her face, down the smoothness of her neck. Her pulse throbbed beneath his fingertips. He continued the path to the top of her gown and tucked his fingertips inside.

Brianna gasped against his mouth. He swallowed the sound. She arched against him, the warmth of his toughened fingertips exciting her.

Heat soared through her, taking her breath away. Startled, she opened her eyes. Around her the carriage was shaded in darkness, but in front of her it was as if gazing through a blurred glass.

It's happening again. No, not now, she wanted to cry out. The images blurred to indistinctness. She moaned her distress. The sudden buzzing in her head increased to cover the noise of the carriage wheels. It drowned out all other sound.

In an instant, pain shot through her shoulder, replacing all other feelings. Her shoulder burned and throbbed in time to the motions of the coach. The same pain as when Ethan was shot, she thought.

Pain and a powerful burning . . . it seemed to want to consume her. She cried out.

Trevor released her at once. "Brianna? What is it, my sweet?"

As she leaned her head against the seat, pain shot through her shoulder anew, and she moaned. She closed her eyes to the blurred images surrounding her. How could this be happening? How could she be feeling the shot again? Was Ethan's spirit in some netherworld between heaven and hell, unable to find peace while she was in the arms of a Yankee?

Trevor caught her close to him. "Brianna? Brianna?" He clasped her hand in his. "Damn, you're burning with fever."

Brianna raised her other hand to her brow and wiped away a sheen of sweat. She stared at her hand in amazement. The evening was fast turning cool. She couldn't be sweating. A lady didn't sweat according to Aunt Harriet. Lady or not, Brianna felt a rivulet of moisture run down her temple.

"I . . ." She trailed off as a fresh pain seared her shoulder again.

"Driver," Trevor shouted. "To the nearest hospital. Hurry."

Brianna licked suddenly parched lips. Water, she was so thirsty. She opened her mouth to ask for a drink, but couldn't speak.

"Driver! Unless you want me taking the reins, hurry."

Brianna heard the shouts around her as if from a long distance away. The pain in her shoulder drew all her conscious thought. She raised her hand and laid it on the spot. The same spot where Ethan's wound had been. She felt only the silk of her dress beneath her fingers.

Brianna blinked and stared at her hand. As the pain vanished, the heat began receding from her body. She drew in a deep breath of the cool evening air.

"Brianna?" Trevor captured her hand in his again.

She turned to him, seeing his face now etched with worry. She let out a shuddering breath. The pain had left as strangely as it had come on.

"I'll have you at the hospital soon, my sweet." Trevor kissed her hands gently, as if he was afraid she'd break.

"No. I'm fine now." At his look of disbelief, she added, "Honestly."

"Brianna, you're feverish and obviously in pain. Your arm?"

"Arm? No, it was my shoulder," she corrected without thought. "The same spot where—" She snapped her mouth closed on the rest of the words.

She had been about to say, where Ethan had been shot. She opened her mouth again and drew in a shaky breath. No one else could know her twin was dead.

"Brianna? The fever—"

"I . . . I just got too warm." She blushed at the memory of what had been interrupted. "That's all. It's nothing. Trevor, please turn the coach." When he only stared at her, she added, "I won't go to the hospital. Either turn the coach or I swear I'll jump out—hoops and all."

"That would almost be worth seeing."

"Trevor. I'm serious."

He laid a hand on her forehead. When he found it cool to the touch, he gave in. "Driver, take us to Miss Devland's home."

The coach slowed to a stop. "Sir?"

"The lady has quite recovered. Take us to the first address I gave you."

"Yes, sir."

The coach sprang forward again and turned onto the next street. Brianna breathed an inaudible sigh. For now her secret was safe.

Trevor paced back and forth across the wood floor outside General Scott's office. The general's loud voice rumbled through the walls. His shouts had been heard throughout the building almost all day long. Old fuss and feathers, as he was not so lovingly called, was in an uproar today. And Trevor was next in line to suffer his outrage.

Trevor's search for the famed Rebel Fox was going poorly. His list of three suspected spies was now useless. Durant had been cleared. Fitzgerald was confirmed as a Southern sympathizer, but he wasn't the spy. That left only Ethan Devland. Rumor had it he'd been seen on the docks more than three weeks ago—then he'd vanished as if into the air around them. There had been no word on him since, nor any record of his departure.

Time was running out. Trevor sighed and rubbed the stiff muscles in his neck. Rumor also had it that General Scott was on his way out, faster than first thought, to be replaced by a younger man.

A loud shout punctuated the air. Trevor spun around.

The door swung open, and a cowed young officer hurried out. Not even acknowledging Trevor's presence, the man rushed past him, obviously intent on escape.

Trevor ran a hand through his hair again and straightened his jacket. He wouldn't even admit to himself his trepidation at entering the roaring lion's den.

"Major!" General Scott's voice rang out loud and clear, belying his advanced years. "What are you waiting on? I don't have all day."

Trevor hurried inside. "Sir."

"You haven't caught that damned spy yet, have you?"

"No—"

"And you know why not?" General Scott slammed his hands down on his desk, scattering papers. "He's not here, that's why."

"Sir"—Trevor spoke up without hesitation—"the Rebel Fox is in the capital."

The general brushed this off with a wave of his meaty fist. "He's been confirmed in Fairfax as late as yesterday. And with him, some damned important troop information."

Trevor only blinked at the news. He refused to let his commander see how much it upset him. "He's been in the city, sir."

"Hell, he's gone now. That's for sure."

"Don't be so sure of that. He seems to move through the lines with uncommon ease."

"Well, Major, you're running out of time." He leaned back in the chair, and it groaned its protest. "We both are. It's going to pour down on us like a hay-rotter. The president is anxious to turn the matter of catching these Confederate spies over to Pinkerton, or Colonel Allen as he's known now."

He sat forward in the chair with a thump. "That information reaching Beauregard makes it look bad for you, boy. And I'm sure you've heard the rumors that I'm leaving soon. McClellan will be taking over. If you don't catch that spy before then . . ." He left the sentence unfinished.

Trevor knew the rest. If he ever hoped to have his own command, he had to give the general what he wanted. And Scott wanted the Rebel Fox as his last hurrah.

"Well, don't stand there, boy. Get on it."

"Yes, sir." Trevor saluted and left the general's office.

All in all he'd gotten off lightly. He wasn't leaving in the same rush as the man before him had left.

Trevor refused to leave the room with the desperate look of a hounded man. He'd catch that spy yet. Too much depended on it.

Trevor strode into his office and dropped into his chair. Swivelling around, he stared at the wall. Right now his leads were about as barren as that wall. Brianna Devland was the only one he had left, and she remained steadfast in her story that she hadn't heard from her brother. Now what?

He swung the chair back around and looked over the pile of papers spread across his desk. On the corner lay the latest copies of the Washington newspapers. As he reached for the top one, a folded piece of paper caught his eye. It hadn't been here when he'd left to report to the general.

The paper crinkled under his fingers as he unfolded it. He spread it out and read the words. He instantly recognized the code his informant used in their communications. Smiling, Trevor reread the message.

The one you seek was at the general's dinner. A message will be delivered across the lines by the Rebel Fox tonight. Be at the Chain Bridge before midnight.

Damn, he'd missed the Rebel Fox last night. He'd been too distracted by Brianna. At the thought of her in his arms, he hardened.

He clenched his fist in an attempt to regain control of his body. He wanted her, and soon, soon he'd have her.

With a smile, Trevor refolded the paper and tucked it into his pocket. Tonight the Rebel Fox. Tomorrow Brianna.

Brianna tucked a stray tendril of hair back under her cap. It wouldn't do for young "Timmy" to be seen with long, blond tresses. She smiled at the thought. Heaven forbid. She slumped and trudged across the bridge. The sentries only nodded at the boy.

The heavy pistol rubbed against her hip, and she readjusted its berth in the pocket of her patched breeches. Tonight the smudges of dirt and mud on her face were real. It had been a long, hard trip across the lines. The full moon proved to be as much an enemy as the Yankees. She'd had to dodge patrols twice by hiding in the shadowy bushes.

The sweet thought of home and a bath beckoned her. Not much farther. She'd left her borrowed horse with the last farmer. He'd been almost as happy to receive the gift as he'd been to help the Cause.

She clambered over the fallen log blocking her path. As she jumped down, a figure stepped partway out of the shadow of a tree. Moonlight glinted off the gold buttons of a Union uniform.

"Halt." A deep, masculine voice rang out in the silence.

Brianna swallowed down the terror that threatened to overwhelm her. She slid her right hand into the pocket of her breeches. The metal of the pistol was cool and reinforcing against her palm, and she curled her fingers around the butt.

Slowly, watching for any sudden move on the part of her Yankee captor, she withdrew the pistol. She bit down on her lower lip. She had known this time would come. Could she do what she had to do?

She raised the pistol and pointed it at the shadowed figure. Her finger rested on the trigger. Could she pull it?

Sweat trickled along her neck and down the center of her back to collect at the waist of her breeches. She forced herself not to wipe her damp forehead or push her hat back. She stood rock steady, facing the Yankee.

The hated Yankee dismissed her pistol with one look and took a step forward into a bright patch of moonlit grass.

Brianna gasped. Major Trevor Caldwell, gun in hand, unflinchingly faced the barrel of her pistol. Her hand shook, betraying her. *Shoot,* her mind screamed for survival when he took another step. Her hand trembled, and she covered it with her other hand.

"Stop," she called out hoarsely.

In the next instant, Trevor lunged.

Chapter Eight

Brianna screamed as Trevor's shoulder caught her full force, sending her backward. The pistol flew from her grasp.

She tumbled back over the fallen log and hit the ground with a breath-stealing thud. Dazed, she struggled to draw air into her lungs. Before she could succeed, Trevor straddled her.

Staring into his hard face, she drew in a shuddering breath. Anything she might have said was frozen in her throat as she watched him reach for her cap.

No. She screamed the denial in her mind, powerless to stop him.

Trevor yanked off the woolen cap, and watched Brianna's long, golden hair tumble down around her face and over her shoulders. The clear moonlit night exposed her fully to his gaze. He felt as if he'd taken a blow to his stomach, almost doubling over with the pain of recognition. *Brianna. His Brianna.*

Her lips trembled under his study. When her

tongue darted out to lick her bottom lip, he felt rage boil through him.

"You're the Rebel Fox?" he forced the words out.

He half hoped she'd deny it, come up with some excuse he could accept. Right now he'd take anything. Anything to cure the pain slicing through him at her betrayal. She'd played him for a fool.

"I couldn't shoot you," she whispered.

Trevor ran his hands over her face, tracing her eyebrows, temples, cheekbones, down to her lips. He trailed the pad of his thumb across her parted lips. They trembled under his touch. Last night she'd clung to him, melting with his kisses. He felt a matching fire burn in his loins. Damn himself for a fool, he still wanted her.

She was a liar, a traitor, and he wanted her with a desperation that couldn't be denied. He shuddered with the intensity of his desire.

Beneath him lay the famed Rebel Fox—the promotion he'd been working toward. All he had to do was turn her in.

Beneath him lay the other half of himself. The woman his blood boiled for no matter how many times he called himself a fool.

As his gaze pinned hers, he fought an inner battle. He'd been raised to put duty above all else. He owed General Scott. His course had already been determined.

A single tear fell from Brianna's eyes to run down her temple and onto his hand. He shivered, watching the drop roll across his knuckles.

It was warm with her life. It was his undoing.

Trevor released his hold on her face, brushing the pads of his fingers across the moisture at her temple.

Her hair lay tumbled over her shoulders. The golden strands sprawled across the grass, shimmering in the moonlight. He brushed through the silken strands with one hand. Her hair rippled and curled around his fingers, as if the tendrils had a life of their own. He eased his hand from her hair and stared down at her. She took his breath away.

Unable to stop himself, he ran his hands over her neck to her shoulders and down her arms. Her skin was velvet smooth under his palms. Capturing her wrists, he raised her arms above her head and held them there.

Brianna stared into his eyes. Fear, defeat and wonder shone through to him. She trembled under his hands. He held her tightly, giving no chance of escape. Another tear trailed across her temple.

Trevor ducked his head and caught the tear with his tongue. It tasted salty, the essence of the woman beneath him. He moaned against her hair, inhaling the sweet scent that he associated only with her. Her breasts were soft beneath his chest, and he rubbed his torso back and forth across her. In spite of the boy's clothing, Brianna was all woman beneath him. He strove to bring his raging desire under control. He would not. He had to turn her in. He could not.

He collapsed on top her, taking her lips in a thorough kiss. Parting her lips, he thrust his tongue into her mouth. Velvet softness greeted him.

He drank of her deeply.

His breath caught in his chest. Pulling back, he brushed his tongue back and forth across her moist lips. Her own tongue darted out to her bottom lip, where he caught it and drew it into his mouth, holding it prisoner.

Brianna sighed against him, and he captured the sound of it as well. His mouth covered hers with a thoroughness that robbed them both of breath.

He felt Brianna shiver beneath him. It took another moment to realize that silent sobs racked her body. His kiss softened, gently touching her lips, her tear-drenched cheeks.

He released her wrists, cradling her in his arms and turning on his side. He held her closely, tenderly.

"Ah, my sweet. What am I to do?"

Brianna wiped her cheeks with the cuff of her dirty shirt like a child. "I . . . I almost never cry," she hiccupped. "I don't."

"I know, my sweet."

"I'm sorry, Trevor." Her voice cracked on his name.

It cut through him, piercing any resolve he might have still held.

"I didn't mean to hurt you," she whispered. "I had no choice."

He thought he heard her murmur the word "promise," but couldn't be sure.

"You have to turn me in." She bit her lip, then added, "I understand."

"I know." He must. He clenched his hand into a

fist. A shudder racked his body in a convulsive movement.

As he stared into her clear, blue eyes, he had his answer.

The only one he could live with.

"I can't do it," he ground out the denial.

Brianna didn't think she heard the words correctly. As soon as he found the message from General Beauregard hidden in her boot, she would be condemned. It held absolute proof of her identity.

"God help me, I can't," he groaned.

"But— "

"You will marry me, Brianna."

Marry him. Marry a Yankee. She couldn't. It would be betraying her promise to Ethan in the worst possible way. How could his spirit ever find rest? No matter how much she craved Trevor's touch, she couldn't marry him. It would destroy what little honor she had left.

She turned her head, pressing her cheek against the damp grass. The earth was moist, musty. She inhaled deeply, trying to draw strength from it to give him her answer.

"No." She shook her head. "No," she repeated.

Trevor caught her chin in his hand and forced her to look at him. "You will marry me. Tomorrow."

When she opened her mouth again, he cut her off. "Marry me or go to Old Capitol Prison."

Brianna swallowed and spoke clearly, pulling on all the strength she had left. "Then, I will go to prison."

Trevor wanted to shake her in frustration. Damn the woman. Did she not have any idea of what awaited her there?

"If the feelings on spies change—and they may soon—you will face a hangman's noose. Are you still so eager to go to the prison?"

Her eyes widened in alarm.

"Oh, no, Brianna." Trevor's hold on her chin tightened until she cried out.

He immediately released his grasp, gently stroking her skin. She trembled under his touch, and he felt himself tremble in return. He wanted her with a fire that could not be denied. He had never experienced this before with any woman. What was so different about Brianna? The word "love," crept insidiously into his mind, and he forced it out. He didn't love her. It was desire, lust, he was experiencing.

He would have her. And keep her safe. His rank would ensure it. She would never survive in prison. He knew it with a certainty that shook him to the core of his being. *He must save her from herself.* He hated himself for what he was about to do. Worse yet, he knew she would hate him as well.

"Brianna." He hardened his voice when she turned her head to face him. "If you refuse to marry me, I will send your aunt to prison along with you."

He ignored her gasp of horror although it tore at him. "Shall I arrest Harriet Devland? The choice is yours. What will it be?"

Silence stretched through the night as he waited

for her answer. *Please, dear God,* he prayed.

In that instant, she hated him. She thought she'd sensed a tenderness in him. But she couldn't have. He was as hard and unyielding as they came. A Yankee through and through. He held the condemning secret of her identity. He could destroy the only person who cared for her. She had no choice. She'd become his wife and hate him all the more for it.

"I'll marry you, Yankee. But you'll regret it until your dying day."

"So be it."

With a mirthless laugh, Trevor stood to his feet, then pulled her up to his side.

"Come, my loving bride to be." Irony tinged his voice.

"Never loving, Trevor. Remember that." She jerked her hand from his. "Where are you taking me?"

"To your new home. By noon, the papers will be in order. We'll be married tomorrow afternoon."

Brianna opened her mouth, but no words would come out. Married. The enormity of what she'd agreed to hit her full force.

"Right now we're going to our new home. First, you'll get cleaned up, and then we will both sleep. In preparation for our wedding night." He sent her a wry smile.

"You know I hate you," she whispered.

"I believe you've already made that clear, my sweet. But you will play the blushing bride. And play it well. Your dear aunt depends on it."

Anger raged through Brianna. She raised her chin and faced him squarely. "You will regret this, Yankee. I swear it."

"I'm sure I will."

He scooped her up into his arms and tossed her on his horse. As he mounted behind her, she thought she heard him groan, "But I'm damned anyway."

Brianna tried to hold herself stiff, refusing to rest her body against his. She would not curl against him like a thankful pet cat.

With every step the large horse took, Brianna bounced. She grasped the saddle, struggling to stay upright and as far from Trevor as she could.

Finally, Trevor swore in disgust and pulled her back against him. "You'll unseat us both."

He held her firmly in his arms. Brianna tried to keep herself stiff in his embrace, but it became harder and harder. The heat from his chest seared through her clothes to her back. It warmed her in a devious way. His breathing rumbled against her ear. It lulled her, soothed her.

Little by little, Brianna relaxed. She was so tired. The last three nights she'd slept little and travelled a lot. The problems she faced seemed enormous, too large to confront. She stifled a yawn and struggled to keep her eyes open. Before they reached the edge of town she was fast asleep in his arms.

"Wake up, sleepyhead," Trevor murmured softly.

Brianna heard the words as if in the distance. She snuggled against her bed. If she ignored the voice, maybe it would go away and leave her sleep.

A feather-light caress at her temple startled her awake, and she snapped open her eyes. Trevor filled her gaze.

"We're home, my sweet," he whispered, his voice husky.

Brianna stared at him, and the memories rushed over her. How she wished it could be different. "You're home," she corrected.

"Ah, Brianna. A Rebel to the end." Trevor dismounted and reached out to her.

She thought she saw sadness in his eyes, but she had to be wrong. He was getting what he wanted, wasn't he? And she was caught in a snare more dangerous than any laid in the woods.

Trevor caught her in his arms and swung her down from the horse. As she knew he would, he slid her body down against his. Pressed between the horse's solid side and Trevor's equally firmly muscled body, Brianna forced herself to stay rigid. He would get nothing willingly from her. This Yankee would have to take everything.

He will, an inner voice warned.

Brianna shivered against the thought. What had she gotten herself into? The jaws of the trap closed more fully around her.

An hour later, bathed and clothed in one of Trevor's shirts, Brianna paced the floor of the bedroom assigned to her. Her mind in a turmoil, she couldn't stay still. Restless, she tugged on a still-damp curl. As she crossed the room another time, she heard the scrape of a chair outside the door.

He couldn't even trust her this much. And why

should he? she asked herself. If the chance would present itself for her to escape and see Aunt Harriet safe, she would snatch at it. Yet there wasn't much chance of that. Trevor held her more tightly bound than if he'd used ropes. She could never allow Aunt Harriet to suffer because of her own actions.

Brianna looked toward the window. The first rays of dawn streaked the sky. Her wedding day. She choked on the thought. It was supposed to be a happy affair. She'd dreamed of it—Papa, tall and proud; Ethan, handsome and teasing. . . .

She shook her head and ran her hands through her damp hair. Those dreams were gone, replaced by harsh reality. She turned away from the window and the dawn. She didn't want to greet the day yet.

Crossing the room, she tumbled into the bed and drew up the covers. Sleep would help the time pass less painfully. Right now she couldn't face the might have beens, the should have beens, the too soon to be.

Hours later, a tap on the door echoed through the room. Brianna sat upright. She grabbed the bed covers tight around her.

"Yes." Her voice sounded timid to her own ears. "Yes," she repeated more firmly.

She wouldn't show fear. She wouldn't reveal her true feelings . . . no matter what. Her pride might be all she had left, but she'd keep hold of it to the last.

Two women entered the room. One, small with pretty features, carried an armload of clothing. The other woman, tall and lean faced, held a tray of food.

"Morning, miss." The smaller woman shifted her gaze to the window. "It's a beautiful day."

"Now, Annie. Give the girl time to wake afore you start talking 'bout the wedding."

"The major said we was to help you dress, miss." Annie nodded to the clothes in her arms.

"Annie. Your manners. Miss Devland's to eat first thing." The older woman sent Brianna a forced smile.

Annie snickered. "With a man like the major she'll be needing her strength."

"Annie. Why don't you go wait on the lady's aunt. I'll be taking care—"

"Aunt Harriet's here?" Brianna jumped to her feet. "Is she all right?"

"And why wouldn't she be?" The tall woman drew herself up fully, the picture of insulted dignity. "She's a guest of the major's."

"May I see her?"

"The major said you was to see her at the wedding. And if you don't get started, you will be late."

"But—"

"Come, miss. I know you're nervous, but you must eat. And you must change out of that . . ." she trailed off, staring at the man's shirt hanging on Brianna.

Brianna pulled the neck of the shirt closer. "I . . ."

"No need to explain, miss. I was young myself

once."

"But it's not—"

"Shush." She brushed off Brianna's denial. "Now come and eat. By the way, name's Sarah Peterson. Just call me Sarah." She drew out one of the two chairs beside the small table and pushed Brianna onto the seat.

The aroma of the hot food tempted Brianna. She was ravenous. She hadn't eaten since around noon yesterday. A whole lifetime away. She dug into the food, forgetting her ladylike manners.

Sarah turned away and began to lay the clothes across the bed. She ran a hand down the creamy gown.

"Beautiful. The major chose you a right pretty wedding dress."

Brianna stared at the gown draped on the bed. The fork clattered to her plate. Before her lay the gown she'd worn the night she met Major Trevor Caldwell.

She'd known he was trouble from the first. She should have listened to her own mind instead of letting Rose convince her to encourage him. Look where it had gotten her.

No, Brianna answered with honesty. She didn't need to blame Rose. She'd known exactly what she was doing when she first allowed Trevor to hold her in his arms. Nothing on this earth could have kept her from him. Did he feel the same way? Did he care for her just a little, she thought, wistful.

She pushed the plate away and walked across to the gown. She remembered it well. She'd worn it the first time he'd held her on the dance floor. And now she'd wear it for this charade of a marriage.

Why was he doing this? There had to be more to it than merely a way to get her in his bed. He'd decided on that almost from the first, she'd bet. What lay behind his proposal?

"Miss?" Sarah touched her arm. "If you're done with eating, you'd best be getting ready. The minister and his wife are downstairs awaiting." She turned away and brushed a dark speck off the skirt of the gown. "It's so nice how the major arranged everything so you could have the wedding here like you asked."

"What?" Brianna choked out the word. She hadn't asked for any of this. It was obviously Trevor's way of ensuring she'd go through with the wedding.

"Listen to me going on." Sarah straightened. "And here it is almost time for the major to come for his bride."

Brianna scurried out of his shirt and into her underclothes, not wanting him to enter and find her half-clothed. She didn't want to give him the idea she was eager for him. But was she? Absolutely not.

Brianna forced herself to stop the jumble of thoughts coursing through her mind. She stood still while Sarah laced her and assisted with the gown. After her hair was brushed and pinned, Brianna stared at the woman in the mirror. Once again questions chased each other across her mind.

At a knock on the door, she whirled around. It

opened to reveal Trevor in uniform. Her mouth went dry, and she stared at her future husband. He seemed taller today, more forbidding, until he smiled. It softened the lines of his face, disarming her.

Brianna found herself starting to return his smile until she remembered her vow. She would give him nothing willingly. She met his warm gaze with a chill one of her own.

"Brianna." Trevor held out his arm. The softly spoken order brooked no argument.

Head held high, she crossed the room. Her hand trembled as she placed it on his arm, and she damned the circumstances that forced her to go through with this.

The walk downstairs seemed endless to Brianna. She wished she could scoop up her skirts and flee the whole unreal scene: Aunt Harriet dabbing at her eyes with a lace handkerchief, the minister and a strange woman beside him, Annie the maid with a wide grin on her face—all waiting for her.

What would they do if she ran? She wouldn't. She'd made her choice, and she'd see it through like she had her promise to Ethan.

Trevor drew her to a halt at his side. Although she felt his hand on hers, holding her in place, Brianna shut everything else out. The words of the ceremony floated past her. She spoke at the right time, said the correct answers. The words that would bind her to Trevor.

At the same time, her mind kept telling her this couldn't be happening. She shut out the minister's voice. She couldn't be marrying Trevor. No, it was impossible. She couldn't be marrying someone she didn't love. And she certainly wasn't in love with Trevor. Was she?

The answer came with the force of a blow as Trevor slipped the gold ring onto her finger. Yes, she loved him. That's why she'd let him force her into marriage. Force? No, if she'd truly wanted to find a way out she could have. Damnation, she loved him.

Chapter Nine

Brianna reeled with the shock of her revelation. She loved Trevor.

"Man and wife." The minister's words penetrated the daze that enveloped her.

She looked up at Trevor. *Her husband.*

His face filled her vision. One lock of midnight hair lay across his forehead. It matched the silken mustache above his lips. But it was his eyes that held her, pinned her in place. His green gaze questioned, sought, found. As she watched his eyes darken, and the golden sheen became more pronounced, she knew his stamp of possession. Her breath rushed out in a gasp.

"May kiss the bride," came from far away.

Trevor needed no further encouragement. Before Brianna could even finish her gasp, he pulled her into his embrace. His arms closed around her, trapping her hands against his chest. Beneath her palms she felt the steady beat of his heart. As he bent over her, the beat increased to match her own.

Eyes wide open, Brianna watched as Trevor's face came closer and closer. Slowly his head descended until his lips were but a breath away from her own.

"Wife," he whispered the word against her lips as his took hers.

This kiss was different. It claimed as surely as if he'd spoken. Closing her eyes against the real world around them, Brianna revelled in his claim and dug her fingers into his jacket.

Husband. The word echoed silently through her mind. Beloved husband.

She returned his fervor as she'd never dreamed possible. Kiss for kiss. Caress for caress.

When Trevor drew his lips from hers, Brianna swayed toward him. Her fingers curled against his jacket. Gently, he caught her hands in his and disentangled them from the cloth. He returned her gaze.

Breath and reality returned at the same time. Flushed, Brianna stepped away from Trevor. So much for her vow to give nothing willingly. She couldn't have returned his kisses more willingly if she'd tried.

Shame rose over her in waves. What of her vow to Ethan? Where was her pride? It was all she had left. That, and her love for Trevor, her conscience reminded her.

"Brianna, girl." Aunt Harriet enveloped her in a hug. "You sly girl. Why didn't you tell me?"

"I . . ." What was she to say? *I married him to keep you safe. I lied to him and to myself.* She couldn't very well tell her aunt that.

"Eloping?" Aunt Harriet drew back and tapped the floor with her cane. "Shame on you. Planning to deny me the pleasure of this wedding." She wagged her finger under Brianna's nose. "Not that I'd blame you."

Brianna blinked and wondered if the whole world had gone crazy.

"I wasn't—"

"Imagine, you and the handsome major. Love at first sight, he said."

"He what?"

"He told me all about it first thing this morning. Dear man, he was standing at the door before I even woke up." She poked Brianna's ribs. "What a sight to wake up to."

Brianna turned scarlet at her aunt's remark.

"Now, girl. Don't go getting maidenly on me. Don't blame you a bit for rushing things. What's one night?" She patted Brianna's cold hand. "If I'd been a few years younger—quite a few—I'd have done it myself." She punctuated the sentence with a sharp nod.

Damn him. Now Aunt Harriet thought she'd spent the night in Trevor's bed. She bet he enjoyed every minute of his lying to her aunt.

"Dear girl. I always knew you could get him if you set your cap."

"I didn't set my—"

Trevor's arm about her waist stopped anything she was going to say. She attempted to step away, but he pulled her against him. Brianna practically had to bite her tongue to keep back her answer.

"Well, I can see it's about time you two were left alone." Aunt Harriet smiled and tapped her cane. "At least you had enough smarts not to marry a gentleman."

Brianna heard Trevor give a choking cough behind her.

"He's a good man, girl. Treat him right." Aunt Harriet caught her close in a farewell hug. "I'll miss you. Come visit when you can."

"I will," Brianna gave her promise.

After another hug, her aunt left the room. As if on signal, Sarah appeared at Brianna's side.

"I'll help you upstairs, ma'am." Sarah winked at Trevor and took Brianna's arm.

Brianna wanted to pull away. She bristled at the implied message from Sarah. Damn the man. He thought all he had to do was touch her, and she'd fall willingly into his arms. With chagrin, she admitted it was close to the truth.

Once upstairs, Brianna was unprepared for the speed with which the older woman helped to undress her. When she tried to protest, Sarah merely shushed her and winked.

Brianna's temper increased with each knowing wink. By the time Sarah had dropped the gossamer-thin nightgown over her head and brushed her hair into a cloud of curls, Brianna was ready to scream. Then the older woman insisted on the crown of flowers woven into her golden hair.

"Enough," Brianna finally snapped, ducking her head.

"Sorry, ma'am. Of course you'd be anxious for your husband to come up." She walked to the bed and pulled back the covers.

"No, it's—"

"No need for apologies." Sarah chuckled. "I understand." She walked back to Brianna, took her by the arm, and led her to the bed. "Now in with you. He'll be here soon enough."

Brianna opened her mouth, then closed it. There was nothing she could say that would convince this woman that she wasn't the blushing bride eagerly awaiting her husband. Right now, she was almost willing to let Sarah believe anything she wanted as long as she left.

With one last wink, Sarah patted the covers, crossed the room, and slipped out the door.

Brianna fumed. Thanks to Trevor everyone thought she couldn't wait for the bridal night. She didn't know who she was angrier with—Trevor, Aunt Harriet for siding with him, or herself. Right now she was furious with all three.

Everyone was so eager to assume she was panting for the man. Well, she wasn't. She would give nothing of herself willingly to a Yankee. And she wouldn't wait meekly in bed for him. She threw back the covers and strode across the room.

The woman in the mirror facing her looked as if she were prepared for her lover. Clothed in a sheer gown, flowers in her hair, and cheeks flushed, Brianna cringed at the picture. She wasn't waiting for a lover. Trevor didn't love her. Did he? Of course not.

Brianna picked up the brush and threw it across the room. It landed with a dissatisfying thud on the braided rug by the bed. Next, she yanked the flowers out of her hair. She wouldn't allow herself to be presented to him as a pretty package just waiting to be unwrapped. She threw the mangled flowers across the room.

She wouldn't play the eager bride for him. Trevor had insisted on this marriage, not her. Why? The question brought her up. Why had he wanted to marry her so badly that he thought he had to force her into it? After all, he didn't love her.

Her breath caught in her chest. He didn't love her, did he? Could he? Her pulse raced. Perhaps? No, it couldn't be. She'd know if he loved her, wouldn't she? Her heart stilled in her breast. Perhaps if he loved her, everything would work out. She had to find out.

Scooping up the equally thin dressing gown, she hurriedly put it on. Tiny covered buttons ran from her neck to the floor. A slow smile spread across her face. Perfect. They should offer appropriate discouragement to any expectant bridegroom. Until she had the answer to her question. Why the marriage?

Her smile widened as she carefully buttoned each one all the way to the floor. Now for a few answers. She slipped her feet into matching slippers and crossed to the door.

As her hand closed over the knob, she paused. Why did she feel as if she were going out to meet a lion in its den armed with nothing more than a twig?

She brushed the thought off and swung open the door. The house seemed shrouded in silence. Her feet made almost no sound on the steps. At the bottom of the stairs she paused. Light shone from under a door down the hall.

Likely a study, she thought. At least a book-lined room wouldn't have a prepared bed in it. Raising her chin and her spirits, she strode to the door.

Her knock sounded timid to her ears, and she pounded the second time. Her knuckles rapped loudly in the stillness.

"Come in," Trevor called out.

Gathering up her courage, Brianna opened the door and stepped inside the room. Trevor sat behind a large wood desk that gleamed from frequent polishing. A matching pair of wing chairs sat with their leather backs to her. She glanced around. It was a man's room, and she felt strangely out of place in the stark masculinity the room emitted. Or was it Trevor who radiated pure maleness?

At her entrance, he set down his glass with a thunk. Dark amber liquid sloshed over the side to puddle in a darker pool on the wood.

Brianna licked suddenly dry lips and searched for her voice. He watched her every move with an intensity that was unsettling. She brushed her hand down the champagne and lace dressing gown. The multitude of buttons provided far less security to her now than they had upstairs.

Trevor's gaze followed her hand and returned to meet hers. His half-closed eyes devoured her from across the room. She took an instinctive step back. He wanted her with a raging desire that shocked her.

Heat radiated across the distance separating them. She felt an indescribable warmth in the pit of her stomach. It inched downward to settle at the apex of her thighs. She took a step forward, then another one. She stopped at the wing chairs.

She slowly released the air from her lungs. Trevor's eyes never left hers. They held both a question and a command. Her first impulse was to run to him, but she held back. She had to know—first.

"Trevor." Brianna paused and swallowed down the building trepidation that caught her. She had to know. "Do . . . do you . . . love me?"

She gripped the back of the maroon leather wing chair. It was cold against her fingers.

"What?" His voice was husky. It almost sounded hoarse from disuse.

She licked her lips. "I asked if you loved me."

He looked away from her. "No." The single word was harsh, cutting.

"Then, I want to know why you married me." The tears welled up, she could feel them, but she would never let him see them. "Why?" Her grip on the chair tightened until her knuckles whitened.

He faced her again, and his gaze had cooled. "To keep you safe from prison."

"You're lying. Why else?" There had to be another reason. She knew that as sure as she breathed.

He clenched his teeth together. "You want an answer. I warn you, you may not like it."

"What? Go on."

Her blood slowed in her veins. Maybe she

shouldn't push it, an inner voice gave warning. She had to know. She tensed waiting for his answer. The leather warmed beneath her hold.

"I would not be played a fool in front of my men and my commander."

"Played a fool?"

"What would you call it, my sweet? I escorted the famed Rebel Fox to the very parties where she collected her information." He turned away from her.

She had her answer. He'd married her because he wouldn't be played the fool; well, neither would she. She spun around and reached for the door. It wasn't there. When had she come so far into the room?

"Brianna." The word echoed Trevor's longing and pain.

She turned around to face him. She could not have refused.

"Come to me," he asked in a whisper-soft voice that threatened to mesmerize her. "My wife." The last was spoken as soft as a caress.

Part of her longed to go to him. Another part of her knew she'd hate herself if she did. The lamplight reflected off the gold buttons of his jacket. He still wore the uniform of her enemy.

Brianna took a step back. She bit her lower lip. "I can't."

Trevor surged to his feet. He shoved the glass of bourbon out of his way. It sailed across the room and clattered against the wall where it shattered, littering the floor with glass shards. The dark liquid dribbled down the wall in rivulets. He ignored it.

She watched the drops roll downward, staining the wall. *He'll destroy you just as surely,* a silent voice warned. No, she shook her head. She wouldn't let him.

"Yes, my sweet," Trevor answered. His voice once again held that lilting, mesmerizing quality.

As he came around the desk and strode toward her, Brianna reacted out of survival instinct. In the next instant she had sprinted to the other side of the desk. The solidity of the wooden desk separated them. She clenched her fists and watched him warily.

Trevor eyed her, his gaze heating with every breath. He lunged to the side, and she jumped the opposite direction. A lazy, sexy smile curled his lips. His mustache turned up at one corner, and she stared at it transfixed.

He reached up with one hand and unbuttoned the top button of his jacket. Brianna's eyes widened. She continued to watch as he freed the buttons one by one. She could no more have looked away than stopped breathing. He peeled the jacket off and dropped it carelessly to the floor. His bare chest glistened in the light of the lamp.

It seemed as if Trevor's body heat reached out to her, calling her, trying to consume her. Her gown was warm, too warm. She felt flushed from her neck to her knees. Hoping to cool her overheated skin, she blew a breath downward. She ached to unbutton the dressing gown. She was smothering in it.

The smile never left Trevor's face. He leaned forward, and his whiskey-scented breath teased her. "Have you tired of your game yet, my wife?"

He tugged off one boot and then the other. They hit the floor with twin thuds of warning.

"How much have you had to drink?" she blurted out.

He stepped to one side, and she to the other.

"Not that much, my sweet." The lazy smile returned. "My second drink." He jerked his head toward the wall where the droplets still reflected the lamp's glow.

So, he wasn't drunk. She didn't know whether to be relieved or sorry. Brianna continued to watch him. He took a step, she another. He took two quick steps, and she retreated the same. The oversized desk stayed between them, separating them. Brianna rested her hands on the back of the large chair. The butter-soft leather was still warm from the press of his back against it. She pulled her hands away.

The supple leather of the chair reminded her of the feel of Trevor's shoulders under her fingertips. She rubbed the palms of her hands together.

"Tired yet, my sweet?" Trevor asked. The soft timber of his voice gave warning.

A second later, he lunged across the desk. Brianna squealed and jumped to the side. She scurried around when he straightened. Cautiously she kept the desk between them. They were both breathing heavily. The game was becoming dangerous. She could sense it.

There was the subtlest of changes in Trevor. For an instant Brianna wondered what it meant. Then her eyes caught his. She stared transfixed. The green-gold depths held her motionless. Tenderness, excitement, and most of all desire reached out to her.

Before she realized what he was doing, Trevor feigned to the left; she jumped to the right. He lunged and caught her around the waist.

Brianna fought him, shoving with all her strength. He held her tight against him, and before she could move he lowered his lips to take hers. His mouth moved over hers, opening her lips, taking all she had, demanding all she could give.

As her hands stilled against his chest, his hands moved up from her waist to stroke her back. The material seemed to melt away, so strongly could she feel his hands caressing her skin. When he stepped away, Brianna felt bereft.

Trevor ran his hands halfway down the tiny buttons of her dressing gown and back up to her neck. Slowly, he stroked her throat. Her pulse beat rapidly under his fingers. Her moistened lips beckoned to him. He took them in a love kiss so sweet it took her breath away.

Ever so slowly he unbuttoned the dressing gown. One by one the fasteners gave way to his fingers. Her breath quickened with the release of each button. She should stop him She should stop. . . .

Trevor knelt before her. He unbuttoned the button at her knee. Then the next. And the next.

The gown lay open to his eyes. The gossamer-thin undergown revealed every curve in the lamp-light. She heard his rush of breath, felt it searing her skin.

He caressed her ankles with his roughened fingertips. Flames lapped at the edges of her senses. She felt ready to erupt into a forest fire.

He ran his palms up her calves, around the back of her knees, up her thighs. Brianna trembled under his touch.

Lowering his hands again, he stroked her legs all the way to her ankles. Bending, he placed a feathery kiss on first one ankle, then the other. His fingers skimmed the backs of her calves and circled her knees.

Trevor raised to one knee and touched his lips to the back of her knee. Turning, he mouthed a kiss on her other knee. Brianna had difficulty breathing. She dropped both hands to his shoulders as her legs threatened to buckle beneath her. She wasn't sure she would be able to stand much longer. Her strength was ebbing away, little by little. It flowed out of her with each new caress.

As he raised his hands higher, she felt the muscles in his shoulders flex. They were hard and slick under her fingertips. Brianna gripped tighter. His roughened fingers made a path up her thighs, stopped, retreated. Once again he placed gentle kisses, this time above her knees. His hands inched upward with agonizing slowness, then circled her thighs.

He rained gentle kisses on her inner thighs. She parted her legs, giving him more access. Once again, roughened fingertips played with the soft flesh of her inner thighs. Moist kisses trailed upward, higher and higher. Bringing her closer and closer to what she didn't know and couldn't even guess at right now. All she knew was she wanted more. More than he was giving.

Brianna moved her hands to the thick curls at his nape. They were crisp and springy to her touch. She curled her fingers in their lushness. Her breath came in ragged spasms.

Trevor's hands stilled. Brianna moaned her protest. He drew back his head, meeting the desire in her own gaze. Slowly he stood to his feet. Swinging her into his arms, he held her against him and lowered his head to place a searching kiss on her lips.

Her mouth opened invitingly to him. Needing no more encouragement, he touched her tongue with his own, then circled hers, darting and tasting.

Unknown sensations raced through Brianna. The velvet underside of his tongue stroked her, and the rough-coated topside intrigued her. She darted her own tongue out, seeking the silken inside of his mouth. Trevor groaned against her lips. She caught the sound and savored it.

Without breaking the embrace, he carried her to the couch. Tenderly he lowered her to the softness. Brianna felt the couch give with the weight of Trevor at her side. She tightened her arms around him, savoring the feel of his bare skin. When he drew back she whimpered.

He returned to take her lower lip in his, then release it. Licking the side of her mouth, he trailed a moist path to her chin. He caught it in his mouth, suckling and kissing. Her chest tightened around each breath she drew.

With agonizing slowness, he lowered his hands from her shoulders to rub his palms across her breasts. The soft flesh swelled under his touch as she arched to meet him.

"Yes, my sweet. Yes." His ragged whisper stirred against her skin.

She felt the heat of his breath on her breasts even through the thin material of her gown. It was heaven on earth.

He took her breast fully into his mouth. His moistness dampened her gown, leaving dark circles around her nipples when he pulled away. The damp material rubbed against her sensitized nipples.

She smoothed her chin back and forth across the top of his bent head. The dark curls were soft against her cheek. She breathed in, relishing his scent.

He traced the outline of her breasts, the pads of his fingertips both rough and gentle at the same time. As she closed her eyes, he moved downward to caress the soft curve of her hip, then ran his palms over her thighs. He covered the triangle of hair between her thighs, rubbing his palm back and forth.

Brianna jerked beneath him.

"Trevor." Her voice trembled on his name. She caught his wandering hand and held it in both of hers.

Searching his eyes, she continued haltingly, "I'm

not . . . I mean I'm . . ." She reddened to the roots of her hair. "I haven't had much experience," she finally blurted out.

"Hell, honey, I knew that the first moment I looked at you." He gently brushed her hair back from her forehead. His fingers glided through the silken strands.

Tenderly, he cupped her face in his hands. He lowered his head, never releasing her gaze. His lips brushed hers, sipped, then drank fully, cherishing.

He eased the gown over her shoulders, his fingers drawing a line from her shoulder to her elbow to her wrist. Downward he continued, drawing the material down to reveal her breasts. He halted, fixing his gaze on the round globes. Flicking out his tongue, he traced around one nipple, then the other. Brianna gasped her pleasure.

His tongue found the valley between her breasts, laving it thoroughly. He alternately licked and kissed his way down to her navel, drawing the gown before his path. Not pausing or giving her a chance to recover from his loving assault, he dipped his tongue into the indention of her navel.

Brianna writhed beneath him. Panting for breath, she kneaded his shoulders and back. The muscles rippled under her fingertips.

Lower and lower he went. He covered her hipbones with damp, heated kisses and then brushed the nest of hair below.

Brianna bucked beneath him as if struck by the white-hot heat of a lightning bolt. The fire raged within her—out of control. She felt as if she were being consumed. Her fingers dug into his shoulders, and she smothered the cry that was building up within her.

"Trevor," she cried out his name.

He raised her hips and drew the gown over them. She felt it glide past her ankles to pool on the floor. She was past caring.

"Trevor," she cried again.

"One moment, my sweet." His voice was roughened with desire.

She moaned when he leaned away, leaving her aching. As he reached for his trousers, she stared, unable to look away. She knew she should, but couldn't. Her gaze was drawn to him as if bewitched. He was magnificent.

Her cheeks burned at the wantonness of her thought. But it was the truth. He took a step toward her, and she trembled with a mixture of desire and misgiving.

Trevor touched her cheek with incredible tenderness. As he bent to join their lips, all else ceased to exist. His lips were soft against hers, gentle. He sipped her sweetness. Brianna felt cherished, loved. She closed her arms tight around him, pulling him down to her.

Trevor cradled her in his embrace. She was here, and she was his. He'd lost count of the number of times he'd dreamed of holding her like this, of making love to her. He settled his chest over hers. She was his life, the other part of him. His wife. His breath hissed out in a ragged groan.

This time it was Brianna who captured the sound.

Drawing his head down, her lips took his, asking for more. She ran her hands the length of him from the cords in his neck to the firm muscles of his thighs.

He deepened the kiss, nearly sending her over the edge. Heat radiated around them, enclosing them in a cocoon of fire. She arched against him. It was all he needed.

Trevor ran his hand down her thighs, parting her legs for him. He dipped his finger into her sweet flesh. She shuddered and convulsed against him. His caress deepened, and she cried out. She ached—for what she didn't know. She writhed under his touch.

Brianna was moist, more than ready for him. He slid one hand behind her, shifting his weight, yet still holding her close. Their breaths mingled together. Instinctively she sought more.

Trevor eased into her, filling her little by little. When he met resistance, he deepened their kiss, plunging his tongue into her mouth. At the same moment, he penetrated her innocence in one shattering, sparkling moment.

Brianna's startled gasp shuddered into a moan of pleasure as he began to move against her. Flames licked up from where their bodies joined to consume her, both mind and body. She held to him tightly, following him into an incandescent place where only the two of them existed.

Chapter Ten

Brianna awoke the next morning with a smile on her face and a sense of anticipation. She blinked against the sunlight streaming through the room. From the angle of the sun it was quite late in the morning. Her smile widened.

She remembered Trevor carrying her up the stairs and collapsing atop her on the bed. She ran a hand through the tangles in her hair. No wonder it was a mess; they'd made love a second time in the bed.

She stretched and rolled over, reaching out her hand. The space beside her was empty. She was alone in the big bed. It was an unwelcome feeling. She shivered with the sudden chill that spread through her.

A feeling close to that of a premonition enveloped her like a shroud of fog. She sat upright and rubbed her arms.

The door creaked, and she jumped, spinning around to face the door. It swung inward slowly. Her breath caught in her throat, and she swallowed down the taste of fear. This was foolish, she told herself. She merely had bridal jitters. Still she eyed the door with growing trepidation.

One booted foot appeared. She tensed. Trevor shoved the door open fully and stepped into the room. Relief made Brianna sag weakly against the pillows. She couldn't say what she'd feared or expected.

Her gaze returned to her husband. He stood before her, resplendent in full uniform. The Yankee blue of his clothing taunted her, calling her a traitor. She yearned for him, and was ashamed of herself. *What had she done? Fallen in love with a Yankee,* her heart answered. *Betrayed Ethan,* her mind accused.

"Morning, my sweet." Trevor's voice held a slight strain.

He stared at her a moment as if awaiting her reaction before he crossed to the bed. He dropped a kiss on her waiting lips and sat down on the edge of the bed.

She fought the urge to curl up against him, to beg him to make love to her again. Shame flushed her cheeks.

"General McClellan is giving a party in our honor two weeks from Saturday." His words were tense.

"Yes?" she asked.

Her mind whirled with the opportunities this could present. Perhaps she could arrange to have Selina invited. Between them, they could. . . .

No, *she* couldn't. Her identity had been uncovered. Worst of all, it had been uncovered by the man beside her. The man who had the power to have her every move watched if he chose.

What of her promise to Ethan? It was not fulfilled yet. She still owed the North for his death. She clenched her hands together.

"You will attend as my wife."

She stared up at him, a question in her eyes.

"You won't be sending any more information South."

His voice was hard, so unlike her lover of last night. The loss pained her.

"I burned the message you were carrying in your shoe. And the clothing."

"What—"

"Brianna, I want your word that you'll stop spying."

"I don't have much of a choice," she spoke bitterly. "My only use was the mystery I presented. Now that it's known who I am—"

"Only I know. And I will keep your secret."

She hadn't really thought he'd reveal her identity, not after last night. However, to be honest, a little doubt had remained.

Trevor swung his legs up and reclined on the bed beside her. He pulled her close.

"Brianna?" He trailed a finger down her arm, traced her wrist, and ran his finger back to her shoulder.

"Humm." Her voice was slow and held a note of returning desire.

A sinuous warmth spread through her. What was this strange power he had over her? Unable to deny him, she cuddled closer against his muscled torso. She tucked her fingers between the buttons of his jacket.

"Dear? Where's Ethan hiding?"

The breath left her in a rush at his question.

"Is he in Washington?"

Pain clamped around her heart. The memory of holding Ethan's dead body close to her tormented her. The pain shattered into splinters, slicing through her.

It was clear to her now. All Trevor wanted was the information she held in her mind about the Confederate spy ring. She saw it all with burning clarity. He'd been telling the truth when he said he didn't love her. He was using her.

"No," she answered, her voice hoarse with pain. "No, Ethan isn't in Washington."

"Brianna—"

She jerked away from him. Scooting to the far side of the bed, she faced him.

"Hadn't you better go back to work? Your work here is finished. I won't answer any more of your questions." She turned her back to him.

The stiffness of her spine said more than words could. It would be useless to try and talk to her now. She had no intention of giving Trevor information.

"Brianna?"

Her chin raised another notch. She refused to

answer him, so he stood.

"I learned this morning that Pinkerton has taken over the search for spies. I wanted you to know," he paused. "I've been reassigned to General McClellan."

She ignored him completely.

"I may be late tonight."

Silence greeted his announcement. Brianna could feel him staring at her, willing her to turn around. She clenched her hands together under the sheet. At last, he turned and strode out the door.

Brianna refused to run after him. If he thought he could come in and question her. . . . She blinked back the sudden rush of tears. She was not crying over last night. *She wasn't.*

All Trevor had wanted of her this morning was the location of Ethan. She blinked, and two tears ran down her cheeks. What was she to say, that she'd held her twin in her arms until his lifeblood had covered her?

A shaft of pain pierced her at the memory. She brushed away the tears from her cheeks.

"Ethan. Oh, Ethan," she whispered in a tortured voice. "What have I done?"

As if in answer, the room blurred before her eyes. She blinked, but it did no good. Surrounding items remained clearly focused, but directly in front was a thick haze. Resigned, she waited for the sensations to start. And start they would; she knew it.

Cool, so cool, the room chilled around her. She

shivered against the cold. Wet, everything about her was layered in dampness. It was as damp and cold as a tomb. The room pitched and swayed around her. She grabbed the edge of the mattress and held on.

This was impossible, her mind cried. The only thing that ever brought on these sessions was when Ethan was hurt while away from her—and lately since his spirit couldn't find peace. Now she'd just been in a Yankee's arms. Guilt racked her.

A second later the room stilled, and the wall came into clear focus. It was over—for now. She held out her hands. They shook with tremors. What was happening to her?

Brianna shivered, wrapping her arms around herself. She had to have answers. As she stood shaken, a single thought rang out.

She had to talk to someone. Rose. Brianna had to get to Rose Greenhow.

She hopped off the bed and surveyed the room. She hadn't seen much of it when Trevor had carried her in last night. Heat suffused her cheeks at the memory. She turned away from the thoughts.

The room was large and centered around the bed. A soft brown canopy the shade of a dun horse draped the bed while darker mahogany-shaded ties held back the panels. A dresser with gilt mirror sat against one wall; an enormous fireplace centered another wall. In a corner stood a colorful screen with a blue muslin gown hung over the side.

Brianna raced across to it and scooped up the dress. She recognized it from her armoire at Aunt Harriet's. Right now she didn't care how it had gotten here; she was just happy it was here. She hugged the gown against her.

She'd have to dress without assistance, but it wouldn't be the first time. Across the room she spotted her undergarments on a chair. The corset would have to stay behind, but she didn't really need it. As quickly as she could, Brianna dressed, using a minimum of petticoats. By twisting and turning she finally succeeded in closing the back of the gown. Minutes later she was ready.

Slipping out of the house proved easier than she'd anticipated. Voices at one end of the house alerted her to the servants, and she tiptoed out a side door. The fresh air of freedom smelled wonderful, even if it did carry with it the stench of the city's overcrowding.

As she left the house and walked at a steady pace, she tapped down the urge to run. She didn't want to draw attention. She was merely out for a stroll. That's what she would say if she was stopped.

Thank goodness Trevor's house was within walking distance of the Capital. Its unfinished dome, hovered over by scaffolding, stood out starkly. After walking another block, she turned away from the structure and headed for Rose's house. An army wagon loaded with artillery rumbled down the street past her.

She was within three blocks of Rose's brownstone when a hand snaked out and grabbed her, pulling her into an alley. A scream bubbled up. Before she had time to release it, her attacker faced her.

"Selina," Brianna gasped.

Her friend covered her mouth with her fingers. "Shh. Can't go to Rose's. Follow me," she whispered.

Brianna caught her friend's hand. "What's wrong?"

"Rose has been arrested."

"No." Brianna was horrified at the news. She knew her mouth gaped open, but she didn't care.

"We have to get away from here. There are men on guard." Selina threw a glance over her shoulder. "This way. I have a coach waiting." She grabbed Brianna's hand and led the way through the alley to the other side.

A hired coach stood at the entrance to the street. The two women hastened to it. Once there, Selina leaned against the side of the coach, obviously shaken. Brianna caught her friend's hand and gave it a comforting squeeze.

"Come on. In with you." She helped Selina into the coach, gave the driver an address, and climbed in after her friend.

Selina sat in silence on the seat. Brianna reached over and took her friend's hands. They were as cold as the ice on a pond. She rubbed them between her own hands. "Are you all right?"

Selina stared at Brianna. "They arrested her."

"When did it happen?"

"Less than half an hour ago. She passed a note to a courier on the street. That's the only thing that stopped me from walking into the trap." Her voice shook.

Brianna shivered. She had narrowly missed that same trap.

"Where are we going?" Selina looked out the window and glanced nervously across the street. Her voice was high-pitched and nervous.

"To a place where we can talk," Brianna reassured her.

"Where?"

"Aunt Harriet's house."

"But—"

"She knows. We'll be safe there."

Selina leaned back against the seat. Brianna watched her closely. What ifs chased each other across her own mind. The coach clattered down the streets and drew to a halt at Aunt Harriet's house. It looked so welcoming and comforting to Brianna. It was home; it was safe.

Before they had reached the steps, Aunt Harriet threw open the door. She'd obviously been at her post at the parlor window. She enveloped Brianna in a hug.

"Land's sakes, girl. I am happy to see you two. I was so afraid for you." She hugged Brianna again, then ushered both women into the house. "I feared you'd be caught."

"You know?" Brianna asked in disbelief.

"Wilkens brought the word just minutes ago."

"He's free?" Brianna questioned.

"By luck, he was returning from an errand when he saw the men."

"How's Rose?"

Aunt Harriet waved her cane in the air. "Enjoying the attention immensely, if you ask me." She pounded the floor with the tip of her cane. "If that woman had boasted a little less, it wouldn't have come to this. She brought it on herself."

"Aunt Harriet."

"It's true." She crossed the room to the parlor, thumping her cane all the way. "I'm just glad you're married now and—"

"Married?" Selina shrieked, grabbing Brianna.

She faced her friend, dreading the answers she would have to give.

"To who?"

"Major . . . Major Caldwell."

Selina's eyes widened almost as much as her mouth. "Well, I'll be . . . Why?"

"Land's sakes," Aunt Harriet gripped. "One look at the man and you have the answer to that."

"Aunt—" Brianna cried.

She shushed her with a snap of her cane on the floor. "Told you that you didn't want a gentleman, didn't I?" Her eyes twinkled with suppressed laughter.

Brianna stared at her aunt aghast. After a minute, her aunt had the decency to blush and look away.

"I'm sorry you didn't give me more warning, though. Didn't think it would be so soon. I had planned on a long talk with you before your wedding night. We never got around to talking much about that part of marriage."

Brianna choked. As Selina patted her on the back, she knew she was blushing all the way to her forehead.

Selina giggled and pushed Brianna into a chair. This time it was Selina who positioned the footstool for Harriet Devland's feet, then perched on the edge of it.

"I can't wait to hear this," Selina muttered under her breath.

Brianna sent her a glance that could strip the bark right off a tree. "Don't encourage her."

"Well, girl, with your mother dead and your father not here, it's up to me to tell you about—"

Brianna's cheeks burned under her aunt's chatter. "Aunt—"

"What to expect. Now Trevor is your husband, and he's going to have urges."

Her aunt was a little late, Brianna thought. Trevor had been having urges since the first night they'd met. A smile pulled at her lips.

Selina looked from one to the other and erupted into a fit of laughter. "Miss Devland, I think you're a bit too late." She almost choked on the last word.

Both women stared at Brianna. She turned scarlet under their scrutiny.

"Oh, dear. I do suppose I am." Aunt Harriet tapped her cane on the floor. "I'm sorry, girl. Was it—"

"I'm not going to discuss—" Brianna sputtered.

"Of course not. A lady never does."

Brianna stilled the impulse to cover her flaming face with her hands.

"That's what got the widow in trouble. She shouldn't have boasted about her conquests. Humph."

"Aunt Harriet."

"I'm sorry, girl. But you know Rose and I never did get along."

"Someone needs to take the word across the lines," Selina spoke up.

They looked at Brianna. She was the obvious choice.

"No, I can't." She'd already been caught once. And today at Rose's house had been too close. Luck had deserted her with a vengeance.

"Much as I hate to say it, you must, girl." Aunt Harriet stood. "Not knowing could cost too many lives. Yours included." She leaned on her cane. "Girl, we can't let the messengers show up at Rose's. No telling who might be exposed. Your major can only keep you safe providing word doesn't get out about you."

"She's right." Selina caught Brianna's hands in hers. "Until word reaches General Beauregard,

ENJOY ALL THE PASSION AND ROMANCE OF... *Heartfire* ROMANCES from ZEBRA

After you have read HEARTFIRE ROMANCES, we're sure you'll agree that HEARTFIRE sets new standards of excellence for historical romantic fiction. Each Zebra HEARTFIRE novel is the ultimate blend of intimate romance and grand adventure and each takes place in the kinds of historical settings you want most...the American Revolution, the Old West, Civil War and more.

SUBSCRIBERS $AVE, $AVE, $AVE!!!

As a HEARTFIRE Home Subscriber, you'll save with your HEARTFIRE Subscription. You'll receive 4 brand new Heartfire Romances to preview Free for 10 days each month. If you decide to keep them you'll pay only $3.50 each; a total of $14.00 and you'll save $3.00 each month off the cover price.

Plus, we'll send you these novels as soon as they are published each month. There is never any shipping, handling or other hidden charges; home delivery is always FREE! And there is no obligation to buy even a single book. You may return any of the books within 10 days for full credit and you can cancel your subscription at any time. No questions asked.

Zebra's HEARTFIRE ROMANCES Are The Ultimate In Historical Romantic Fiction.
Start Enjoying Romance As You Have Never Enjoyed It Before...
With 4 FREE Books From HEARTFIRE

AFFIX
STAMP
HERE

HEARTFIRE HOME SUBSCRIPTION
SERVICE
120 BRIGHTON ROAD
P.O. BOX 5214
CLIFTON, NEW JERSEY 07015

we're all in danger. If too many are caught going to Rose's . . ." Her words trailed off.

As much as Brianna hated to admit it, they were right. Rose's entire spy ring was in danger at the moment. Word had to reach the South. Meeting places and routes had to be changed immediately. Many lives hung in the balance.

"Very well."

Brianna pressed her body against the tree. The rough bark cut into her back. She stood motionless, hardly daring to breath in the early twilight.

Minutes later, two soldiers walked past. She feared her heart was beating so loud that they would hear it. Luck had definitely deserted her. Why, in the last hour alone, she'd had to hide from three different patrols.

The woods teemed with Union troops. They meant to intercept any person who dared to take news of Rose Greenhow's arrest; Brianna was sure of it.

She leaned her head back against the tree trunk and gulped in air. The first half of the trip through the lines had been easier than she'd hoped. The Yankees must not have expected anyone to attempt to cross the lines so soon. But now, two hours later, her message safely delivered into a courier's hands, things had changed. The Yankees stalked the woods with a singular purpose.

Fear lapped at the edges of her resolve. She

wouldn't give in to it. She'd make it out of here.

As she stepped away from the tree, a twig snapped under her foot with the sharpness of a rifle shot. She held her breath, sure it would bring a passel of troops down on her.

When nothing happened, she crept away from the tree. Ducking low, she sought the shelter of another tree a few feet farther on. If she had to sneak from tree to tree, she'd do it.

Minutes later, she ran out of trees. Before her lay a wide clearing. She gnawed on her bottom lip, weighing her chances of slipping across unnoticed. They were slim.

She curled her hand over a low-lying limb and thought over her options. She could chance going back deeper into the woods and circling around, but she might run into even more patrols. Backtracking would take at least another two hours. Washington lay tempting her on the other side of the clearing. She had to risk it.

Brianna took several deep, calming breaths in preparation for the dash across the open space. She licked her lips, swallowed, and ran for it.

"Halt." The shout rang out in the stillness.

She ignored it and ran faster. Her breath burned in her lungs, but she kept running.

"Halt." The crack of a gunshot accompanied the order.

At the terrifying sound, she glanced over her shoulder. Several soldiers on horseback thundered across the clearing. Fear became a living thing, eating at her. It threatened to devour her. She panted for breath. She turned her head back, and that's when she saw him.

A single rider burst through the wooded expanse to her right. Leaning low, the rider came straight at her. She clamped down on her scream of terror.

She refused to surrender and forced her legs to keep pumping. There was nothing else she could do. Her mind screamed an endless litany of escape.

The lone rider neared her, and Brianna altered her course, veering to the left. It did no good. He changed with her, bearing down on her.

Seconds later, he drew even. A muscular arm snaked out and caught her around the waist. With a heave, he swung her across his mount.

The saddle slammed into her stomach. The force of the move robbed Brianna of her breath. She gulped in air, then fought him. Kicking out, she tried to turn on her side. When it didn't work, she attempted to throw herself off the horse.

An arm slammed across her with the force of an iron band. The only thing she could move was her feet, and they hung useless in the open space. She wiggled against the hold.

"Be still. You damn fool."

Brianna's mouth snapped open. *Trevor.* It couldn't be possible. She yanked her head upward and glimpsed his determined face. There was no mistaking him or the anger set in lines across his face.

"I—"

"Shut up," he growled out the command.

Brianna fell silent immediately. Her mind churned with questions. How had he appeared here?

The horse shifted beneath her, and Trevor's grip tightened. Brianna could scarcely breathe in her upside down position.

Shouts pursued them. As Trevor's powerful mount's hooves pounded the ground, a shot echoed behind them. Disbelief crowded her brain. The Yankee soldiers were shooting at them. Didn't they know Trevor was a Yankee?

Another shot rang out, and Brianna flinched.

Trevor flicked the reins in front of her, and the horse responded with a burst of speed. A wooded area loomed before them, and Trevor raced for it. His mount responded to his every command.

At the trees, Trevor veered down a path. Moments later another path intersected, and he turned the horse sharply to the right. Brianna lurched with the sudden turn.

She thought she heard the thud of riders behind them, but couldn't be sure it wasn't their own mount's hooves beneath her ear. She lost track of the number of twists and turns that they took. The ground passed in a blur of speed.

Suddenly, Trevor pulled his horse up shortly. Brianna would have tumbled off if it hadn't been for Trevor's firm hold. Scarcely before she'd taken in that they had stopped, he swung her upright in front of him. She sprawled in a sidesaddle position.

"Not a sound," he growled against her ear.

She looked around and recognized the streets of Washington. Had they really made it safely? She peered over his broad shoulder for any sign of pursuit. It looked clear.

The remainder of the ride to their house was made in tense silence. She half expected to be stopped at any second. A servant stepped out of the shadows at their approach, and Brianna's breath caught in her throat.

Trevor handed the reins to the man, dismounted, and held out his arms for Brianna. She swallowed and leaned toward him in trepidation. He merely lifted her down, keeping her a wide distance from him.

In silence he led her through the door and into the lamplit study. Brianna stepped into the room and was swamped by heated memories of the night before. She forced herself not to look at the couch where they'd made such passionate love.

"Sit." Trevor eased her into one of the wing chairs. "I don't know about you, but I could use a drink."

He unbuttoned his jacket and tossed it on the back of the second chair. As he strode to the liquor cabinet, Brianna couldn't tear her gaze from his back. His muscles bunched and rippled in the glow of the light. Her lips parted, and she stared.

He poured two brandies and returned to her,

holding out one glass. She took it from him, but didn't taste it yet.

"Drink it," Trevor ordered in a low voice and dropped into the chair beside her.

He leaned his head back, closed his eyes, and sighed deeply. Brianna watched him warily and took a tentative sip of the liquor. It burned her throat all the way down to her stomach. She resisted the urge to cough. Silence reigned in the room.

The more the silence stretched between them, the smaller the room became.

"When, Brianna?"

The sudden question startled her, and she jumped, sloshing a splatter of brandy onto her skirt. "What?"

"When are you going to quit?"

She took a quick swallow.

Trevor surged to his feet, setting his glass on the desk. He turned to face her.

Brianna felt every muscle in her body tense. His very stance warned her that her time had run out. Her throat became dry in spite of the recent swallow of brandy.

"Brianna, it's time to go upstairs." The words were softly spoken in a tired voice.

No matter how soft his voice was, she recognized the command it held. Rebellion sprang up in her.

"I'm not finished with my brandy."

Trevor grabbed the glass from her hand and set it on the desk beside his glass. "You are now."

Something in his manner warned her better than any words could have. She pushed herself to her feet and preceded him out of the room. What now, her mind screamed.

Head high, she strode up the stairs. There was only one way to find out. The thud of his footsteps echoed hers.

Brianna entered their dimly lit bedroom and crossed to the fireplace. No welcome glow awaited her. She heard Trevor stop, and she turned to face him. He stared at her from across the room.

As the door clicked shut, she jumped and stepped back. He didn't pursue her. She stepped back another step for safety anyway.

She screwed up her nerve. "I haven't thanked you for saving me."

"It's the least a husband could do. Your bath is ready." His voice was deceptively soft and low.

She met his gaze with a level one of her own. She wasn't going to bathe with him looking on, and she might as well make that clear to him.

"Not now."

"Why not, my sweet?"

Brianna saw his eyes darken as if he'd just had a picture of her sitting nude before him. A sweet longing stirred in her. She skirted the large enameled tub before the fireplace, putting a few more steps between them. "How did you know where to find me?"

"I could say that I followed the nearest commotion."

"Did you?"

"No. I followed you."

"You followed me?"

"Since the moment you left this house."

How had she not known he was there? How had she missed seeing him? "You're lying."

His jaw clenched before he spoke. "You narrowly missed Pinkerton's men at Mrs. Greenhow's house."

Brianna's eyes widened.

"Is she who you worked for?" Silence fell between them. "I didn't really expect you to answer that. Someday we'll talk about it."

Brianna gritted her teeth in frustration. He thwarted her at every turn.

"Your friend saved you that time. Selina James—I believe that's her name. Right?" He paused. When Brianna didn't answer, he continued. "Next you had a lengthy visit with your aunt. How is dear Harriet, by the way?"

"Enough." She threw out her arms.

"Brianna, how many chances are you going to take?"

"I . . ." her voice trailed off. She didn't know. As many as she had to, she supposed.

"You're not quitting, are you?"

His voice had lowered on the last words. To her ears, it almost sounded like defeat she'd heard. But that wasn't possible.

Trevor's eyes locked with hers, and he held her gaze trapped in his. His face tightened in anger before he swung away from her. His boots rang out on the wooden floor as he strode to the door. He opened it, then looked back at her.

"Next time I should let you rot in prison."

The door slammed behind him.

Chapter Eleven

Brianna stared at the closed door in shock. *He wouldn't, would he?* A cold shroud of fear enveloped her. She'd married him like he wanted, hadn't she? What more did he want?

She couldn't surrender her promise to Ethan. She was honor bound. That was something a Yankee couldn't understand.

She stood in the dimly lit room and waited. Part of her was sure Trevor would return at any moment; then the slam of the front door echoed through the still house. He was gone.

Her breath rushed out, and she wrapped her arms around her waist. She hadn't realized how stiff she'd been holding herself until that very moment. She stepped back. Her knees bumped the tub, and they almost buckled beneath her.

She regained her balance and spun around. Warm tendrils of steam wafted up to her from the enameled tub, offering warmth to her suddenly chilled body. She gave in to the invitation. Stripping off her grimy clothes, she dropped them to the floor.

The warm water called to her with its own siren song. She dipped a toe in, testing the water. Perfect.

It had cooled just enough to be a comfortable and soothing temperature.

She stepped into the scented water and sank down. It enveloped her in a world of warmth. Leaning back, she rested her head on the edge of the tub and inhaled deeply, savoring the scent of lilacs. Her favorite. Was it a coincidence? It had to be.

Straightening her leg, she cupped her hands with water and poured it over her knee, then ducked her leg back down into the water and drew up her other leg.

Suddenly the bedroom door swung open. It slammed against the wall and bounced back to stand ajar.

Trevor stood in the doorway. Light glistened off his bare chest, making her all the more aware of her own nudity. She sank lower under the water until it sloshed against her chin.

He stepped into the room, reached behind him, and closed the door with a quiet thoroughness. Brianna swallowed and stared. He must have left his jacket downstairs. She couldn't resist running her gaze across the breadth of his chest. A dark pelt of hair invited her to rub her fingers across it. He was beautiful. He reminded her once again of a sleek cat in the forest, especially with his gleaming, hungry gaze.

His eyes never leaving hers, he dropped his hand to the waistband of his trousers. He unfastened them with a smooth movement and pushed them downward. She knotted her fingers together beneath the water.

Brianna watched as the pants slithered down his

legs, revealing tightly corded thighs and calves. He stepped out of his trousers and left them in a pool on the floor. He was fully revealed to her gaze. Her heart raced as she saw how ready he was.

As if under a spell, she didn't move a muscle when he walked toward her with quiet, decisive steps. He was going to make love to her, and heaven help her, she wanted him.

Trevor stopped at the side of the enameled tub. Brushing his mustache with one finger, he leaned over her and pressed his lips against hers. She ceased breathing.

He caressed her mouth, rubbing his lips back and forth across hers. Bracing his hands on the edge of the tub, he climbed into the warm water. His mouth never left hers.

Brianna raised her chin as the water rose, sloshing over the side in a wave when he immersed his body. She unclenched her hands to run them up his back. It was slick and wet from the bath water.

She shifted her legs as Trevor sat down between them. His legs brushed hers, the hairs tingling against her inner thighs. She tightened her hands against his back.

"Ah, Brianna." His hoarse whisper was a prayer.

He clasped her waist in his hands and drew her toward him. She couldn't have resisted even if she'd wanted to, but resisting was the farthest thing from her mind.

Raising her as if she weighed nothing at all, he lifted her until her face was above his. His tongue darted out, stroked her lips, then plunged into her mouth.

Brianna moaned her surrender. She couldn't fight him when he did that to her. She didn't want to fight him.

She returned his passion, kiss for kiss. His hands stroked her back to the indention below her waist, then back up to her neck. He slid his hand beneath her cloud of damp hair.

With agonizing slowness he lowered her. Her breasts rubbed his chest, and she thought she'd scream out with pleasure when his thick, wet pelt covered her breasts. She pressed against him, the sensation intense as he shifted his shoulders, rubbing back and forth across her nipples while the water lapped around them.

His hands on her waist, he drew her downward, closer and closer. She bit her lip to still her cry.

"Oh, yes," she moaned her need.

Mere inches separated their joining. He lowered her until she felt him prodding against her. Then he filled her.

Her velvet warmth sheathed him, and Trevor forced himself not to shout with the pure pleasure of it. Never had a woman created this unquenchable desire, the essential need he had for Brianna. He rocked her back and forth, sliding her away and pulling her back to him. Wisps of steam swirled around their bodies in a silken mist.

He mouthed silent words of love against her hair. The words were lost amidst the steam and heat that enveloped them. He pulled her tighter on top of him.

Brianna dug her fingernails into his shoulders and

cried out in ecstasy. His own cry of release mingled with hers.

She collapsed against him, breathing heavily. His ragged breath matched hers.

"Ah, my sweet," he murmured against her temple. He brushed the damp tendrils of hair back with his cheek.

Brianna moaned in answer. She couldn't have voiced a coherent thought if her very life depended on it.

"Come, let's go to bed." Trevor kissed her temple, her cheekbone, and trailed his tongue across to her lips.

Of their own accord, her lips parted to give him access. He dipped the tip of his tongue in, savoring her invitation. Slowly he entered, deeper and deeper until their mouths were sealed together.

Brianna felt his flesh harden against her. In that instant, her own strength returned. Her tongue darted into his mouth. This time it was she who sought, tasted, savored.

Trevor clasped her tightly in his arms and lunged out of the water. Without loosening his hold, he stepped over the side of the tub and carried her to the bed. Water dripped from their bodies as he laid her atop the coverlet and followed her down. He took her again with a desire that surprised them both.

Later, Trevor eased her out of his arms. Brianna moaned her protest.

"One moment, my sweet."

He lifted the covers from the floor. Smiling, he

glanced her way. "Don't know how they got there, do you?"

Brianna giggled. She remembered exactly how they'd gotten on the floor.

A wide grin on his face, Trevor joined her in the bed. He drew the cover around them.

The space beside her was cold and empty when Brianna awoke the next morning. A twinge of pain rushed through her. Why did he have to slip away each morning? Just once she'd like to wake up with him in the bed beside her. She didn't even know when he'd left or where he'd gone off to today.

A knock sounded at the door, and Brianna smiled. He'd come back.

"Come in," she called out in invitation. As if Trevor needed an invitation.

Sarah bustled into the room. "Glad to see you're awake. Major said to let you sleep a bit."

Brianna tried to hide her disappointment. Even the servants knew when he'd left the house. It seemed everyone but his wife knew. She clamped down on the building fissure of anger.

"I would have let you sleep, but you have a visitor downstairs." Sarah's voice brimmed with disapproval. "A very insistent visitor," she added.

"Who is it?"

"Said his name's Captain Lewis. And that you'd be wanting to see him."

"Grant." A smile broke over Brianna's face. "Please, hurry and help me dress."

"As you wish." Sarah strode to the armoire and

yanked out a gown. "It isn't proper," she muttered under her breath.

The rest of Brianna's toilette was completed in heavy silence. She could feel Sarah's disapproval. She started to explain her friendship with Grant, but thought better of it. The older woman would never understand.

A short time later, Brianna descended the stairs with Sarah close on her heels.

Grant strode out of the parlor to meet Brianna. He caught her hands in his and drew her forward to place a light kiss on her lips.

A loud cough sounded behind them. "I'll be bringing in some refreshments soon," Sarah spoke coolly.

Brianna couldn't help but smile at her mother-hen attitude. She led Grant into the parlor and took a seat in one of the wing chairs. Beside her a small table hosted a bouquet of colorful flowers.

Grant sat across from her. Leaning forward, he recaptured her hands. "Brianna? Married? I can't believe it."

"It's true."

A small smile lifted the corners of her lips. She clamped down on the grin that waited to bud as memories of last night rushed over her. She withdrew her hands from his and smoothed the folds of her skirt.

"What does Ethan say?"

Her head snapped up at the question. Pain ripped through her, but she covered it with a pale smile.

"He doesn't know yet," she answered in a low, soft voice.

He'll never know, she thought. She couldn't very

well tell the news of her marriage to his unmarked grave—wherever it was hidden.

"I . . . I haven't gotten word to him or Papa."

She flinched at the thought of her father's reaction to the news that she'd married a Union officer. Papa had held firm views on the right of the South to choose its own destiny. Ethan, ever his father's son, had shared those views in a stronger way than she'd ever imagined—until his death showed her. Now it was up to her to carry on. But how could she since the Rebel Fox had been uncovered? Of course, the answer was clear. She'd find his killer herself.

"Brianna?" Grant tapped her arm.

She started and looked into his concerned face. His concern reminded her of Ethan. Grant and her twin had been so close, like brothers. That's how she had often felt about Grant, too. He'd always been a pleasant enough escort. He couldn't help it if he didn't take her breath away with just a look the way Trevor could.

"Why, Brianna?"

She flushed guiltily at the course her thoughts had taken. What was she to answer? She hardly thought Grant wanted to hear that Trevor thought he'd forced her into marriage, or that she'd married him because it was what she wanted.

"Am I supposed to congratulate you?" he asked. The bitterness in his tone startled Brianna.

"Grant—"

"Surely you knew how I felt? I was waiting until after the war was over." He stared at her, his gaze intense.

"I'm sorry, Grant." She laid her hand on his arm.

"You were Ethan's best friend. My friend. I . . . I never thought of you in that way."

The look of pain that briefly crossed his face hurt her as well.

"I would have given you the world." Grant shook off her hand and surged to his feet. He crossed the room and leaned back on the fireplace mantel.

"He doesn't love you, you know."

The words sliced into her with the suddenness of a knife thrust.

"I'm sorry, Brianna. It's just that I've heard rumors. Did you know that McClellan's taken over?"

"Yes."

"I suppose you would've already heard. Did you know he has a reputation for promoting married men faster? Guess he must be missing his wife too much or something."

He leaned his arm on the mantel and turned his gaze to the bouquet of flowers. "Quite a stroke of . . . luck for Caldwell. You and a promotion." He laughed without humor. "Guess we'll have to wait and see how fast that promotion comes through."

Brianna paled and gripped the arms of the chair. Her fingers dug into the fabric.

Grant turned to her. "Oh, I'm sorry. I never should have said that to you." His face colored with shame. "I didn't mean to imply that's why Caldwell married you. Forgive me?"

A lump closed off her throat, preventing her from answering. Had there been any truth in what Grant had said? One part of her mind reminded her of Grant's temper; the other part whispered the fact that her husband had never yet mentioned love.

She swallowed and found her voice. "I—"

"No, I'm sorry. How could he not love you?" Grant apologized. "Anyone would."

But did Trevor, her heart questioned.

Contrite, Grant crossed to her and caught her cold hand in his. "Please forgive me, dear?"

How could she not? Grant had been Ethan's best friend and her avowed protector. She gave him a trembling smile. "Of course."

"Promise me one thing, please?"

Brianna sensed his need of her to agree and nodded.

"If you ever need anything—anything," he repeated, "you will let me know." He closed his fingers around her hand.

"Yes." Her smile became sincere.

"If he hurts you . . ." The words faded. Grant pulled her to her feet and hugged her to him. "You only have to let me know and I'll be here. Goodbye, Brianna."

He released her and strode to the door, almost knocking Sarah over as she entered the room with a tray.

"Well, I never." Sarah drew herself upright with a huff. She turned on her heel and left the room with the tray.

No matter how hard Brianna tried over the next two weeks, she couldn't put Grant's words out of her mind. The question of Trevor's real reason for marrying her ate at her relentlessly.

The days passed uneventfully. She came no closer

to finding out who had betrayed Ethan, and the inactivity nagged at her. She should be doing something. Every time she left the house she had an escort of either Sarah or Annie. She knew it was Trevor's way of keeping her from spying. She grew restless and more agitated as each day ended.

Although the days may have bored her, the nights didn't. Each night she lost herself in Trevor's lovemaking. All thought of war abandoned her, and she surrendered her heart to him in the darkness of night.

Each time they made love, she waited for him to say the words she needed so desperately. But she waited in vain. Not even the whisper of "love" passed Trevor's lips.

By the time the night of General McClellan's party arrived, Brianna was on edge. With Sarah's assistance, she had dressed in a gown of silk muslin with flounces worn as disposition. Woven embroidered bands ran across the full width of the skirt while narrow frills of the same floral pattern trimmed the fitted bodice. They emphasized the low neckline—so low it made her blush—which formed a wide, deep curve over her shoulders. Nervously she pulled up her shawl.

"No, leave it."

She whirled around at the words, her gown swinging in a small arc. Trevor leaned against the open doorway. Admiration warred with desire on his face.

Brianna knew how he felt. The dark jacket of his uniform fit his chest snugly, molding itself around his shoulders. She ached to unbutton it and release his chest to her touch.

Trevor walked with agonizing slowness toward her. She ceased to breathe as she watched his approach. Finally, she sucked air into her lungs.

"Ah, my sweet."

He pulled her to him, and she went into his arms willingly, not caring that the hoops of her skirt flew up in the back. His lips took hers in an act of possession. She clung to him, reveling in the magic of his mouth.

When he lifted his head, ending the kiss, she was filled with emptiness.

He stepped back and pulled a box out of his breast pocket. He flicked it open to reveal a perfect cameo on a velvet ribbon. Pulling it from the case, he tossed the box aside and lifted the necklace to her throat.

"May I?" His eyes burned into hers.

Brianna lifted her hair. "It's beautiful."

"Like you."

She smiled and knew he was sure to see the love reflected there. "Thank you, Trevor."

He leaned forward, placing the cameo at her throat, and fastened the ribbon behind her neck. His arms were warm on her shoulders where he'd rested them.

"Shall we go?" He stepped away and held out his arm.

She closed her fingers on it in disappointment. Damn the party, she'd much rather stay here in this room with him. Here she'd found a safe cocoon of love, and the outside world couldn't intrude. Even if he hadn't said the words yet, she knew something special was growing between them.

A chill of premonition swept over her like a faint breeze. If they left this room, something would happen to destroy the fragile bond between them. Her steps faltered.

"Can't we stay here?" she whispered the request.

Trevor stopped and stared down at her. Was that a hint of fear he heard in her voice? It couldn't be. His Brianna feared nothing and needed no one. He balled his free hand into a fist. When would she realize she needed him as much as he needed her?

"No." His voice sounded harsh even to his own ears. "This party is in our honor," he added more gently.

"Of course," Brianna said without feeling.

As he started toward the steps again, she followed him in silence. Surely this unease, this foreboding, would come to nothing. She'd make sure it did.

The carriage awaited them when they reached the door, and she wished they'd had to wait. All too soon they arrived at the general's house. It was as brightly lit as the time before. Had the dinner party really occurred less than a month ago? So much had happened.

She jumped when Trevor took her hand to help her from the carriage. She pulled her wandering thoughts back and put her hands over his. Even though he lifted her from the coach with the strictest sense of decorum, the thrill of his touch swept over her.

Scarcely had he released her when the first well-wishers approached. She'd had no idea that Trevor was so well respected and liked. Looking up at him, surrounded by his peers, she could understand why.

Once inside, General McClellan himself was the first to offer a toast. Brianna glanced around her at the predominately Yankee guests. She spotted only one or two Southern sympathizers in the midst. A sense of being out of place enclosed her. What was she doing here in the middle of her enemies?

Trevor slid his arm around her waist, and she leaned against him instinctively. The warmth of his hand penetrated her clothing and her thoughts. With it came the knowledge of being torn between two things. Her love for Trevor vied with her promise to Ethan.

She shut her mind to the battle within her. If she was to make it through this evening, she had to think on something else.

She tried to concentrate on the people around her. The guests paraded through the rooms in a sea of colors and fabrics. The Union blue of the men's uniforms stood out, so she fixed her mind on the women instead. Ivory, yellow, pale green, deep copper—the colors were endless.

Minutes later, the lilting strains of a waltz filled the room. Conversation eased to a stop.

Trevor caught her hand. "May I have this dance, Mrs. Caldwell?"

Taking her smile for consent, he led her to the dance floor. When he turned toward her, she stepped into his arms willingly. Their bodies blended together, and they moved as one.

Brianna closed her eyes and let Trevor lead her around the ballroom. His hands were strong and sure, and she had an almost overwhelming urge to rest her head on his broad chest. She drew in his scent. It seemed to envelop her—spicy and tangy and fresh.

All too soon the dance ended, and Brianna was claimed by another partner. Three more dances with three different partners passed before she pleaded thirst. Her latest partner went in search of refreshments.

Relieved to be alone for a moment, Brianna tapped her foot to the music. She let the voices around her blend together, ignoring them for the space of a few moments. Scattered words penetrated.

"Sherman . . . Kentucky."

"Grant . . . Missouri."

"Marching on . . ."

"The *Monitor's* keel was laid only last month."

Training took over, and her head snapped up. She listened to the conversations around her.

Talk of the war filled the air. It swirled and ebbed around her. For a moment Brianna wondered if the people of Washington never tired of the discussions. The war had already gone on months longer than the three months people had expected it to in the beginning. As the weather threatened to turn bad, she questioned if perhaps Trevor was right in his prediction of a long war. She shivered against the thought.

Uneasy, she glanced around the room. Instinctively she sought Trevor. Their eyes met across the distance, and he flashed her a smile. She returned it, but it widened to a grin when she saw him start in her direction.

"Congratulations, ma'am." Secretary Cameron gave his infamous thin-lipped smile.

"Thank you, sir." She returned his greeting. She'd

always admired the canny Scot, even if he was Lincoln's secretary of war.

They were joined by Gideon Welles. The secretary of the navy reminded her of Neptune with his gray wig and long gray beard.

"What's this I hear of the *Monitor?* When's steam to be applied?" a senator strolled up and asked.

Before anyone answered, Brianna felt her elbow caught in a viselike grip.

"Excuse me, gentlemen." Trevor cut into the group, never releasing his hold on her. "I'd like to steal my wife for a few minutes."

Laughter greeted his request.

He drew Brianna away from the group and strode across to an open door. She had no choice but to follow in his wake.

She tripped on the hem of her gown and jerked back. He proceeded on, his grip tightening on her arm.

"Trevor, I—"

"Shut up," he growled at her.

Open-mouthed, she stared at his profile. Anger radiated from him in waves. It reached out to enclose her.

He stepped through the terrace door and pulled her after him. Stopping abruptly, he backed her against the outside wall and faced her. He raised his hands to plant them on the wall, one hand on either side of her shoulders. He leaned forward until his face was inches from hers. Light from the doorway showed the fury he held in check.

Trepidation grew into fear that closed its icy tentacles around her heart. Something was deadly wrong.

What had happened?

"You are not to relay that information," he ordered.

"What—"

"The *Monitor,* and heaven only knows what else you enticed out of those men."

"I enticed?" She raised her chin and returned his angry glare with one of her own. She'd done nothing wrong. She wouldn't back down or cower before him.

"Yes, you—"

She knocked his arms away. "I didn't entice anything. The senator started that discussion."

Trevor's single expletive shocked her.

"You won't lie your way out of this one. I know you're up to your old tricks. Now I know why you were named the Fox."

His eyes narrowed on her, and she refused to flinch under his scorn. She met this with a look of disdain. "If you had the brains of a fox—"

"Marrying you was a mistake. Nothing's worth this." He spun around and strode away.

Chapter Twelve

Brianna had known if they left the house tonight something would happen to destroy the magic.

What magic, her mind jeered.

The air grew so still, Brianna was sure she could hear the crickets breathing. She sagged back against the outside of the house. If the wall hadn't been there, she would have fallen.

The rumors Grant had heard were true. Trevor had confirmed them with his own admission.

"Marrying you was a mistake. Nothing's worth this." His words taunted her, tortured her.

She shook with the force of the blow. Silent sobs racked her body.

Trevor didn't love her. He'd only married her for a damned promotion.

"Ma'am?"

She whirled around at the unfamiliar voice. A servant stood in the doorway. "Yes."

"The major said you were ill. He is saying your goodbyes and wanted me to see you to your carriage."

She just bet he did. As she agreed to follow the

waiting servant, she tapped down her anger. She'd save it for Trevor.

When the major joined her in the coach, the aura of suppressed fury still enveloped him. She decided to remain silent—for now. No sense in pulling on an enraged animal's tail.

The tense ride home lasted an eternity for Brianna. She bit her tongue innumerable times to keep from speaking. As soon as the carriage stopped at the house, Trevor threw open the door and dismounted, leaving her in the carriage.

Brianna sputtered her anger. He'd left her. Why, the low-down son of a—she bit off the rest of the thought. Well, let him go. She'd show him she could manage fine without him.

She attempted to clamber out of the carriage with more determination than grace. The hoops beneath her skirt had a mind of their own. First, they rose up in the front, and when she pushed them down, they flew up in the back. She flushed at the amount of skin she was surely revealing.

Finally, she gave up holding on to her dignity and let her skirts do as they pleased. She descended the carriage in a flurry of silk and petticoats.

She was breathless and madder than a. . . . She searched for a fitting phrase. She was madder than a rooster in an empty henhouse. She nodded in satisfaction and arranged her gown.

With as much shredded dignity as she could pull together, she walked up to the house and threw open the door. To her left the lights to the study shone from under the closed door. *Well, let him stay there if he wants.* She was going to bed.

Brianna mounted the stairs, her steps echoing her ire. As she swung the bedroom door open, Sarah jumped to her feet, one hand on her chest.

"Ma'am, you nearly scared the life out of me." Sarah crossed to her.

"I'm sorry. Sarah, please shut the door and help me undress." Brianna was in no mood to dawdle. She had no intention of being half-naked when Trevor walked in the room.

Minutes later, Sarah left the room muttering under her breath. "The hurry of some people."

Brianna buttoned the top two buttons of her dressing gown which had been left undone. At the feel of the covered buttons, memories of their first night together swamped over her, taking her breath away. Anger returned her breath in a rush.

If he thought he was crawling into her bed tonight, he had a surprise in store for him. Striding across the room, she dragged the straight-backed chair over and propped it against the door. She didn't entertain the idea that it would stop him, but it might make him think twice.

Smiling, she climbed into the big bed and pulled up the covers. How odd, the bed had never seemed this large before. Or this lonesome. She tossed and rolled until she found a semicomfortable position where she had a good view of the door.

It stayed closed. She lay watching the door and waiting. Her eyes became heavy, and she blinked to stay awake. Gradually, her lids closed, and she drifted into a fitful sleep.

The next morning dawned overcast with scattered clouds. The gloomy day suited her mood perfectly.

She checked the other side of the bed. It was undisturbed. Trevor hadn't come to join her. She didn't know whether to be angry or relieved.

She hopped out of bed and pulled the chair back across the room. He hadn't even tried to come in. Her pride stung from the insult. Well, she'd never let him know that it mattered. Not in the least.

An hour later, a commotion arose at the front door. Brianna rushed to see what was happening.

Harriet Devland stood in the hallway swinging her cane back and forth.

"Who do you think you are?" she accused the red-faced servant. "I will not wait to be announced."

"Aunt Harriet."

She turned at Brianna's voice. "Oh, girl, it's good to see you." She toddled over to give her a jarring hug. "Help me to a chair, will you? That nearly wore me out."

Laughter flowed from Brianna's lips for the first time that day. "Come on."

She led her aunt into the parlor. Searching the room, she located a small footstool, scooped it up, and placed it in front of a chair.

"How are you, Aunt Harriet?"

"Land's sakes. You've had a spat."

Brianna stared at her aunt in amazement. "How—"

"One look at you. That's all it took. You don't have the look of a well-loved woman. And a spat is the only thing that would stop that man."

"Aunt—"

"I'd think you would be over being shocked by me by now." She sat in a chair and eyed Brianna. "Well, what happened?"

Her aunt's concern was her undoing. Brianna sniffed once, then dissolved in tears. Her aunt waited until the flood slowed, then held out a handkerchief.

"Well, tell me about it."

"Last night at the general's party there was talk of—" She remembered Trevor's warning. "Of a Union ship. I didn't ask questions."

"Uh huh. Go on."

"I didn't do anything. Didn't ask questions like before, but he came up and overheard the talk. He said I *enticed* the information. Enticed." Anger flared briefly only to be snuffed out by hurt. "He said our marriage was a mistake."

"Humph."

"Oh, Aunt Harriet, he only married me to get a promotion."

Her aunt stamped her cane on the floor. "Are you three bricks shy, girl? Anyone with eyes can see he's crazy over you. Wanted you in his bed so bad he couldn't wait for a proper betrothal."

"No, it wasn't like—"

"Don't tell me. I have eyes. Well, what are you going to do now?"

"I—"

"Have you apologized? Explained it to him?"

"Of course not."

"Well, let me know when you've come to your senses." Aunt Harriet sprang out of the chair and crossed the room with remarkable speed.

Why did she never get the last word with her aunt? Brianna started at the slam of the door.

The rest of the day dragged on for what seemed like forever. It brought no other visitors, and Trevor didn't return until dinner.

Brianna refused to greet him lovingly. The meal passed in stiff silence with only the clatter of knives and forks for conversation. As soon as the meal ended, Trevor strode off to his study, shutting the door behind him. She stuck her tongue out at the door and climbed the stairs for bed.

Tonight she didn't bother to drag the chair to the door. He obviously didn't intend to join her this night either. Sleep finally claimed her after an hour of tossing and turning.

She woke suddenly as a shaft of light shone in the room. Sitting up, she turned to the door. Trevor stood, a lamp in one hand. Her heart knotted in her chest at the sight of him.

Without a sound, he blew out the lamp. She heard the rustle of clothing. Seconds later, she felt the bed give under his weight. She stayed stiff. Waiting.

"Brianna," he whispered.

The single word stroked her, caressed her with a siren's call. It cost her every bit of determination she possessed, but she ignored it.

Strong, yet gentle arms drew her into his embrace. Trevor's lips brushed hers once, twice, then found the hollow in her throat. In spite of herself, a tiny moan escaped her lips.

His mouth returned, capturing the sound. He nipped at her lips, teasing, tempting. When she parted them at last, he slid into her mouth. He rubbed his tongue back and forth across her teeth, then dipped into the moistness behind her teeth.

Brianna's resolve fluttered away. She raised her arms, gripping his powerful shoulders. The skin was smooth beneath her fingers, but the muscles rippled at her touch. She sighed against his mouth.

He stroked her body, sliding her gown off as his hands roamed. When there was nothing left between them but skin, he rolled her over and slid between her thighs. Their joining was intense and desperate, leaving them both shaken when it was over.

Each day followed the same pattern. They rarely saw each other or spoke during the day, but when darkness came, they surrendered to the passion between them.

As the morning sunlight filtered through the room, Brianna felt the other side of the bed as she did each morning. It was cold and empty like it had been for the last week.

She clenched her fists in the sheet. She didn't know how much more of this she could stand. Lovers by night, enemies by day.

Even Sarah had taken to barely speaking to her, obviously blaming Brianna for the rift between her and Trevor. She still helped her dress, but with sullen silence.

At lunch, Brianna picked at her food with disinterest. The lukewarm meal wasn't one of the cook's better efforts. She wondered for a moment if Sarah and the cook were in league together.

Less than an hour later, Sarah surprised Brianna with a rap on the bedroom door.

"Ma'am."

Brianna turned from the flowers she'd been arranging on the dresser.

"You have a visitor." Sarah turned abruptly and left the room before Brianna could even ask who.

Checking her appearance in the gilt mirror, Brianna tucked back a stray curl. The strain of the last week showed on her face, and she tried to pinch some color into her cheeks. Satisfied that she looked better, she crossed the room and hurried down the stairs, anxious to see who the visitor was.

As she stepped into the parlor, a feminine bundle of dark hair and pale green silk threw herself into Brianna's arms.

"Selina." Brianna returned the hug.

Her friend drew back, looked askance at her face, and said, "You look awful."

"Never one to flatter, were you?" Brianna straightened the skirt of her aqua gown. "How have you been? Come, let's sit down."

Selina caught her hand and stopped her. "I have a better idea. Let's get out of here."

"Selina."

"How about lunch at Willard's? Like we used to do?" She flashed an impish grin.

How could she refuse, Brianna thought. Especially when the idea sounded so inviting. "I'd love to go."

She felt like a criminal as they sneaked out of the house. Once in Selina's carriage, they erupted in giggles. By the time they reached the front door of Willard's Hotel, the weight of depression had slipped from Brianna's shoulders.

The moment they stepped inside the bustling hotel, center of Washington's gossip and political maneuvering, Brianna was enveloped by a roar of voices and movement. The noise welcomed her after the terse silence that reigned in the house. She grinned and looked around.

Selina caught her hand and pulled her toward the dining room. "I'm starved. Are you?"

"Yes, as a matter of fact I am." Her appetite returned with the flow of people around her.

Brianna followed on her friend's heels, anxious to savor once again the well-known fare of Willard's cooks. After they were seated at a table and had ordered, she looked around the room. The bustle and noise beckoned to her, bringing along memories.

She'd overheard many secrets here in the past. She smiled at the memory of a most productive lunch with a news correspondent. He'd given her more troop strength and movement facts than she could have gotten elsewhere in a month. Rose had been very pleased.

A frown creased Brianna's face at the thought of her friend.

"What's wrong?" Selina leaned across the table.

"I was reminiscing. What's the latest news of Rose?"

"She's doing as well as can be expected. What with being a prisoner in her own home. She's surrounded by detectives and soldiers. But, she still sneaks out messages now and then."

The delivery of their food temporarily stopped any conversation. Once they were alone again, Selina leaned forward.

"No one's seen Wilkens since Rose's arrest." Selina lowered her voice in spite of the surrounding noise. "He disappeared the day Pinkerton's men captured her."

"What?" Brianna gasped. She'd lost track of her fellow spies since the night Trevor rescued her from being captured by the soldiers.

"I'd bet he's the one."

"The one?" Brianna repeated cautiously.

"The traitor." She continued over Brianna's amazement. "Rose warned me to be careful my first night back from Boston. She told me we had a snake in our midst."

"Rose was right."

Brianna thought of Ethan, and the traitor's hand in his death. She remembered that Wilkens had been out the night she brought Ethan to Rose's house. So many things fell into place now. Why couldn't she have seen it earlier? In time to stop him?

"I'd bet he's long gone." Selina speared an oyster with her fork.

Brianna frowned. Selina was likely right. Wilkens had moved on, to another game. His latest betrayal had culminated in Rose's arrest, forcing his own departure. Everything pointed to Wilkens. Her quest was ended.

The satisfaction at finding the identity of Ethan's killer eluded her. She'd wanted a part in stopping the traitor. She deserved that much, didn't she? He'd killed Ethan as surely as if he'd put the Yankee bullet there himself.

Hatred, hot and violent, rampaged through her. The unfairness of it railed her. She'd wanted to put an end to the traitor herself.

"Brianna?"

She glanced across at her friend.

Selina toyed with her fork a moment, looked away, then faced her. "How much have your loyalties changed?" she blurted out the question.

Brianna raised her chin and returned her friend's

steady perusal. "I may be married to a . . ." She couldn't say the hated word "Yankee" aloud. "To an officer, but I am no different from before." The words came out sounding stilted even to her own ears.

"Are you sure?"

"Yes," Brianna answered without hesitation.

Although she'd stopped actively spying, her convictions hadn't changed. "I still support the Cause." She bit her lower lip. "I'm honor bound . . . to Ethan."

"I'm sure he's fighting in his own way back home."

Brianna tried not to flinch at her friend's assumption. She couldn't blame her since she didn't know the truth.

Selina knotted her hands together. "Brianna, I need your help."

Brianna's stomach lurched, then righted itself. She knew what was coming next.

"I have to get a message across."

She couldn't. The last time, Trevor had caught her and barely kept her from being captured by the soldiers. Now she was sure he had her followed. She plucked at the tablecloth.

"I can't. I'm watched. There must be someone else—"

"Not that I can reach today. You're the only one who can do it."

"You don't understand."

"I can't get anyone else right now. Lives depend on this getting through." She caught Brianna's hand and stilled her nervous movements. "A regiment has been moved out, leaving a gap in the city's defenses. Don't you see what this means?" Her voice rose.

Selina leaned closer, whispering now. "This mistake

leaves an opening for the Confederate forces. If they could capture the capital—the war would be over."

Brianna's heart jumped. The war over. The wonder of it held her speechless.

"Our forces have been waiting for this. It's our answer. Don't you see? We have to get the word across. And by someone who knows how to cross through the lines. By someone who's done it before."

Brianna closed her ears to the fear that nagged at her, whispering she'd be caught. She had to do this. She owed it to Ethan.

"Very well." Her answer carried a ring of defeat.

Selina squeezed her hand tighter, and Brianna felt the crisp edge of a square of paper between her fingers. She curled her hand around it. With natural, unhurried movements, she slid her hand from under Selina's.

As Brianna drew her hand back, she knocked her spoon onto the floor. Picking up the utensil from the carpet, she quickly slid the note into her shoe. She glanced at her friend and received a wink of confirmation.

"This is my last time."

"I understand. A disguise is waiting in the second room on your right, second floor." Selina sipped her water. "A servant is waiting to help you dress. I'll give you ten minutes; then I'll pay the bill and leave."

"No," Brianna took command. "Harvey Tillman is sitting in the corner; he'll be a perfect decoy. Go talk with him about his newspaper work. I'll slip out. In ten minutes, act like you're looking for me, pay the bill, and check the lounge. Then take the carriage and leave."

"Very well. Good luck."

Brianna hid her grimace. She had the feeling she was borrowing trouble. Her luck had already run out.

Ten minutes later, Brianna stared in open-mouthed amazement at herself in the mirror. It reflected a young soldier in a Union uniform. Her hair was hidden under her cap. Up until now, she'd always avoided the disguise of the enemy uniform. It carried too many extra dangers if she were caught.

She tugged the cap more securely on her head and gulped down her fear. With the added Union patrols watching for spies, the blue uniform offered the best chance of success. Besides, this was the last time, she reminded herself.

Brianna slipped through the posted sentries with surprising ease. The blue uniform provided access as if by magic. So far the trip had taken less than two hours. She'd passed the lines into Confederate territory mere minutes ago. Nervously, she fingered the uniform buttons. Maybe she should take off the jacket now. She wore a white blouse beneath. She'd unfastened the top button when a sound to her left alerted her.

Diving to the side, she crouched behind a tree. The sound drew nearer. She tensed as it continued to approach.

Silence fell. Brianna stayed hidden, waiting. A twig snapped, and she jumped. If a Rebel soldier found her now, he might shoot her on sight.

She squeezed her eyes tightly shut, willing the sentry away. Another twig snapped. The footsteps stopped even with her. Swallowing, she opened her eyes, turned her head, and stared into the wide eyes of a deer.

The animal leapt off and ran in the opposite direction. Brianna laughed with relief. A deer. Only a deer. She laughed until she had to hold her sides.

Even Trevor would see the humor in this. Her laughter died on her lips.

"Trevor," she whispered.

He'd be furious with her for going on this mission. For spying. But this would end the war sooner.

The boom of a cannon echoed in the far distance—a reminder that a battle raged within a couple of miles of her. A much larger one would rock the capital after she delivered her message.

She buried her head in her hands. How many lives would her message cost? Maybe Trevor was right that the spies only lengthened the war. Her heart leapt. Trevor. What of Trevor? He'd been reassigned since their marriage, but he hadn't spoke of his duties. In fact, he hadn't talked of military matters at all. She lowered her hands. The message she was carrying, the battle it would bring—it could endanger Trevor.

A chill flowed throughout her body. Another boom resounded. She closed her hands over her ears, trying to shut out the sound, but she couldn't stop the pictures that formed in her mind. Trevor, wounded or dead because of her.

No, she closed her eyes. She couldn't do it. She couldn't endanger the man she loved.

Dazed, she stood and made her way back the direction she'd come. She trudged along, torn by the two sides of her decision.

"Halt, or I fire," a soldier called out.

Brianna froze where she was standing. Without Rose's help, she lacked any official papers to show. She turned around and stared open-mouthed at a soldier. He wore a blue uniform. Blue, not gray.

"Hey, boys. I think we got ourselves a Rebel," he shouted.

How had he known? What had given her away?

The sound of approaching soldiers rang in her ears. She had to get out of here.

Brianna spun around, and her heart dove for her toes. Rifles centered on her. As if hypnotized, she counted them. Five. She fought the impulse to run. She knew with certainty the rifles aimed at her would cut her down if she moved. Fear held her immobile.

Her heart returned to pound against her rib cage. Luck had deserted her with a brutal vengeance.

"Take him to the colonel." A sergeant stepped forward.

He shoved Brianna in the other direction, and her hat fell forward over her face. Several strands of hair slithered to her shoulders.

She knew it was too late to try and tuck her loosened hair up under the cap. A second later, the sergeant grabbed the cap in one hand and pulled it off. Her hair tumbled down around her face and shoulders.

"A woman spy." He shoved the cap back on Brianna's head. "Get her out of here."

This couldn't be happening, Brianna thought. But the rifle poking in her back was all too real.

At the camp, she was led to the commander's tent. Head high, she faced the officer. He stood close to six foot and looked weary. Streaks of gray shot through his brown hair. At first glance he seemed like the grandfatherly sort, but one look at his thin, mirthless smile warned her.

"Sir," the sergeant reported. "We caught this woman sneaking around. She didn't know the password. And she's wearing the blue."

"I can see that, Sergeant."

"What do you want me to do with her, Colonel Chambers."

Brianna paled at the name. She'd heard many tales of Colonel Chambers. His hatred of Southern women and the Confederacy was legendary. Luck had more than abandoned her. It had turned on her.

Under the colonel's questioning, she fell silent, refusing to answer. Her actions enraged him. For a moment, she thought he would strike her.

"Search her. Take her boots and hat and tear them apart. If you don't find anything, come back and strip her. I want to know what message is so all-fired important."

The men jumped to follow his orders, dragging Brianna off. After a degrading hand search, they took her shoes and hat, then bound her. A guard was posted.

The ropes cut into her wrists, but she ignored the pain. Fear and despair alternated within her. They would surely find the note—the proof they needed to declare her a spy and convict her. They might even hang her because of her stolen Yankee uniform. The lump in her throat threatened to close off her air.

Each minute stretched out into the next. A flurry of activity across the camp alerted her. A group of men came toward her, Colonel Chambers in the lead. The soldiers behind him muttered in lowered tones. All fell silent when the colonel stopped in front of Brianna.

"Look what I have here." The colonel held up the pieces that until a few minutes ago had been her boot. In his other hand, he grasped the folded message.

Chapter Thirteen

Brianna paced the confines of her cell. The stone floor was cold beneath her sock-clad feet.

She looked around the small room deep inside Old Capitol Prison, and a chill of fear shook her. She rubbed her hands up and down her arms. The wool jacket was coarse under her fingers.

They'd left her in the Yankee uniform, shoeless. Her boots and the folded note had been retained as proof of her guilt. She resumed her pacing. If she paused to reflect on her possible fate, she'd go mad. If Colonel Chambers had his wish, she would surely hang. It was like a nightmare come to life, and she couldn't wake up from it.

She didn't know how long ago Colonel Chambers had delivered her here. It had been several hours at least. She'd watched the light from the tiny, high window in the room change from bright to golden to darkness.

At first, she'd held the fear at bay by assuring herself that Trevor would come. He'd saved her twice before. He'd save her again.

She'd rehearsed over and over what she'd say to him. In her mind, he'd understand. He'd forgive her when he knew she'd been caught saving him. He'd take her home to the safety of his love.

Hour after hour passed, and he didn't come. She feared he didn't care enough to save her this time. Would he ever know she'd turned around to save him or would she hang before he knew the truth?

Fear caught in her throat, and she couldn't swallow. She could almost feel the rough rope around her neck. She forced herself to breathe naturally, and to hold on to her one hope.

Trevor would come to save her. She recited the phrase over in her mind like a litany. He had to.

Damn her. Trevor stood outside the cell door, fists clenched. Fury surged through his body, and he tried to control it. If he didn't, he knew he'd be tempted to see how his hands felt around her throat. Her betrayal ate at him.

White-hot anger flooded over him in torrents. With it came the memories of loving Brianna. His breath hissed through his teeth in ragged jerks.

"Damn you, Brianna," he whispered. "For you've surely damned me."

When word of her arrest had reached General McClellan, he'd immediately summoned Trevor to his office and given him an ultimatum. Brianna had been sentenced to hang. The sentence could be reversed only if Trevor swore to personally deliver Brianna across the lines. It was his to choose.

Choice, he scoffed. She'd destroyed any choice they might have had. He'd hoped against hope that someday she'd come to love him. Now it was too late.

Forcibly, he shoved all thought of their lost future aside. He was here to take his wife home, and see she didn't escape before he sent her out of his life. If he put her across the lines, she'd only find a way to resume her spying. Next time he wouldn't be able to stop the hangman's noose. The only choice he had was to send her far away—to England.

He didn't know where he'd find the strength to send her away from him. But he had to. For the life of him, he hadn't been able to devise an alternate plan.

Trevor called the guard and stood aside while he unlocked her cell door. It took all his concentration to prepare himself for the meeting he faced.

She spun around when the cell door opened. Like a man ready to die of thirst, Trevor drank his fill of her. She stood proud before him in spite of the fear reflected in her eyes. Red-gold curls framed her pale face and tumbled down her back. They gave her the look of an angel—a look he knew to be a lie.

Even dressed as she was in the breeches and coat of a soldier, the fact she was a woman couldn't be denied. The pants fit her snugly, emphasizing each curve he knew so well. He didn't trust himself to speak. He stood silently, watching her every move.

Brianna blinked against the bright lamplight.

Trying to see through the halo of light, she made out the figure of a man. A tall man.

She narrowed her eyes, trying to see better. He stood silent, waiting it seemed. Her vision cleared, and she recognized Trevor.

The next instant, she flew across the floor and threw herself into his arms.

"I knew you'd come," she whispered, her voice hoarse from her fears.

She clung to him tightly. A moment later she felt him stiffen under her hold. A chill like an icy hand scraped down her back.

"Trevor?"

Silence engulfed the room. It was worse than the darkness had been.

"Trevor?" Brianna trembled and caught his arms. She clung to him tightly.

He pushed her from him.

"Trevor, I can explain—"

"Not here." His voice was as carefully controlled as the anger that radiated from his body.

Brianna stared at him. He was a stranger. He stood before her, cold and rigid. If he were any stiffer, he would snap in two. Despair reached out its tentacles for her.

"I know you think you have a right to be angry," she spoke quickly. If she kept talking, he would surely listen. He would have to.

"I said not here." His hard voice brooked no arguments.

A tiny hope flickered, unwilling to be snuffed out. Perhaps he only meant that this wasn't the place to talk. Brianna grasped this minuscule hope with her whole being. Of course not here. That's what he'd said over and over. He was protecting her, keeping her from confessing anything the prison guards could overhear. She strove to convince herself.

Deep inside she knew she was lying to herself. But she needed that lie. She grabbed hold of it tightly and refused to relinquish it. Trevor had come for her. Everything would be all right.

She pressed her lips tightly together as if to keep the flicker of hope safe within.

"You're to come home with me."

A brilliant smile lit her face. "I'm going home. With you."

"This is not my choice."

His grim look of disgust silenced anything else she might have said. Slowly, the glimmer of hope she'd held to was snuffed out. A chill, like a January wind, enveloped her inch by inch. She followed him from her prison cell in numb resignation.

He'd only married her to keep her true identity secret and for his damned promotion. She'd spiked both for him. It gave her no thrill of victory. Only a hollow feeling of defeat filled her.

The distance between them grew through the carriage ride home. She might as well have been alone in the coach for all the notice he gave. An unsettling fear of the future haunted her.

The wheels rolled through the rutted streets. The monotonous clacky-clack lulled her in spite of her unease. Her head nodded, and she jerked up. With all the strength of will she possessed, Brianna held herself upright. She would never collapse before him.

The silent ride culminated at the house. This time Trevor helped her from the coach, but he did it with a determined and firm detachment. There was no sensuous sliding of his body against hers. The instant her feet touched the ground, he released her and stepped away.

The chill of his attitude toward her frightened Brianna. It was as if he had no feelings at all. Wary of opening a conversation, she followed his lead into the house.

Trevor closed the door behind them. "We'll talk upstairs." He turned away as if he didn't care if she followed him up the stairs or not.

The steps had never seemed so endless to Brianna before now. Their bedroom door stood open, and a lamp lit the room in preparation of their arrival. She stepped into the room and glanced around.

The naked bed caught her attention instantly. She stared at it. Even the brown panels and satin ties had been removed. She turned to Trevor in puzzlement.

"What—"

"I won't be sleeping here tonight."

His words startled her. She knew she should be thankful for her release from prison, but she couldn't say the words. Not when he faced her like this. A cold anger such as she'd never seen in him before shut him off from her.

"I'm going out." He turned away from her. "I'll speak with you in the morning."

"Where are you going?" The question rushed out before she could stop it.

Trevor hesitated, then looked back at her. "To find more pleasant and trustworthy companionship. You needn't worry—I'll be warm and comforted."

Brianna felt as if she'd been slapped. He was going to the arms of another woman.

"Go ahead. Go to her."

"If I am, you can have the assurance that I'm going to a woman who doesn't dress like my men."

She struck out in instinctive retaliation for the hurt.

"Go ahead. Why shouldn't you? Maybe she can get you the promotion you can't get yourself. The one you married me for."

He gave a mirthless laugh. "You don't believe that."

"It's true."

"Brianna." He said her name wearily, as if he'd tired of the discussion.

"Don't deny it."

"Marriage to you has cost me a promotion. More than that, it may cost me my position and self-respect." He turned away and stared out the window at nothing. "I married you because I loved you."

Brianna's mouth dropped open. Her heart soared at his admission, and she reached out her hand. "You love me?"

His next words brought both heart and hand

crashing down. "I said I *loved* you. It's over. You destroyed that with your constant betrayal."

"Trevor, I—"

"Don't. I don't want to hear it. It's over."

Brianna took a tentative step forward. In a flash, he grabbed her shoulders, halting her. She felt none of the warmth she associated with his touch. Cold—forbidding cold—emanated from him in icy waves.

Trevor set her from him. "You damn fool. Wearing a Union uniform. How long did you think I could keep protecting you, Brianna?" He slammed his fist against the wall. "It's all over. I'm putting you on a boat for England tomorrow."

Her world crashed down around her with the ferocity of a twister. "England?"

"Yes. I want you as far away from here as I can get you."

She gasped at the harshness of his words. She was to be banished from him, from her country, from all she held dear.

"Trevor, don't do this. I beg you." She clutched his sleeve.

He removed her hand with deliberate movements. "Don't push me. I could have let you hang. Instead the sentence has been reversed."

"I . . ."

"And don't try escaping. I'd hate to see your pretty, deceptive neck broken. I've had the linens removed so you can't use the window."

Not waiting for her answer, he strode out of the room. For the first time, Brianna heard a key turn in the lock.

At the sound, something within her snapped. The shock and sense of loss that had held her immobile released her. He was sending her away to England. A flood of tears threatened to choke her. It was over between them. She covered her face with her hands and gave into the hot, salty tears, grieving for what she'd lost.

A heavy sense of hopelessness swept over her. She'd lost Trevor—as surely as if she'd killed him. She'd killed their love.

She couldn't wait around for his return, wait for him to send her away. The room's memories engulfed her: the enameled tub; the first time they'd made love in this room. The sight of one of Trevor's shirts tossed carelessly across a chair brought fresh tears to her eyes.

She couldn't stay. He'd made that clear. And she wouldn't meekly be put on a boat or sail out of his life. She'd not leave her country willingly.

A desperate plan formed. She could make it across the lines without his help or knowledge. She'd been doing it successfully for months. The time had come for one final trip south.

Crossing to the window, she glanced down. The ground fell steeply before her. She'd likely break her neck in a jump. It would save Trevor the satisfaction of sending her away, but she wasn't a quitter.

She whirled away from the window and circled the room like a caged animal. No way of escape presented itself. She paced back and forth for the better part of thirty minutes before the seed of an idea caught hold.

"Could it work?" she asked in a whisper.

She rushed to the armoire. Her gowns still hung inside. She grabbed up an armful and carried them to the bed. Once there, she released her bundle. The gowns fell to the bed in a sea of color. Searching through the clothes, she pulled out her dark blue riding habit.

It took a surprisingly short time to change from the hated uniform to the velvet riding habit. She crossed to the armoire and pulled out her boots. Instead of putting them on, she set them to the side. Later.

Brianna returned to the armoire. Step by step, she emptied it. Pawing through the clothing she separated the items she would need into a small pile.

She needed one thing more. Back to the armoire she went. There it was. She drew out a small travelling case. Not too heavy, but it would hold what she'd need.

As soon as she'd packed, she set the case beside her boots and returned to the clothes-laden bed. She gathered up two gowns, tying the arms together.

She tugged on the dresses and smiled when they didn't give way. Her idea would work.

She picked up another gown, tied it to the two, then reached for the next one on the stack. Her chain grew. She paused to test each new link.

Satisfied at last with the length and sturdiness,

she looped one end around the bed and tied the arms of the first gown to the bedpost. She carried the remainder of her makeshift rope to the window, opened it and tossed the clothes out. They fell downward in a graceful arc and came to rest against the building.

She leaned out and looked down. The last garment barely touched the ground. A knot rose in her throat. What if the makeshift rope gave way? What if. . . .

She refused to consider the possible flaws in her plan. She refused to go to England. She was going home—home to Tennessee—and nothing would stop her.

Allowing herself one last glance around the room, Brianna grabbed up her case and pushed it through the window. It landed with a thud. Next, she pulled on her boots, fastened her cloak, and climbed onto the window ledge. *Let it work, please,* she prayed.

Brianna grabbed the clothes rope with both hands and slipped out the window. She hung suspended in air. Emptiness grabbed at her feet, and she kicked frantically, trying to find a toehold. Her foot connected with the side of the house, and she clung to the rope. Hand over hand, she lowered herself, hardly daring to breathe. At any moment she expected to hear the sound of ripping garments and plummet to the ground.

At last her feet touched the earth. She wanted to bend over and kiss the dirt. Instead, she released her deathlike grip on the rope and turned her back on the house.

Wishing she dared stop to say goodbye to Aunt Harriet, Brianna knew she couldn't. She'd have to wait until she was safe in Tennessee before she sent word. With resolution she picked up her case and turned toward the woods surrounding Washington.

Trevor tossed back another swallow of brandy. The amber liquid had long ago ceased burning on the way down. He'd tried many a night to bury himself in drink in the month since Brianna left.

"Brianna." He whispered her name almost reverently.

The dimly lit study echoed back the hiss of her name.

He stared at the far wall, and a picture of a temptress with red-gold hair and luscious lips formed before him. Eyes as blue as calm water beckoned him. How well he remembered those eyes darkening in passion when he caressed her smooth skin and ripe breasts. His temptress held out her arms to him. Unable to stop himself, any more than he could stop breathing, he stood and took a step.

The picture vanished into cold reality. With it the numbness of the brandy.

Trevor threw the glass against the wall. It shattered, the brown liquid running down the wall in crooked streams. He rubbed his hands across his face.

He ached. It had been a month since he'd held her in his arms. A month of hell. He ached for her and knew it was more than desire.

She was the other half of himself. He'd loved her from the beginning, but hadn't realized it until it was too late. He'd been unable to stop the best part of himself from fleeing in the dark of night.

Why hadn't he told her the truth? That her name had been placed on a special list of dangerous persons. One slip of any kind guaranteed her death at the hangman's hand.

Instead he'd allowed hurt and despair to drive him from her that night. Her betrayal had cut him to his core. She'd vowed to never love him; now he knew she'd meant it. She'd kept that vow. If she'd cared the smallest amount for him, she'd never have continued spying. This last time she'd been carrying information on the defense of Washington.

He dropped his hands and leaned his head back against the top of the chair. Where was she? Was she safe? His mind refused to accept the possibility that she was dead. Not knowing ate at him.

Even Aunt Harriet blamed him for Brianna's disappearance. Rightly so, he admitted. He'd gone to the elderly woman, had asked for Brianna, and been told she wasn't there. He believed her. How could he not when he'd witnessed the anguish on Harriet's face when he told her of Brianna's disappearance?

He hadn't even been able to learn the location of Brianna's father from her aunt. The little woman had given him a severe dressing down, ending with calling him all kinds of a fool for not stopping

Brianna from leaving.

Since the day of that first visit, he'd heard a sermon from Aunt Harriet on a weekly basis. Couldn't she understand that a Union officer couldn't just up and go off to Tennessee looking for a rebellious wife? He'd definitely get himself shot or captured if he tried. Not that he'd been much of a soldier since the night Brianna left.

Trevor lunged out of the chair and crossed to the liquor cabinet for another drink. Harriet Devland and her foolish notions. He poured a generous portion of brandy in the glass and gulped it down. His throat caught fire, and the inferno raged all the way to the pit of his stomach.

Tears streamed down his cheeks. He gasped for air. He'd been a fool for tossing down good brandy that way. Almost as bad a fool as he'd been to lose Brianna, his heart jeered.

He set the glass down and stared over the room. Maybe there was a way for a soldier to find his wife. He leaned back against the wall and planned.

Chapter Fourteen

Chattanooga, Tennessee
Spring, 1862

Brianna held the tin cup of water and helped the young soldier to drink. Gently, she eased him back down on the cot. He was scarcely older than she.

"Rest a while. I'll be back to change your bandage later," she promised.

The all too frequent sound of artillery fire rumbled in the distance. She froze a minute, listening. It was a ways off, and not too intense. Another skirmish. There'd be more wounded by sundown from it. No matter how small the battle, it always took lives.

The fighting seemed to be all around them. Even Shiloh had fallen to the Union. Johnston had bled to death after the battle. Good men were dying on both sides in greater and greater numbers.

A picture of Trevor filled her mind. Was he safe? He had to be. She held to that conviction.

Brianna continued on to the next bed. One

glance at the man's ashen face confirmed her fears. The sergeant would not make it through the afternoon. After giving him a sip of water, she sponged the man's forehead. He burned with fever.

As she straightened, he caught her hand in his and struggled to sit up.

"Sally? Is that you, Sally?" he asked. His voice faded away, and he stilled.

Brianna fought her gathering tears as she eased her hand from his motionless fingers. She'd never get used to the suddenness and finality of death. It haunted the makeshift hospital like a specter. She'd done what she could to help during these last two months since she'd come home, but it was never enough.

Lifting the sheet over the dead soldier's face, she turned away from the cot. There were others who needed her more.

A low moan from the other row of cots drew her attention. She crossed over to the wounded man. The stench of vomit hit her, and she attempted to ignore it. Too weak to sit up, he had retched all over his shirt and the sheet.

"Everything's going to be fine," she assured him. "You'll feel much better after you're clean again. Do you feel like a sip of water?"

She held the cup to his cracked lips. He drank greedily. She drew the cup away.

"Easy. That's enough for now. I'll go and get you those clean sheets."

She rolled up the top sheet and took it with her to the back of the room. She'd never been squeamish, and she wasn't about to start now.

In a moment she returned with fresh linens. Once she'd finished and had the man settled, she carried the remainder of the soiled linens away.

"I'll take that. Lose another one?" a gentle voice asked.

Brianna turned to meet the concerned gaze of Rachel Crane. Her bright red hair coiled atop her head like a coronet. Intelligent green eyes that too often reminded her of Trevor shined in a startling, beautiful face. Her open acceptance and friendship had been a healing balm.

"Does it ever get any easier?" Brianna asked of the friend who'd taught her all she could about nursing in the last two months.

"Don't think so. Why don't you go on outside for a spell?"

"Will you join me?"

"Yeah, I will."

The women sat together under the shade of a tree. The warm sunlight of early spring bathed the earth while the low thunder of battle rolled in the distance, a striking contrast to the beauty of the day.

"Honey, when are you going to quit pining for that man and do something about it?"

Brianna leaned her head against the broad tree trunk. She and Rachel had few secrets between them. The long, hard hours tending the sick inspired confidences.

"Oh, Rachel. I wish to heaven I could."

Dreams of Trevor and the magic of his touch haunted many of her nights, robbing her of sleep. Often she woke in a sweat.

"But, you know it's not that easy. Don't forget he was going to send me away from my country." *And him,* she added silently. That part hurt the most of all. "I can't forgive him for that," Brianna whispered.

"You never know until the time comes what you can forgive a man for."

"I know."

"Honey, if you don't take life by the hand, it's going to pass you by."

Better to pass her by and leave her alive, Brianna thought. She still had nightmares of the hangman's noose tightening around her neck.

She picked up a leaf and slowly shredded it. Trevor didn't want her anymore. He'd made that abundantly clear.

"It wouldn't do any good." She tossed the remains of the crumpled leaf onto the ground. "It's over. And besides, if I go back to Washington, they'll complete the hanging sentence."

"Honey, I sure am sorry. I wish things could work out for you."

"A Yankee and a Rebel spy. Maybe it never stood a chance."

"Listen here, when you're in love, color of the uniform don't matter. The heart can't see what color a man's wearing."

Memories of a similar conversation with Aunt Harriet swamped over Brianna. If only there were some way to make it right between her and Trevor. The only way that could possibly happen would be if the past hadn't happened. She'd meant it when she'd said she couldn't forgive him for his plan of banishing her to England. He'd wanted her out of his life forever.

"Have you heard from Brett?" Brianna changed the too-painful conversation to her friend's concerns.

A wide grin lit Rachel's face. "Got a letter yesterday when I got home. He's safe. He's gone to California and is putting in for a stake there. In about a year, I'm going to join him." She stood and brushed the dust from her skirt. "And you'd better believe nothing's going to stop me from going to my man."

Rachel reached down and pulled Brianna to her feet. "Take a lesson from that, honey. And think on it some."

Brianna kept recalling Rachel's words throughout the remainder of the day. If only her path could be so clear.

At last, she left the hospital and its ever-present smell of death behind her and started the walk home. She enjoyed this part of the day. The warm glow of sunset never failed to soothe her after her time at the hospital. The walk to their home on the outskirts of town took her over half an hour, but she needed every moment of the solitude and the memories of Trevor it brought.

Her father stood at the door of the large house, waiting, as he did each day. The sight of James Devland in his tailored clothes brought back memories of happier times. Horseback rides, picnics, hours at Papa's secret fishing place, and even a birthday circus—signs of caring from an indulgent father. His indulgence had only been tempered by Aunt Harriet's sternness on her annual visits.

He'd been the best father anyone could ask for. Brianna had never known her mother, who'd died giving birth. Papa had been both parents.

How often through the years had he stood at the same door calling her and Ethan? Life had been so simple before Papa had become Senator Devland three years ago. Before Washington, before the election, before the war. She and Ethan had been inseparable. Now it felt strange to hear only her name called. Brianna dug up a smile for his benefit.

"It doesn't do any good." He looked down at her with love.

"What?"

"That smile. I can see right through it and you, too. Always could."

This time her smile was genuine.

"Was it rough today?" he asked.

"Yes."

"Thought so. A hot bath is waiting for you. Go on upstairs. We'll talk later if you feel like it."

She planted a kiss on his leathery cheek. "Thanks. What did I ever do to deserve you?"

"Why, you got born, girl." He patted her shoulder and shooed her upstairs.

Over dinner, her father fell serious. "Have I ever told you how happy I am to have you home?"

"No." Brianna swallowed the bite of golden cornbread she'd taken.

"Well, I am." He reached across the table and patted her hand. "I never should have left you behind in Washington. I thought you'd be safer there."

"I understand."

"I thought Harriet could keep you out of trouble. I should have known better. If I'd used better sense, maybe I'd have both my children home now."

His words struck her like a blow. She stared at him. Her father looked as hurt as she felt. It was time to put her pain aside and help him with his.

"Don't blame yourself. No one could've stopped Ethan from doing what he felt was right. If we'd come home, he would've enlisted."

"Maybe you're right." The lines on his face cleared a little.

"You know I am."

Brianna smiled across at him. His hair had grayed while they'd been apart, and he still had to be careful not to exert himself; but his body had healed. She'd feared what the news of Ethan's death would do to him. Her father had at first appeared to crumple before the news, but he'd rallied and gone off for a walk alone. When he'd returned, he'd held her and shared their grief.

"Jeff Davis wants me to join his cabinet."

Her father's announcement startled her. "What? When?"

"As soon as I can. Will you come with me?" He waited for her answer.

Brianna stared at him a moment. Could she face going back to Virginia? Being that close to Washington and Trevor?

"Well? What will it be?" Her father's eyes twinkled with love and a little excitement.

She could tell that he couldn't wait to go back into politics. She couldn't refuse him—any more than she'd been able to say no to Ethan. *And look where that had got her.*

"Of course I'll go," she answered with a false smile. "When do we leave?"

"In a week's time. Or less, if we can get everything closed up here."

"I'll tell them at the hospital tomorrow morning." She pushed her plate away. "I think I'll try to get some sleep. There was a skirmish today—a distance away. We'll be sure to still have more wounded tomorrow from it." She rubbed her hands over her arms. "It never ends, does it?"

One glance at her father's face confirmed that he no longer believed the war would be but a few months long. Trevor had been right.

The thought of him sent a pain through her. It was still there—the pain. It hadn't lessened at all since the night she'd fled. She missed him so much it was almost unbearable. Where was he right now? Was he all right?

Trevor reined his horse in. The air was crisp and cool with just a hint of woodsmoke from a campfire in the distance. Faint strains of music drifted across the night, but it didn't lend a peaceful feeling. Together the smoke and music confirmed the apprehension he'd been feeling for the last half hour. He'd steered too near the Confederate camp outside Chattanooga.

The moon shone brightly, giving no excuse for his error. If he'd concentrated more on reaching his own Union camp and less on Brianna Devland Caldwell, he wouldn't have strayed so far.

Was she still here? Could he convince her to return home with him?

He knew there were ways a person could get a message to someone in town. And he planned to do just that as soon as he reached the Union camp.

Thoughts of her had helped to push the horror

of Shiloh from his mind since the battle. He brought his mind back to his present task. He should have known better than to risk coming this close to town in order to avoid the pickets. The information he carried from General Halleck was too important to endanger it. He patted the saddlebag, checking to see it was still securely fastened and the papers safe inside.

Now all he could do was hope to skirt the Rebel site without being spotted by the pickets. It would be a tedious job. His horse was built for distance, not for silence.

Leaves and twigs snapped underfoot. Trevor eased his mount onward, trying to stay near the center of the rugged path. In the moonlit night, his blue uniform shone a beacon to any watchful sentries.

Trevor leaned low over the saddle, one hand on the reins, the other on his pistol. Every new sound took on the pose of a threat. Capture now would mean death or a Confederate prison. He didn't know which one would be worse.

Either would keep him from Brianna. It had taken him months and more battles than he could count to get this close to her. He wasn't about to give up without one hell of a fight.

If he could make it past this far edge of the Rebel camp, he'd be safe. The pickets wouldn't come out much past this point for fear of running into Union sentries.

Trevor began to relax his hold on the reins. Almost there. The neighing of a horse to his right alerted him, but it came too late. He'd already been spotted by the pickets.

Shouts broke the night calm. Damn, he'd been so close to making it. Four mounted riders galloped for him. He sent his own horse racing through the night. The sounds of pursuit resounded behind him.

Trevor urged the horse on, all his hopes pinned on the stallion's great speed. Flecks of mud rose from the horse's hooves.

As he glanced over his shoulder, his horse stumbled on the rough terrain, almost throwing him. He slowed his mount. He'd only be worse off if his horse threw him. Damn. The Confederate pickets were closing in on him.

Trevor jerked on the reins, and the stallion wheeled to the left through the border of trees. At the jerky motion, Trevor's breath whistled through his clenched teeth.

He cursed his own stupidity. In trying to stay out of sight, he'd gotten too close to the Confederate camp ringing Chattanooga.

The shouts behind him intensified, and a shot whizzed past him to thud into a nearby tree. Another shot echoed, and he bit back the cry of pain as the ball sliced into the meaty flesh above his shoulder blade.

Leaning low and gripping the horse's mane, he

begged the stallion for just a little more speed. His horse pulled ahead with a good lead. Maybe. . . . Trevor sucked in a breath, and pain stabbed through his chest, stealing the breath back.

His grip on the coarse hair between his fingers loosened. Before he could seize the mane again, he shifted in the saddle. As he struggled to stay astride and right himself, his mount reared. Trevor grabbed for a hold and missed. He hit the ground with a cry of pain.

Dazed, he blinked and looked around. His horse galloped out of sight. To his left a large clump of brush lay in the shadows. Gritting his teeth against the burning pain, he rolled to the dark cover. He gave himself a second to catch his breath from the exertion, then crawled into the concealment of the undergrowth.

He yanked off his kerchief, wadded it up and pressed it against the back of his shoulder to staunch the flow of blood. Warm, sticky liquid trickled over his fingers, and he tightened his grip on the hastily fashioned bandage spread across the wound.

The thundering of approaching hoofbeats alerted him. He pressed himself deeper into the brush and waited. The riders galloped past. After several minutes of silence, he pushed himself upright. The world spun around him.

He was so tired. After what he'd seen and been through at Shiloh, he was weary of the war and all it had to bring. But if it hadn't been this campaign he'd been involved in, it would have been another just like it. War engulfed the nation. It had for a year and would continue to do so. Sleep beckoned to him, tantalizing him with welcome darkness and peace.

"Brianna," he whispered, aching for her as he had since the night she left.

Darkness threatened, and he fought it almost violently. *The saddlebag.* Instinctively he reached out for it; but the darkness won, and he sank to the ground.

Brianna inhaled the early morning air. Although the day promised to be warm, she was glad she'd worn her cloak against the morning chill.

She'd refused her father's offer to escort her to the hospital. She needed the peace and quiet of her morning walk to prepare her for the day ahead. The hours would be filled with too many moans of pain. She relished the peaceful silence around her and drew strength from it.

She took her usual route, veering around the outskirts of town. She smiled and waved her greeting to the group of soldiers stationed to guard the main crossing.

A short distance later, she heard what sounded like a moan. She stopped and listened. Very few people were out yet, and virtual silence reigned.

She waited and strained to hear the sound again. Nothing.

She'd gotten used to hearing too many moans at the hospital, Brianna chided herself. Now she heard them everywhere. She started off for the hospital.

There it was again. She froze in place. She'd recognize a groan of a man in pain anywhere, and what she'd heard had been just that.

The groan came again. Brianna cocked her head and listened, trying to trace the sound. It seemed to be coming from a clump of bushes near the old deserted slave cabin.

She crossed over to the brush. Sure enough, one boot-clad foot stuck out from under the leaves. She'd bet it was a soldier from one of the camps outside town. Likely, he'd had too much drink last night and was suffering the after effects this morning. The bright sunlight would add to his discomfort considerably.

It would serve him right if she left him. She really should, but she couldn't. Even a soldier recovering from a drunk needed some compassion. He might even have injured himself last night.

She bent down and pushed the branches aside. The man lay facedown on the ground. From the back of his head to well past his shoulder was covered with a copper-colored stain.

Blood, so much blood. The poor man was covered with it. She pulled back and had to draw up her strength to touch him again. Was he even still alive?

She pressed her fingers against his neck and felt the beat of a pulse. Weak, but steady.

Afraid to roll him over until she knew the extent of his injuries, she left him on his stomach. She checked for the wound, careful not to cause him more pain. As she touched above his shoulder, fresh moisture soaked her fingertips.

She pulled her hand back. It was covered with blood. She immediately felt under his chest for an exit wound. There wasn't any. That meant that the ball was still in him. He'd need attention right away. She'd send a hospital litter back for him.

Gently she brushed the dust and leaves off his sleeve. A touch of blue was visible. She caught back her cry of alarm. Beneath the dirt and blood was a Yankee blue uniform.

What on earth was a Yankee doing here? The fool man. After he received treatment at the hospital, he'd be taken to prison. She shuddered at the stories she'd heard about the prisons on both sides of the war.

Gently, she rolled the injured man over onto his back. Leaves stuck to his face from his night on the ground. She took out her lace handkerchief and brushed the leaves off.

Dark stubble covered his chin. His lips were crusted and dry. Above them was a mustache. A shiver ran through her.

She was acting foolishly. She forced herself to sit back on her heels and draw in several deep breaths to clear her mind.

No, it couldn't be. It couldn't, she repeated.

Cautiously, she brushed aside the remaining leaves, afraid of what they might reveal.

"Trevor." Brianna mouthed the word, but no sound came out.

A whistle pierced the morning stillness. She jerked, recognizing the sound of the "Bonnie Blue Flag" that signalled the approach of the Confederate sentries.

Horror suddenly struck Brianna, leaving her immobilized.

Chapter Fifteen

The whistled strains of the Confederate song grew louder. Nearer. The men were only blocks away.

Brianna looked around. She had to hide Trevor. She couldn't let the soldiers capture him. With his wound, he'd never survive.

Frantic, she sought an escape. The sentries strode nearer with each wasted moment.

She hugged Trevor close to her breast. She wouldn't let him be taken, she vowed.

From the corner of her eye, she spotted the old slave cabin and murmured a prayer of thanks. The cabin had been deserted even before the war. If she could only get him inside.

She caught his arms and tried to lift him. She couldn't.

"Trevor, wake up." She patted his cheek. "I need you to try and help me."

He didn't respond. She struggled with his inert body. Despair rose up, but she refused to listen to it. She'd be damned if she'd give up.

Ignoring the blood and the additional pain she

might cause, she caught him under the armpits and pulled. Her muscles strained, and his body moved. Only a few inches, but she'd moved him. She smiled triumphantly.

Brianna blew her hair out of her eyes, and pulled again. This time she dragged him farther. She glanced over her shoulder. The cabin still lay a fair distance away.

She filled her chest with air, braced her feet, and pulled with all her strength. Her shoulders and arms screamed out from the strain, but she kept going. The gap between them and the cabin closed.

At last she bumped into the outside wall. She kicked the door open, refusing to release her hold on Trevor. If she let go, she'd never have the strength to pick him up a second time.

She dragged him into the dreary cabin. When she finally eased him down on the dirty floor, her arms were numb. She collapsed beside him, leaning her head back against the wall, and struggled to even her ragged breathing. Oh, but the man was heavy.

As the numbness left her arms, prickles of pain ran from her neck to her fingers. She straightened her arms and bit her lip against the ache. Sweat ran in rivulets down her back, and her neck chafed where her cloak clung to her damp neck.

She reached to lift her hair off her neck and saw the blood and dirt on her hands. Without pausing to think, she wiped her hands down her cloak. She felt a moist spot on the front and looked down. The light blue material was streaked with blood and dirt.

She couldn't let anyone see her like this. Quickly, she yanked off the cloak and wiped her hands thoroughly in its folds. It was beyond repair. A few more stains wouldn't matter. At least it had protected her gown from any telltale marks of blood. She shook the cloak out and draped it over Trevor.

Forcing herself to her feet, Brianna stared down at him a moment before she turned to the door. He would be safe enough alone for a few minutes. Her act of dragging him inside had left an obvious trail. She had to dispose of it before anyone spotted it—especially the soldiers.

Once outside, she made quick work of destroying any signs of a wounded man's presence or their trek to the cabin. She'd scarcely finished when the sentries rounded the corner. She tucked the more bloodier hand in her hair and waved at them with her other hand.

The men returned her greeting with a salute and continued on their patrol. Brianna had to force herself to stand still. She wanted to run back to Trevor, but she made herself wait until the soldiers passed out of sight.

Grabbing up her skirts, she ran back to the cabin. Trevor lay where she'd left him. Half-afraid of what she'd find, she checked for signs of life. His pulse still beat with a steady rhythm.

She ripped a strip off her petticoat, raised him up slightly, and pressed the material against his wound. Gently she eased him back down. With any luck, the weight of his body and the additional padding would stop any bleeding, at least for a short time.

Something had to be done about his wound and soon. Without proper treatment or supplies, he'd bleed to death. The only thing to do was to go on to the hospital. Once there, she'd make her excuses, gather a few necessities, and return to Trevor.

At the door, she paused and looked back. She'd tried to make him as comfortable as possible. He looked so weak and defenseless.

"Don't you dare die on me, Trevor Caldwell."

She turned and slipped back out the door. The sunlight was bright, marking the passing of time.

She scrambled down the hill to the small stream and plunged her hands into the icy water. The copper stains dispersed in the water and floated downstream. Using her lace handkerchief as a towel, she wiped her hands, then cleaned her face. Satisfied her appearance wouldn't cause questions, she climbed back up the hill and set off for the hospital.

He'd be all right; she kept reciting the promise throughout her trip.

At the hospital, Rachel greeted her warmly, and Brianna inwardly cringed at the lie she'd prepared.

"Oh, Rachel, it's just awful."

"What's wrong?" Rachel drew her to the side.

"One of the servants was injured this morning," Brianna paused, then rushed on. "I know we can't spare the doctor. If you can spare me, I'm needed at home. Papa isn't strong enough to take care of Jeb."

"Of course, go." Rachel glanced around the room at the cots of injured men.

Brianna felt terrible at her lie. These men needed her, too. It wasn't fair to leave Rachel shorthanded, but she couldn't desert Trevor.

"Rachel . . . I–"

"Go." She steered Brianna toward the door. "We only got three men from yesterday's skirmish. Not nearly what we expected. It'll be fine. You come back when your household is taken care of."

Brianna hugged her friend. "Thank you." Gratitude almost overwhelmed her.

"No need for thanks. You've already done more than your share around here."

Guilt swept over Brianna. She had to grab hold of her courage in order to do what she needed.

"Rachel? Would it be all right if I took a few things? Not much, just a couple of things for him," she assured.

"Of course. You've earned it. Go get what you need."

Her back to the room, Brianna gathered up a small knife, some pads, and a roll of bandages from a cabinet. As an afterthought, she added a package of sewing thread and a needle into her reticule. She hoped she wouldn't need to use it.

Waving to her friend across the room, Brianna hurried out of the hospital. Every second that passed nagged at her. She prayed she was making the right choice in treating Trevor herself instead of surrendering him to the sentries for hospitalization. *And prison,* her mind added. *Don't forget what awaits him in a Confederate prison.* She shivered.

Brianna kept her pace to a rapid walk. She dared not arouse undue interest. The slow pace chafed her. Already she'd been gone longer than she'd planned. Had Trevor's bleeding started up again?

"Don't let him die like Ethan," she whispered her plea.

At the cabin door, she paused to gather her courage together. She feared for what she'd find inside the room. She shoved the door open a crack and peered into the dusty interior.

"Trevor?" she whispered.

Silence.

She stepped into the cabin, closing the door behind her. The stench of disuse assailed her. For now, cleaning the cabin would have to wait. Dust layered everything in the one-room building. Everything except for the man lying on the floor.

Brianna rushed to Trevor. Kneeling beside him, she felt for life. His pulse pounded against her fingertips, and she murmured her thanks to God.

"Trevor?" she asked softly.

She received no response. She hadn't truly expected one.

Perhaps it was best for now. The act of removing his clothes would be painful enough, but it was nothing compared to treating his wound. It'd be better if he remained unconscious a little while longer. She didn't possess the strength needed to hold down a fighting man and cut into him at the same time.

She stood and surveyed the cabin for anything of use. Her gaze took in the rickety table and chair, a small bed, and a wooden cabinet. She crossed the room to the fireplace and picked up a piece of wood from the stack on the floor. The brittle wood broke apart in her hand, and she smiled in gratitude. Dry wood. A very small fire with dry wood wouldn't smoke.

She stacked a few pieces of wood together, searched along the fireplace, and found a cluster of matches. One struck on the first try. She babied the fire until it flared into a healthy glow. She'd need those flames in a few minutes.

Next she checked the cabinet. It yielded several faded cloths and a half-full bottle of whiskey. She gathered the items up and returned to Trevor.

She pulled back her cloak, wadded it up, and set it aside. As she leaned over him again, she noticed his shallow breathing. It stressed the need for urgency. Without hesitating, she unbuttoned his jacket and checked his chest. No exit wound marred his skin. She cringed. The ball must be lodged in his shoulder. Her hands shook as she rolled him over onto his stomach.

A low groan left his lips. Brianna brushed damp curls back from his forehead and felt a lump. Gently, she ran her fingers over and around the swelling. He must have hit his head during a fall, either before or after he was shot. Catching up her discarded cloak, she tucked it under his cheek, then placed a light kiss against his skin. The stubble of several days' growth scraped her chin.

"I'll be right back," she whispered, even though she knew he wouldn't hear her.

Fighting back the rush of memories the kiss brought, she grabbed a pan and ran out of the cabin. Hurry, hurry, her mind ordered as she filled the pan with cool, clear water at the stream and returned to Trevor.

She placed the pan on the floor and sat down beside him. The first thing she had to do was get his jacket off. She pulled away her makeshift bandage. Beneath it, the jacket was caked with dried blood. She scooped water into her hands and poured it on the crusted jacket. Once it had softened, she picked away the torn cloth.

Her hands trembled when she reached for the knife. She caught the lower edge of his jacket in one hand and drew the knife upward. The sharp blade sliced through the material. She pulled what remained of the jacket off and tossed it aside.

Tearing off another strip from her petticoat, she wet it and dabbed at the edges of the wound. Blood oozed and trickled down his arm. She wiped it away.

Brianna grabbed up the whiskey bottle. She poured a generous amount over her hands and over the gaping wound. Trevor jerked on the floor, then lay still.

Her heart rose in her throat. She tipped up the bottle and took a swallow. Her eyes teared as liquid fire seared her throat, and she blinked her eyes. Now she was ready.

Gently, she eased her index finger into the hole in Trevor's back. Warm, sticky blood squished, then oozed around her finger. She gritted her teeth against the feelings, but it did no good.

Her stomach lurched, and she pulled her finger back out, fighting down the rising bile. She turned her head away and gulped in several calming breaths. Scooping up the whiskey bottle, she took a swallow to steel herself. Fire seared her throat again, and she sputtered.

Brianna screwed up her courage and stuck her finger into the wound again. She closed her eyes against the blood oozing under her hand. Gingerly, she probed for the ball. She had to get it this time. At last her fingertip grazed something round. *That's it,* she thought in triumph. She eased her thumb alongside and brought out the ball.

Swallowing, she set the blood-covered ball on a cloth on the floor and repressed a shiver. Her work was only half over. Before she could lose her courage, she picked up the small knife. The blade shone from the firelight. She stuck the blade into the flames and held it there until it glowed with heat.

She pulled the knife out and returned to Trevor. In spite of the fire and the warm day, chills coursed through her body. She grabbed the whiskey bottle, pouring the amber liquid over the heated knife. Her hands shook as she raised the bottle to her lips for one last sip.

Quickly, before she could change her mind, she lowered the hot blade and pressed it to Trevor's torn skin. His whole body jerked, and beads of sweat covered his brow.

Brianna gagged at the smell of burning flesh. Nausea threatened to overcome her, and the room swirled around her. She gritted her teeth, fighting it off, and threw the knife across the room.

Her stomach heaved, and she swallowed repeatedly.

"I will not be sick. I will not," she ordered herself.

With shaking hands, she unrolled the hospital bandage and wrapped it tightly around his shoulder and upper chest. Her breath rushed out in ragged gasps. She'd done it.

Brianna staggered to the door. Once outside,

she leaned against the wall, then promptly lost her breakfast.

As she neared the house, her steps lagged. Brianna tried to calm her growing trepidation. This was Papa; he'd understand. She hoped.

She'd stalled as long as she could, washing down the inside of the cabin. Trevor had slept through her efforts. When the room passed for livable, she'd run out of excuses. Papa had to be told where she'd be for the next few days. She couldn't wait any longer and allow him to check with the hospital, so she'd headed home.

The house loomed before her. For the first time in her life, it looked foreboding. She mounted the steps and opened the door.

"Brianna!" Her father stood in the doorway and gaped at her. "What on earth happened to you?"

"Trevor's here."

"That Yankee did this to you?"

Her father stiffened, and Brianna saw him clench his fists. His face turned a mottled shade of red.

Immediately, she caught his arm. "No, Papa."

He shook her hold off. "Where is he?"

"It's not what you think. He didn't touch me."

"Then, what in blazes is going on? You come here looking like you've been through heaven knows what, announce your husband is here, and—" He snapped his mouth closed, leaned closer, and sniffed. "You've been drinking."

"Only a few sips," she confessed. "I had to, to get through it."

"That scoundrel—"

"Papa, he's been shot." Brianna bowed her head and blinked back tears of fear and exhaustion. "He . . . he's," she stammered. "I don't know how bad he is. If he's going to live or die."

Her father grabbed her by the shoulders. "Brianna, tell me what in the devil you're talking about."

"I found him this morning. He'd been shot. I did the best I could, but I don't know if it's good enough. I couldn't let him go to prison."

"What did you do?" His voice warned that maybe he didn't really want to hear an answer.

Brianna drew in a deep breath. "I borrowed some supplies from the hospital, and I treated him myself. The ball was lodged and . . . and I got it out." She shuddered. "There was so much blood."

Her father slipped his arms around her and drew her close. "Hush, it'll be all right."

"Papa." Brianna pulled back to look into his face. "I can't let him die. And I can't turn him in." Her lower lip trembled. "I hid him in the old Blackthorn cabin. I told Rachel that Jeb had been hurt. She thinks I'm here. Please, don't tell anyone the truth?"

"It means a lot to you, doesn't it?"

"Yes. Oh, Papa, I still love him."

She could read the war going on in her father. His eyes showed it clearly.

"Very well. We'll bring him here," he said in resignation.

"No, we can't. I don't think he should be moved right now. Besides, President Davis could send an escort to you at any time. We can't chance any soldiers."

The danger of the situation hit them both. Her father clasped Brianna's hands in his.

"We'll just have to be careful then, won't we?"

"No. I won't let you do this. He's my husband, and the risk is mine alone."

"Brianna—"

"It would put everyone in this house in danger. Do you want that?" She rushed on, intent on dissuading him. "It could ruin your career. It could send you to prison."

"Brianna—"

"No, I won't have it. All I want is for you to cover my absence for a few days."

"Of course, but I think you're making a mistake. We've got plenty of room here."

She shook her head. "All I need is some clothes. For both of us."

"Both?"

"Papa." She smiled at his expression. "He's wearing a Yankee uniform." She explained Trevor's need of clothing.

"We can take care of that."

"And I need another petticoat." She drew up her skirt to show a large rip. It was one of several.

"Brianna."

"I needed padding and bandaging for him."

"How bad is it?"

She shuddered and dropped her skirt. "He took a ball in the back. In the shoulder. It looks real bad."

Her father drew her with him into the house. "We'd best work while we're talking. What did you do for him?"

Quickly, she explained her treatment, ending with, "I left him on the floor."

"That's fine. We'll get him into bed in no time."

She stopped and turned. "We? You're not coming with me."

"Try and stop me." He laughed. "I want a look at the man who married my only daughter, and I'm going to get it."

Brianna gave in and smiled. When her father took that tone, it was best to give up.

"You go on upstairs and gather those clothes. I'll get some food."

"Thank you." She hugged him.

"Ah, it's nothing. Now, hurry up. I want to see this young man."

Minutes later, Brianna returned downstairs with a bundle of clothes and bed linens. "Ready."

Her father held up a basket. He winked and

tucked in a bottle of whiskey. "He'll be needing this for the pain when he comes around. And you leave it alone." He shook his finger at her.

Brianna laughed. "Yes, sir."

They walked to the cabin with only an occasional word between them. Brianna opened the door and led her father to where Trevor lay on the floor.

"So, this is him?" He bent over the wounded man.

While her father looked Trevor over, she made the bed with fresh linens. Hesitantly, almost afraid of what he might find, she walked over to where her father was checking Trevor.

"How is he?"

"You did a good job, girl. A real good job."

She gathered her courage in both hands and asked, "Will he live?"

"I'm not promising anything, but I think so. He's healthy and built well."

Brianna felt her face redden. Her father didn't seem to notice.

"If that bed's ready, let's get him up there."

Together, they lifted Trevor onto the bed. His body filled the mattress almost completely.

"Don't worry if he stays out awhile. With that lump on his head and the wound, it'll be likely he'll be out the better part of a couple of days."

Relief made her legs weak.

"I'll bring you some laudanum. It'll be best if you can keep him sleeping for several more days.

That way he won't tear that wound open again. And he looks like he needs some rest."

"Thank you."

"I'll be back tomorrow. With a poultice for that wound. It'll keep out infection. I'll also bring more food. It's too risky for you to do much cooking here. Might draw attention to the place. You keep that fire low, you hear?"

Brianna hugged him and kissed his cheek.

After he'd left, she crossed the room to Trevor. She tugged off first one boot, then the other. Her hands paused at the waist of his pants. Above the band, dark hair tapered down to disappear beneath the clothes. Memories of the nights they'd lain together swept over her in waves, leaving her weak. She closed her eyes and body against the desire that engulfed her and pulled his trousers down. She drew the sheet up to his chest. It was going to be a long night.

Trevor slept through the night with only a slight tossing of his legs. Brianna administered the laudanum each day mixed in the broth she poured down his throat. He slept for two days before he stirred, calling out in delirium, then lapsed back into unconsciousness.

The next two days passed in a blur for Brianna. Trevor barely roused, only enough to take the broth she fed him. Papa visited daily.

Brianna bathed Trevor, kept cool cloths on his brow for the nagging fever that persisted, and worried endlessly. Each night she donned a nightgown and slept fitfully in the narrow bed with him. When he tossed and moaned in his sleep, she held him as if to keep death from taking him from her.

The fifth day dawned clear. Before midday, Trevor began thrashing around on the small bed. Brianna rushed to his side and tried to calm his movements. He kicked, and the sheet slithered to the floor.

She replaced the sheet, pulling it up to his chest. His skin was too warm under her fingers. She grabbed up the bowl of fresh stream water and dipped a cloth into it. Wringing out the cloth, she placed it on his fevered brow. Throughout the day, she sat by him, refreshing the cloth, dipping it in the cold water. Still his fever raged, and Brianna fought it for him, sponging him and begging him to fight it, too.

By nightfall, he shivered with cold. She joined him in the narrow bed and put her arms around him. She held him close, hoping to infuse his body with some of her own heat.

Much later, Brianna drifted between wakefulness and sleep, haunted by erotic dreams of Trevor. Hands eased down her arms from shoulder to wrist and back up, stroking, caressing. She reveled in the sensations, keeping her eyes closed against reality.

It wasn't until she felt the tickle of fine hair against her ear that she woke fully. This was no dream.

She jerked back. "Trevor?"

"Brianna, my sweet. Is it really you?" He nuzzled her neck. "Ah, love, I want you so badly. How I've missed you. Did you miss me?" He nibbled her ear.

She sighed her answer. "Yes."

"My sweet, tell me you love me?" He licked and suckled the sensitive spot behind her ear.

She quivered in his arms. "Yes."

"What, my sweet love?"

"I love you," she whispered.

"Come, let me make love to you." He rolled her onto her back with one swift move.

She gazed up into fever-bright eyes. Gently, she felt his brow. It was cooler than it had been in days. A smile tipped her lips and grew. Now he burned for her.

"Brianna. Please?"

She couldn't refuse any more than she could will herself to stop breathing. Sitting up, she drew her nightgown over her head and dropped it on the floor.

Trevor pulled her back into his embrace with his one good arm. Brianna sighed against his throat. It was heaven. He breathed her name against her mouth, then followed it with his lips.

As he leaned over her, she eased him back. "Your shoulder."

"Is fine. Your love is the only medicine I need."

"But—"

"Come, Brianna, my love. Heal me."

She pushed him down onto his back. Leaning over him, she covered his chest with her kisses, loving the white bandage as well as the skin. She rubbed her nose back and forth across the pelt of hair on his chest, alternately kissing and licking.

Gradually, she worked her way to his waist. His groan stopped her. She looked up at him.

"I don't know how much more I can stand. My sweet, you're killing me."

He caught her wrists and drew her up to him. Breathing a kiss on her mouth, he murmured. "Are you ready?"

Her need of him had been building the last five days, intensifying each time she touched his body. Now it exploded in a flood of desire.

"Yes."

He caught her waist and lifted her, then lowered her atop his flesh. She cried out in ecstasy. They made fevered love, each trying to make up for the time apart.

The next morning dawned as bright as Brianna's mood. *He loved her.* Brianna repeated the words over and over to herself.

As she remembered last night, heat suffused her cheeks. She hadn't known she could be so wanton, or so well loved.

She rolled over and watched Trevor sleep. Smiling, she was tempted to run her fingers across the stubby growth on his chin. It was so unlike him to look unkempt.

She slipped out of the bed, dressed, and eased out the door. The early morning air held a chill, and she scrambled down to the stream. Once her pan was full, she returned to the cabin. Papa had brought a razor yesterday, and she planned on presenting it to Trevor this morning. She grinned at his upcoming surprise.

Brianna set the water to heating, withdrew the razor, and crossed to the bed. Trevor lay sleeping like a contented cat. She reached out her free hand.

Suddenly, Trevor sat up and knocked her hand aside. The razor slid across the floor. A second later, he clasped his hands around her throat.

Chapter Sixteen

"Trevor," Brianna called, her voice tight. "Stop it. It isn't funny."

Fear lapped at her mind, but she pushed it down. This was just a silly game. It had to be.

His lips lifted into a cold smile.

"You're hurting me." She pulled at his hands.

He stared into her eyes in silence. She could feel his animosity.

"What kind of game are you playing?" she asked.

"Honey, I'm through playing."

A chill shook Brianna. What had happened? She clung to his wrists.

"What have you been drugging me with?"

"Papa gave me a bottle of laudanum to—"

"So your dear father is in on this. I won't give you any secrets you can use. What did you think keeping me from my mission would accomplish?"

"Mission?" she repeated the word.

His hands tightened slightly; then he loosened

them again. "You think you're the only spy? Where are the papers? Or have you already sold them?"

"Trevor, let me go. You're delirious."

"That's a laugh. Where are they?"

"I don't know."

She released her hold on his wrists and laid her hands on his chest. He sucked in his chest as if she'd burned him.

"You traitorous liar."

She flinched as if he'd struck her. In fact, it felt as if he had. She searched his face. He was flushed. The fever had returned. That's what was wrong.

"Trevor," she spoke softly. "You're delirious. Let me get you back to bed."

"Why, so you can use that razor on me?"

"How can you say such a thing after last night?"

"What about last night? Tell me."

"You made love to me. You told me you loved me."

"Liar."

Brianna blanched. She could feel the blood drain from her face.

"You're even more deceitful than I thought."

"No."

He released her and strode away. He scooped up the razor and stuck it in his back pocket. "How long have I been here?"

For a second, she wondered where he'd gotten

the time to dress. She'd only been gone a couple of minutes for the water.

"Five . . . five days. And today. Since I found you," she answered.

He glanced around the room as if running the information over in his mind.

"Trevor? What were you doing here? In Tennessee?" she asked, her voice tentative with beginning doubts.

"My dear, I'm fighting Rebels."

No, she argued, *it's the fever talking, not Trevor.* She walked toward him. He didn't stop her. Standing next to him, she reached up and laid her palm on his brow.

He jerked his head back, but not before she'd felt the cool skin.

"What are you trying?"

"You're not feverish." She muttered the words in shock.

If he wasn't, then what was going on?

"Trevor, last night—"

"Nothing important happened last night."

She recoiled from him. How could he say nothing important? He'd made love to her. He'd told her he loved her. He'd. . . .

The truth struck her. He didn't remember last night. Her mouth dropped open. He'd been delirious then, not now.

She knew he'd spoken the truth last night. He did love her. She'd just have to make him remember.

The sound of singing outside halted her planning. She recognized "Dixie." Damnation, another Confederate patrol. She whirled around.

Trevor snaked out his hand and pulled her to him. He pressed a pistol against her side. Brianna opened her mouth, then snapped it closed. The cold metal bit into her ribs. What did he think he was doing?

"Not one sound," he hissed against her ear.

Did the fool think she wanted to be caught harboring him? Much less have him captured? Oh, no, she had better plans in store for him. She was tallying the score, and once he remembered their night together and his words of love, she'd pay him back—in full. He'd wish she'd sent him to prison before she got done with him.

The heat of his body warmed her back. She relaxed against him and felt him stiffen. A smile curled her lips. He wasn't immune to her no matter what he said or thought. Not any more than she was to him.

The off-key singing retreated, then faded away completely. Trevor removed the gun and slipped it into his waistband.

Brianna turned to face him and watched his movements. If she could somehow get that gun away from him, she could force him to go across the lines to a Union encampment. She wouldn't let him stay here and put himself in danger trying to complete a foolish mission.

She took a step forward and slowly raised her

right hand. Trevor stopped her with his next words.

"My dear, it's time you packed."

"Why?" Her heart pounded in her chest. She'd been so close to his gun.

"Because you are taking me back across the lines. Back to Washington."

Her smile threatened to burst through, but she hid it. She'd take him back all right. And she'd make him remember their night together. Before they reached Washington, he'd be back in her bed, too.

She turned away, not trusting herself to speak. Talk about spiking your guns. He'd certainly done that. She'd been all set to steal his pistol and convince him to leave. If he'd refused, she would've used that gun to force him back to safety.

Oh, she'd lead him back to Washington. With pleasure. But Trevor Caldwell had a few surprises in store for him.

"Very well," she answered meekly. Her mouth split in a wide grin, and she was glad she had her back to him.

"And don't try to escape."

She wouldn't dream of it. Wiping the smile from her face, she turned back around.

"We'll leave at dawn. Is my horse outside?"

Trevor flexed his shoulders, working out the stiffness, and grimaced.

She followed the play of muscles across his chest. Last night, he'd overexerted himself, but she wasn't going to bring it up again. She sighed at the memory, and her gaze strayed to the bed.

"Brianna?"

She snapped her attention to his face, avoiding his naked torso. She wished he'd put on a shirt.

"Hum?" She blinked, trying to remember his question. "No, there wasn't a horse around when I found you."

Trevor reached for the shirt draped across the bed. The white dressing stood out starkly against his skin.

"Your bandage needs changing."

Brianna licked her lips, nervous at the prospect of the closeness the task would involve. There was quite a difference between wrapping a bandage over the rippling muscles of an unconscious man and a fully conscious one. Not to mention him being the same man who made love to her the night before, and who now watched her with searing intensity.

"Very well." Trevor pulled out the straight-back chair and straddled it.

With shaking hands, Brianna removed the old bandage. A bruise discolored his back, but no infection colored the wound. Papa's remedy had worked. And thankfully, she wouldn't have to use the needle and thread.

As she wrapped the strips over Trevor's shoulder and around his chest, she stroked the smooth skin beside the cloth. Trevor sucked in his breath at her touch. She pulled the bandage slowly, using her fingertips to smooth it, prolonging the sensuous contact as long as she could.

When she finished, she didn't know whose breathing was more ragged—hers or Trevor's. No, he wasn't immune to her. Hiding a smile of satisfaction, she vowed to touch him at every opportunity. It would be a mixture of torture and pleasure for her, as well as him. Her fingers still tingled from the contact with his bare skin.

Brianna stepped back and balled her hands into fists. Satisfaction warmed her when she saw that Trevor had his own hands clenched over the top rung of the chair.

"We'll need horses." His voice was strained. "Can you send a message to your father to bring them here?"

"Yes," she answered with a pretense of reluctance.

"Then, do it now."

Brianna wrote out a brief note to her father, using the childhood code she and Ethan had invented as children. She knew only Papa would understand the hidden words, telling him of her willing return with her husband.

Once she was finished, she handed the note to Trevor. She watched as he read it.

With a jerk of his head, he signalled his approval. "That should take care of it."

Brianna stared at him. "You'll need a disguise of some sort."

"What?"

"Surely you can't expect to travel like that?" She gestured to his body.

"And what's wrong with me?"

"You're a healthy adult male. A war is going on. And you're not wearing a uniform." She ticked the points off on her fingers.

"I will not wear a Rebel uniform." Trevor's eyes narrowed in warning.

"Of course not. You'd be shot as a spy."

"Then—"

"It will have to be a common sight," she continued, ignoring him. "I've got it. With a wig and walnut dye. And the right clothes, you could be my maidservant."

"Absolutely not," he roared. He stood and the chair rocked.

She flinched at his yell. "Very well. It was just an idea."

Brianna bit her cheek to keep from laughing at the insult written across his face. It was too much. She turned away and looked at the wall to hide her face while she fought down her laughter. Once she'd succeeded, she faced him again.

"We'll change it to a male house slave," she suggested.

"I will not be your slave."

"You will be if you want to get to Washington alive." She propped her hands on her hips. "It would be perfectly natural for me to travel with a slave through the South. We would not attract unnecessary attention."

"How do you plan on pulling that off?"

"I know a mixture for a walnut dye. It will last for a couple of days if you don't wash it off. Or with a little silver nitrate added, you'll stay dark until it wears off."

As soon as she said the words, she realized just what she'd revealed. It wouldn't take long for him to put the facts together and remember her masquerade that one night long ago. When he did, he'd be furious.

A frown knitted Trevor's brows together. Brianna watched him closely. His brows arched, and she knew he'd added up her revelation and remembered that night when his horse had knocked down a serving girl.

"The slave girl. That was you." He caught her arm. "Wasn't it?"

Brianna swallowed. "Uh huh."

She waited for his explosion. It didn't take long. Anger tightened his jaw.

"I bet you enjoyed quite a laugh out of that escapade."

"Not really," she answered truthfully. "I was terrified."

"And to think I let you go." He shoved his hand through his hair. "I even tried to stop you and give you money. To think I felt pity for you."

"I'm sorry."

"What other masquerades did I meet you in?"

"None. That was the only one." She garnered her courage and decided to try a tactical maneuver. "See how effective it is? It would work for you."

As the chill of his anger remained, she placed her hand on his arm. She felt the play of his muscles under her fingers. His muscles tightened all the way from his wrist to his shoulder.

"Trevor? It's the only sure way I know of. Please, give it a try?"

When he met her request with silence, she added, "Unless you have a better idea." Her voice snapped, demanding an answer.

"Very well. But it had better work." He frowned down at her. "And don't think for a minute I'll let you get away with treating me like your slave."

"I wouldn't dream of it," she lied.

She recognized the time for a tactful retreat and dropped her hand from his arm. She didn't want to push—yet.

"I'll send the message to Papa. I heard some children playing down the way earlier. One of them will take the note to the house for us."

Trevor gave an abrupt nod and crossed to the small fire. "I'll shave while you do that."

Brianna stepped outside and leaned against the door. She wasn't sure how well her plan was going.

Sunset had long since painted the sky when Brianna heard her father's whistle. She fired a glance to Trevor and was relieved to see the even rise and fall of his chest. He slept undisturbed.

She tiptoed to the door and slipped outside into the moonlit night. Immediately, she searched the shadows and spotted her father beside a thick tree. She ran the short distance to him. He enveloped her in a firm hug.

"Papa." She returned his embrace.

He held her a moment, then set her from him. His concerned gaze examined her face. "Are you sure this is what you want?"

Tears caught at her throat. "Yes, it is. I love him, Papa. Enough to do anything to win him back."

"You do that." He caught her hands in his. "This war won't last forever. Don't let it stop you from holding on to love with both hands, girl. He's a good, strong man. Do what you have to do."

"I intend to."

"I've brought everything you asked for. The horses are hidden behind the cabin in that old rundown barn about half a mile to the north."

Brianna felt the tears building again and tried to blink them away. They trickled down her cheeks.

"None of that. Once this is all over, I want grandchildren to bounce on my old knees."

"I'm already working on it," she said with an impish grin.

"Promise me you'll be happy?"

"I'll try. And you?"

Her father glanced away, and she saw a tinge of a blush on his cheeks in the moonlight. It made him look at least ten years younger.

"Papa? Out with it."

"I've been seeing a bit of Mrs. Preston. She's a widow now, for the past three years."

"You sly fox." Brianna grinned. Years ago, her father and Betty Preston had been quite an item before she married a riverboat gambler.

"Since I came home from Washington, she's been keeping me company."

Brianna's grin widened. She threw her arms around her father. "I expect to hear news of a wedding within the year, you hear me?"

Her father laughed. "It'll be a lot sooner than that if I have my say. I'm thinking of asking her to go with me."

"Do it, Papa."

After a tearful goodbye, Brianna watched her father until he was out of sight. She dried her cheeks with her hands, picked up the bundle he'd left, and walked back to the cabin.

Trevor stepped back from the door and eased it closed before Brianna was halfway across the yard. The last thing he wanted was for her to know that he'd been out of bed before the door had even clicked shut behind her. And dressed before she'd reached her father. He'd watched the touching scene between her and her father, and hated himself for his part in it.

He called himself ten kinds of a cad for what he was doing, but she'd left him no choice. The missing papers changed everything.

The information he'd been carrying revealed critical Union plans for an upcoming move south. If that information fell into Confederate hands and the Union wasn't aware of it, the battle that would follow would make the horror and deaths at Shiloh seem like children playing in comparison.

The fighting at Shiloh had been so fiercely intense that the bullets had stripped the trees to skeletons, leaving the landscape stark and desolate. The bloodstained ground was scarred with artillery. Men had been cut down and in places lay two deep. The dead had carpeted the fields—Yankee and Rebel side by side.

Trevor shut his mind against the memories. Suffice it to say that he could not let that battle be refought.

Had Brianna delivered the papers yet? He'd searched the cabin while she was out, but hadn't found either his saddlebag or the papers. Was her brother even now delivering them to some Rebel general?

A third question shook him to his sock-clad feet. Dare he believe her that she knew nothing of the papers? If only he could.

Trevor wanted her at his side. He ached to have her in his life again. However much he desired her luscious body, he wasn't fool enough to trust her again.

Once a spy—always a spy. He feared it was true in Brianna's case.

His throat tightened, and he slammed his fist into his palm. He couldn't live without her, and he couldn't trust her one bit. She held the power in her hands to crush him with another betrayal.

Was he taking her back to Washington to hang after all? The pardon he'd obtained for her from President Lincoln wouldn't be any good unless he could make her quit spying.

The door swung open with a creak, and he faced her. When Brianna walked into the cabin, she avoided meeting his gaze, but her attempt to hide her tear-stained face from him failed. He'd seen the traces of tears the instant she walked in the room.

He watched her cross to the table and drop her bundle on it. He ached to go to her and hold her in his arms and take on some of her pain. First, he had to deal with his own demons.

"Papa brought the dye mixture." Brianna unpacked the bundle. "But he couldn't get the silver nitrate. That means we'll have to reapply the dye a couple of times on the trip."

"That's fine." Trevor stayed where he was, observing her actions.

"It would be best if we applied it now."

"Very well."

Brianna held back her smile of triumph at his

answer. Trevor didn't know what she had in store for him. By the time she'd finished putting the dye on him, he'd be ready to make love to her. Her stomach quivered at the thought of applying the dark dye to Trevor's bare skin. Her hand trembled as she poured the mixture into a bowl.

She concentrated on the dark liquid in the bowl and studiously kept her gaze from Trevor.

"You'll have to take off your shirt," she told him in a voice that oozed innocence.

The rustle of fabric behind her informed her of Trevor's compliance. Brianna smiled to herself. Everything was going exactly as she'd hoped.

"Um, would you like to sit in the chair or on the side of the bed?"

"The chair will be fine."

Trevor strode to the chair, clad in only his pants. Brianna noted how his pants molded to his hips and thighs. As he straddled the chair and crossed his arms on the top rung, she watched the play of muscles across his shoulders. Her breath hissed out in a rush.

Resolutely, she squared her shoulders and dipped her fingers into the bowl of liquid. She shook the excess from her hand and stroked across his shoulder.

As her fingers touched his warm skin, she almost sighed out her pleasure. His skin was firm under her fingertips. Her touch became soft and caressing. His bare skin began to radiate his body heat, and her fingers caught it and held on to the warmth, savoring it.

She caught up his right arm and applied the dye from shoulder to fingertips, smoothing the stain so that it wouldn't streak.

Across his neck and shoulders, down his back, then up again, her fingers stroked his skin, leaving it dark under her ministrations. He leaned forward, and the muscles rippled, the dye glistening in the firelight.

Brianna swallowed and licked lips that had suddenly gone dry. Her breath rushed out, and she tried to even it before he could notice.

At last his skin was darkened down to the line formed at the waist of his pants. Brianna stared at the divider for several moments.

"Um . . . I need you to remove your pants."

Trevor's eyebrows rose. His expression clearly asked why.

"I need to . . . Your body must be colored with the dye."

"Everything?" he asked, his voice feather soft. He drew in a breath; it was irregular.

"Everything," she whispered. Her heart skipped a beat.

Without another word, Trevor stood and unfastened his pants. He drew the pants down, stepped out of them, and tossed them on the chair. He remained standing and faced her.

Brianna's breath lodged in her throat. He was as magnificent as she'd remembered. She forced her eyes away from his body and dipped her hand into the dye.

Starting at his feet, she rubbed the coloring over his ankles and up his calves. When she reached his knees, she was engulfed with the memory of the first time he'd made love to her. Every kiss, every nibble, every caress was branded into her mind.

She skimmed his knees and started up his thighs, pausing every now and then to scoop more dye into her hands. Any rubbing motion had long since turned into a caress. As she approached his upper thighs, she slowed her movements.

"I think that's enough," Trevor spoke in a rush. "I can finish it."

He reached out and caught her hand, stopping her. "I said leave it." His voice was terse and ragged. "I'll do the rest myself."

Chapter Seventeen

Brianna shifted in the saddle and glared at Trevor's back. Trevor had insisted that he take the lead, not caring a whit that as her slave he should be following her. These were her woods, and she knew them far better than he. Twice before, they'd had to pull their mounts off the rutted road and hide from approaching soldiers.

Besides that, he'd been insufferable—ignoring her since they'd started out. If a patrol came along this instant, she'd happily turn him over to them.

She nudged her horse to catch up with him. What did he think he was doing? Trying to leave her behind or lose her? *Not by a long shot, Yankee.*

As she flicked the reins, her mount burst into a gallop, bringing her up to Trevor's horse. Brianna slowed and proceeded to glare at Trevor's broad back again.

She was still simmering from his rejection last night. After his abrupt dismissal of her assistance with the dye, she'd climbed into bed, and waited. The fool man had chosen to sleep in the chair. Stubborn Yankee. He'd left her to the sleep of the frustrated—hot, restless and unfulfilled.

She watched the rhythmic move of his body and began to make plans. Tonight they'd share a blanket . . . and much more. A slow smile spread across her face.

"Halt! Dismount off them horses." A shouted order came from the side.

Brianna caught back her scream. To the left, a group of soldiers stood ready, rifles in hand.

"What seems to be the problem?" Brianna asked, trying to keep the tremor out of her voice.

"We're looking for any Yankee stragglers. A full unit of 'em pulled out several days back."

"Do I look like a Yankee soldier to you?" she asked with a laugh.

"Have you seen any strangers about, ma'am?" another soldier asked, obviously ignoring the presence of the black man riding with Brianna.

"We—"

The look she shot Trevor told him to stay quiet.

"We're riding to—"

"I didn't ask you nothing." The corporal turned his gun on Trevor.

"I—"

"Uppity slave. One would think you don't know your place."

Brianna intervened before Trevor could speak again. "I apologize for Nathan. He's used to running my father's house. He's just being protective of me for my father's sake."

"Ma'am, you'd best be keeping an eye on him. My pa had one just like him. He ran off to join the Yankees." The corporal's face showed his hatred.

"Well, thank you, sir. I'll do that." Brianna smiled at the men. "I feel a lot safer knowing our fine soldiers are protecting these roads."

The corporal tipped his hat to her. "Be careful, ma'am."

"Thank you. I intend to be."

Brianna flicked her reins and sent her horse ahead of Trevor. She glanced back at him. "Come along, Nathan. You know Father's starting to worry about how long we've been gone."

She could feel the glare of Trevor's stare cut through the clothes covering her back. She resisted the urge to look around at him. The silence stretched between them, making her more and more uncomfortable.

After several minutes when she figured it was safe enough, Brianna motioned Trevor to stop. She reined her horse in, and Trevor drew up even with her. He glared across at her.

"Next time let me do the talking," he ordered.

"That's what got us into trouble in the first place," she shot back.

"If you're quite through playing the lady of the plantation, I'll take the lead." He nudged his horse and rode ahead.

With a wave of his hand, Trevor took the lead. Brianna was back to shooting glares at his backside.

That night was spent in the woods. Trevor insisted on separate bedrolls, much to Brianna's disgust.

The week followed in much the same pattern. They rode long hours on rutted backwoods roads, surrounded by Johnny-jump-ups and other wildflowers in bloom. Occasionally they cut through the woodlands to avoid Rebel pickets.

As the distance to Washington grew shorter, Brianna grew more frustrated. So far, Trevor had thwarted her every attempt at renewing their relationship.

Her back ached, her legs even with the protection of her riding habit were chafed, and she was hungry. She began to study the passing scenery in earnest. A short time later, the ditch alongside the road gave way to a wooded area. Her horse snorted, and Brianna knew there was a stream nearby.

Brianna pulled her horse to a stop. Even if Trevor was made of untiring steel, she wasn't. It was past time for a rest.

"Trevor," she called as he continued riding down the road.

He glanced over his shoulder, then reined his mount in. "Yes?"

"It's past noontime. Let's stop for a while and eat."

"We need to—"

"I'm stopping," she declared.

Brianna drew her horse off the narrow road and turned down an overgrown path. She let her mount have its head, knowing it would lead her to the water.

Trevor had no choice but to follow.

"Whatever happened to obedient wives?" he muttered to her back.

Brianna merely smiled.

Within minutes, the wooded growth thinned, and before her lay a rushing stream. Clear, fresh water bubbled over jutting rocks, sending out an invitation she couldn't refuse.

Brianna dismounted and led her horse to the water. It was so crystal clear that she could see the bottom of the stream bed.

"Trevor, isn't it beautiful?"

She let her horse drink its fill. Giving in to the lure of the tempting water before her, she sat down in the grass and removed her boots and socks. Rolling up her riding skirt so that it wouldn't get wet, she strode to the stream and plunged her feet into the icy water.

Her squeal of delight drew Trevor, and he joined her at the stream.

"Come on," she invited, kicking water at him.

"No."

"Afraid to get wet?" She hit the stream with her

hand, sending up splatters of water.

Trevor's eyes narrowed, and slowly he took off his boots and socks. Rolling up his pants, he stalked Brianna. She squealed and turned to run. He caught her and swung her up.

"Afraid to get wet?" he repeated.

She threw her arms around his neck and held on. "Don't drop me."

"Tempting."

Trevor lowered her, taunting her, then stood her on her feet.

The second she was safely down, Brianna kicked up a spray of water. They splashed in the water like children.

Finally, Trevor scooped Brianna up in his arms and carried her to the grass. He gently lowered her down.

"I'm starved, woman. Are you going to keep me from eating all day?"

"Me?" she sputtered. "Why, you're the one who kept plodding down the road on one of those beasts of torture." She gestured to where the horses lazily grazed.

Trevor looked at her in puzzlement. "I thought you liked riding."

"I do. A civilized ride—a short, civilized ride," she corrected. "This is neither short nor civilized." Brianna rubbed her backside for emphasis.

Trevor's deep chuckle sent skitters along her spine.

"I'll go get our food," he said.

She watched him stride to the horses. He moved with sure, confident steps, and an inborn grace of movement. Once again she was reminded of a sleek cat in the forest.

When he returned, he tossed a blanket onto Brianna's lap.

"Well, don't just sit there, woman. Do your share," he teased.

Brianna stretched and jumped to her feet. She spread the blanket over the soft cushion of grass.

"Satisfied?" she asked, her hands on her hips.

Trevor turned and looked at the blanket. He stared at her bare feet a moment; then his gaze trailed, ever so slowly, up to her face.

Brianna's heart gave a thud. She felt as pulled to him as if she'd been caught in the stream's rapid-moving suction downstream.

Trevor straightened his shoulders and bent back to the task of pulling out the food.

Lunch was eaten in a sexually charged silence. Brianna couldn't help but wish that he'd kiss her then and there and get the waiting over with. Both her nerves and her temper were wearing thin. She wanted him back as her husband, in her bed and her life.

Once the meal was finished, Trevor strode to the water's edge and stared out across the ripples. Brianna watched him. The slight breeze ruffled his hair, and he raised his hand and brushed it back.

She shifted her eyes to the water and concentrated on its hurried movements. At least the water was uncomplicated and didn't ooze distrust at her. Gradually, the steady movement of the rushing water soothed her. Her eyes fluttered closed, and she struggled to keep them open.

Stretching her arms over her head, she reached back, and her fingers brushed against the rough bark of a tree. It offered a tempting chance for a nap. Brianna leaned back against the tree trunk, scooted her shoulders into a comfortable spot, and wiggled her bare toes. It felt good to sit on something that didn't move under her with a rocking rhythm.

She concentrated once again on the soothing sound of the nearby stream. Her eyes fluttered closed again, and she drifted off to sleep. A low sigh left her lips.

At her sigh, Trevor turned. Brianna lay curled against the tree. Her lashes posed dark crescents against her skin. He watched her hungrily, aching to take her pliant form into his arms.

If only things could be different between them, he wished. If only he hadn't been carrying those papers. If only Brianna hadn't taken the papers.

Trevor sank down onto the blanket and watched over Brianna. She looked so vulnerable in sleep, so trustworthy, but he knew it was a lie.

Brianna woke slowly. She blinked against the sunlight reflecting off the water. Gradually, the scene before her blurred. The water and grassy bank became inseparable, indistinct. It was happening again, she thought.

Next, the pain came. Only this time it was more of a dull ache. Her shoulder stiffened, and she reached her hand up. Then the nausea hit with the force of a blow. Everything around her rolled and swayed. She continued to hold her shoulder. It throbbed beneath her fingertips. She staggered to her feet and cried out.

Trevor was on his feet in an instant. Brianna saw him in her side vision. As another wave of nausea hit her, she turned away and was violently sick.

She leaned against the tree and gulped in deep breaths of air.

"Brianna?"

Trevor touched her shoulder lightly.

Both the nausea and dull ache in her shoulder left instantly. She turned around to face Trevor. She knew the questions were coming. There was no way she could ward them off.

"Brianna, what's wrong with your shoulder?"

"Nothing. It's nothing."

"This isn't the first time this has happened."

"It's—"

"Brianna?" His voice was insistent, demanding an answer.

"It's . . . it's foolish; I can't explain it."

"Try."

"Ever since Ethan and I were children, I . . . I've felt things."

"What kind of things?"

She shrugged. "When we're apart, I feel when he's hurt." She lifted her hands, then dropped them to her sides. "I hurt."

She saw the doubt in Trevor's eyes.

"I know it sounds crazy. And no one can explain it. It just happens."

"How?"

"I don't know. For instance, the time Ethan fell out of a tree and hit his head. My head hurt for days."

"What's happening now? Where is your brother?"

Pain flashed across her face. "Nothing's happening now. I . . . I must have been dreaming. And I imagined it when I woke up."

"Where is Ethan?"

She fell silent.

"Brianna, where is Ethan?" He repeated the question.

She turned to him. What good would continuing the lie do now? Her throat tightened on the words. She forced them out past the constriction.

"He's dead. Ethan's dead."

"Dead?"

"A Yankee shot him. Last year."

"How do you know—"

"I saw it. I held him in my arms until he died."

"My sweet," Trevor's voice broke.

"He made me promise."

"Made you promise what?"

"He was the Rebel Fox. And I swore to take his place." She caught his shirtfront in her hands. "I promised."

Brianna crumpled against him and burst into tears.

"It's all right. I understand." He closed his arms around her. "Go ahead and cry if you want."

She sobbed against his chest, releasing the pain she'd held in for so long.

Trevor held her until she stopped crying. He felt like joining her tears. Now not only was he fighting her convictions, he was fighting a ghost as well.

At last, Brianna raised her head, and tears shimmered in her eyes. She uncurled her fingers from his shirt.

"Thank you," she whispered.

He kissed her forehead.

She stepped back out of his embrace. "Shouldn't we be going?" She looked around the wooded retreat. It no longer held happy memories for her.

"Do you feel up to riding?"

"Yes." She wiped her tears with the back of her hand. "I want to leave here. Please?"

"Sure." Without another word, he retrieved the horses, then tied their picnic blanket behind a saddle. "Ready?"

Brianna jerked her head and climbed on her horse. She followed Trevor away from the stream and back to the rutted, narrow lane.

They rode in near silence until shortly before sunset. Trevor pulled his horse up and waited until Brianna came up alongside.

"What is it?" Her chest tightened in fear. Had he heard a patrol ahead?

"Why don't you start looking for a good place to camp tonight? We've had a long day."

Brianna released a sigh of relief. Nothing was wrong. "Sure," she answered.

Trevor nudged his horse and took the lead again.

Less than half an hour later, Brianna spotted evidence of an old pathway to the right.

"Trevor?" she called softly.

When he turned, she motioned to the overgrown trail. He flashed her a smile and turned his horse back. They followed the remnants of the trail for a couple of miles before the woods and brush separated to reveal a small clearing. A narrow brook ran nearby.

The water was heavenly to Brianna. Cold, but so refreshing. She took advantage of the water while Trevor cared for the horses. She luxuriated in the feeling of being clean again after a day of riding.

Returning to the camp, she prepared the meal while Trevor took his turn at the brook to wash off the day's grime. After they'd eaten, Trevor spread out the two bedrolls, one on either side of the small campfire.

As Brianna eyed the separate bedrolls, she

fumed. They were steadily nearing Washington, and he'd yet to touch her. How was she to bring back his memory of their night in the cabin and his profession of love if he wouldn't cooperate at all?

Did she have to do everything? She slipped behind a bush and changed into a thin nightgown, then strolled back to her bedroll. She could feel Trevor's gaze on her. As she raised her arms and gave a languorous stretch, he coughed.

Brianna smiled to herself. Maybe it was working. She slowly sank onto the blankets. Angling her head so that she could see him from the corner of her eye, she began to run her fingers through her hair, working loose the tangles. She rolled her head back and sighed.

The silence of the woods surrounded them, and she listened for the sound of Trevor's breathing. It had quickened—a sure giveaway. Her smile widened a little. He was in for a big surprise.

Tonight she needed him. And she intended to have him.

She needed to belong to someone, to be a part of someone again.

Stretching out her arms, she leaned back, bringing her breasts into prominence. She raised her arms, then clasped her hands behind her head.

"Ouch." She cried out.

Trevor sprang to her side. "What's wrong? Brianna, are you hurt?"

"I'm sorry."

She gazed up at him. She nibbled on her lower lip, her teeth grazing the skin.

"It's my hair. There's a tangle in the back I can't reach. Could you?" She turned her back and looked over her shoulder at him.

"Ah, what do you want me to do?" His voice was hoarse, and he cleared his throat.

"I need my hairbrush. It's in the pack over there."

She pointed to where the packs lay to the side of his bedroll.

"Sure. I'll get it."

As soon as he strode off, Brianna gathered up the blanket and followed him. At his bedroll she stopped, dropping the blanket to the side.

When Trevor turned around with the brush, she slowly sank down onto his bedding. Her eyes never left his as she brought her hair over one shoulder.

Trevor walked back to her slowly. As he reached her side, he extended out the brush.

Instead of taking the hairbrush from his hand, she caught his wrist and drew him down beside her. Beads of sweat stood out on his upper lip. She leaned forward and licked them away.

Trevor pulled back. She tilted her head and stared up at him with a small pleading smile.

"Please, would you mind terribly? Brushing my hair, I mean."

Without waiting for his answer, she turned her back and flung her hair over her shoulder. She held her breath. Would he refuse her request?

Brianna felt his weight shift on the bedroll. The brush touched the top of her head, then trailed down the length of her hair. Again and again, he brought the brush through her hair.

"Umm," she murmured. "That feels good."

Behind her, Trevor cleared his throat.

Brianna scooted closer to him. When her hip touched his thighs, she heard the sharp hiss of his breath. She paused, then eased a little closer into the vee of his thighs.

Her own body grew warm cradled between his legs. Liquid heat crept up her back to her neck. Trevor's fingers skimmed her nape, and the heat from his touch coursed down her to settle deep within her.

Brianna forced herself to stay still, resisting the almost overwhelming impulse to turn toward him. She slowed her own breathing and listened for his.

Trevor eased her hair to the side, and she felt the warm moistness of his breath on the sensitive skin of her neck. Of its own volition, a sigh escaped her lips.

Behind her, Trevor stiffened. She wanted to cry out.

A shudder shook his body, and he pulled Brianna back against him. She moaned as he nestled her tightly between his thighs.

His tongue skimmed her nape. Licking, sucking, he trailed his tongue to the hollow of her ear.

"Ah, my sweet. My sweet Brianna," he whispered against her ear.

She melted against him.

Trevor tossed the brush down and turned her into his embrace. His lips teased hers, begging entry.

She raised up on her knees and leaned into him, her breasts grazing his chest. At his groan, she pressed closer.

He held her tightly, pulling her against him. He molded her to him, from knees to chest. She felt him hard and pulsing against her.

She opened her lips to him, but her tongue touched only the air of their mingled breaths. The next instant, his tongue plunged into her mouth, mating with hers.

He ran his hands down her back, cupping her buttocks in his hands. He drew her more snugly into his embrace, cradling her between his open thighs.

Brianna curled her fingers into the thick curls at his neck. She sank her hands into the luscious pelt. Snuggling against him, she released his hair, and caught at the thick cords of his neck.

His hands slid upward to catch the straps of her gown. Leaning back, he eased the material down her shoulders, over her breasts, and down to her knees. His fingers followed each inch, branding her.

Brianna loosened her hold on his neck and ran her hands around to his chest. She worked the buttons loose, one by one. Trevor shrugged out of his shirt, and she unclasped his pants.

He shrugged out of them, then kissed her forehead, her eyes, her cheeks, taking his time until he reached her lips. Lightly, he brushed his lips across hers. The fine hairs of his mustache tickled while the stubble on his chin scraped. The two sensations combined to send a flame through her that burned much hotter than the campfire casting its glow across their bodies.

Gently, Trevor eased Brianna back on the blanket. He balanced his weight on his elbows and looked into her eyes. Brianna knew without caring that her love had to be written in her gaze. Smiling, she pulled him down to her.

He entered her gently, treating her like a breakable object, but Brianna would have none of it. She clung to him, surrendering everything. Trevor cried out his release, holding her tightly as she joined him.

Afterward, he drew the blanket over them and cradled her in his arms. She snuggled against his warm body.

"Brianna?" Trevor murmured against her neck.

"Umm?"

"What did you do with the papers?"

For a moment she thought she'd surely heard him wrong. He couldn't—

"Brianna?" Trevor waited for her answer, then repeated, "What did you do with the papers?"

She recoiled from him, drawing up the blanket to cover her nakedness.

Trevor reached out to play with a tendril of hair that draped over her shoulder.

She pulled away and sat up, the blanket drawn to her chin. The warmth and contentment from their lovemaking left her in a rush. Anger replaced it.

Those damn papers. How could he dare to ask her about them after what had just happened between the two of them? He *still* didn't trust her. The sense of betrayal and pain cut deep.

"Papers?" she asked in disbelief.

"Yes, the papers from my saddlebag. Where are they?" He watched her every move, his gaze wary. "What did you do with them?"

Each question accused her. Each question struck her like a blow. She met them unflinchingly, silently. Shock and anger warred in her.

Her eyes narrowed, and she raised her chin. She wouldn't give him the satisfaction of seeing how he'd hurt her. And she wouldn't answer his damned accusations.

She'd taken all she was going to take for tonight. He could just wonder about those all-important papers.

Brianna grabbed up the blanket from the ground and strode across to the other side of the campfire. She stopped, her body so stiff she felt as if she might break into pieces if he touched her. She glanced back over her shoulder at Trevor.

"If you ever ask me that again, I swear I'll shoot you myself."

Turning back, she tossed the blanket onto her bedroll, dropped down on top of it, and pulled the rough blanket up to her chin.

Chapter Eighteen

As the days on the trail passed, the silence between Brianna and Trevor grew. Neither spoke during the tiring ride unless it became necessary. The few words were short and sharp.

Each night separate blankets lay on opposite sides of the small campfire, emphasizing the growing distance between the two. Brianna felt that Trevor and she were as divided as North and South.

At last they reached Washington, the Capitol standing out starkly. The city of Washington seemed even more crowded and dusty to Brianna upon their return. Clouds of dust layered everything and hung in the air like a fog.

Trevor's home came into view, and Brianna's stomach knotted. The memory of her last night in the house arose like a specter. The harsh words spoken that night still held the power to hurt.

The servants rushed out at Trevor's shout. Sarah and Annie greeted him warmly with hugs. Cool stares were all that Brianna received. Exhausted and unwilling to deal with the situation, Brianna dismounted, handed the reins to Trevor and strode into the house. As on the trail, she spent the night alone.

Brianna's first morning back, Sarah informed her that she had an early morning visitor in the parlor.

"Your aunt, ma'am." Sarah's voice was curt.

Brianna hurried down the stairs. She'd missed Aunt Harriet so much. She rushed into the room.

"Aunt Harriet." Brianna flew into her aunt's arms.

"Glad you're back, girl. How's your papa?" She clasped an arm around Brianna's waist.

"He's fine. Thinking about marriage." Brianna grinned.

"Land's sakes. That Preston woman finally ran him to ground, did she?"

"Just about." She joined her aunt's laughter.

"Well, let me look at you, girl." She set Brianna away from her.

"You still haven't made things right with him yet?"

Brianna couldn't believe her aunt's powers of observation. She avoided her probing gaze and searched the room for a footstool.

"Well?" Aunt Harriet persisted.

"Let's sit down and then talk," Brianna suggested, stalling for time.

She led her aunt to a comfortable chair and rounded up a footstool. Once her aunt was settled, she sat in the chair facing her. "But how could you tell?"

"It's in the eyes. Yours are shadowed, girl. Well?"

"I tried."

Oh, how she'd tried, Brianna remembered.

"He still upset over you leaving?"

"He's never spoken of it."

"Well, he followed you, didn't he?"

"I don't know." Brianna wasn't sure of much right now. She twisted her ring around on her finger.

"Fool girl. Of course he did." Aunt Harriet pounded her cane on the floor.

Brianna sat forward in her chair. "I honestly don't know. When I first found him wounded, all I thought about was keeping him alive and safe. Then . . ."

"Well, come on. Out with it."

"He accused me of stealing papers from him while he was wounded."

"Well, did you?"

"Aunt Harriet."

"I had to ask."

Her aunt rolled her cane back and forth across her lap, deep in thought. After a minute, she snapped it on the floor with a thud.

"Did you tell him you didn't take them?"

"Yes. Several times. He doesn't believe me."

Her aunt chuckled. "Can't say that I blame him myself."

"Aunt Harriet." Hurt rang out in Brianna's voice.

"Now, don't go getting cross-legged on me, girl. Put yourself in his place. Would you trust him if things were reversed?"

"I suppose not," Brianna answered thoughtfully.

"Give him time, girl. The man's been hurt mighty bad. And a wounded animal always lashes out."

Brianna thought over her aunt's words. Perhaps she was right.

Scarcely had the door closed on Aunt Harriet's visit when there was another knock at the door. A sullen Sarah announced Selina James.

Brianna embraced her friend. It felt good to see her again.

"How are you?"

"I'm fine. I've missed you. Of course, I heard a report on everything from your aunt. How are you recovering from your trip?"

"Well enough."

"Enough to slip through the lines for us tonight?"

Brianna's breath froze in her throat. Either way she answered, she'd betray one she loved.

"Since Rose has been returned to the South, and now that she's nearly on her way to England, we need you."

"Selina," she paused.

"Brianna, you're needed now more than ever."

"No, I'm through spying."

"Won't you reconsider?"

Brianna clasped her hands together. "No. I won't."

"So, will you turn me in?" Selina asked in defiance.

"You know I could never do that." Brianna was horrified at the thought.

"Then, why?"

"I'm on a special list now. If I'm caught again, they'll hang me."

Selina faced her friend. "There's more, isn't there?"

"Yes," Brianna answered truthfully. "I love Trevor. I can't chance hurting him."

"But what of the Cause?"

"There's two sides to this damn war. Unfortunately, I'm on both sides."

"May I still visit?" Selina stood tense.

Brianna threw her arms around her friend. "Of course. Always."

Selina returned the hug. "I hope he makes you happy."

"He will."

They embraced again, and Selina left.

The days passed with agonizing slowness for Brianna. Her aunt's advice dogged her every step. Her relationship with Trevor had worsened. He still mistrusted her and hadn't touched her since their return to Washington. She was frustrated, alone, and lonely.

By the end of the week Brianna's temper was short. She knew she couldn't go on like this much longer. Out of boredom, she rearranged the vase of multicolored roses on the parlor table for the fifth time that morning. When a knock sounded at the door, she jumped. *Now what,* she grumbled to herself. She walked into the foyer.

"A message from your aunt, ma'am." Sarah held out the note. "She wants you to come for a visit today."

"Thank you for your," Brianna paused, "observance," she added. Anger edged each word.

The servant woman had even taken to reading all her messages. Brianna fumed. That was another thing she and Trevor would have to talk about—if he ever came home from the Capitol long enough for anything. He'd practically lived there since they'd returned to Washington.

"Sarah, I'll be going to visit my aunt now. If Trevor asks for me, tell him I'll be at her home."

"Yes, ma'am." Sarah sniffed her disapproval.

Brianna knew without asking that the woman would relay her every action to Trevor. She could feel his distrust, and it ate at her.

She knew it was going to take all her love to rebuild what they'd once had together. However, it was worth it, and this time she wouldn't throw it away.

Trevor paced the smaller, outer office like a caged animal. It had been over fifteen minutes since he'd been summoned to the White House by President Lincoln, without being given the reason for the appointment. Running a hand through his hair, he strode to the window and stared out across the expanse of lawn.

Washington sprawled before him. A multitude of Federal encampments surrounded the city. It was too bad it hadn't been done early enough to stop the Confederate spies from the damage they'd caused.

The connecting door to the office creaked open, and Trevor turned at the sound.

"The president will see you now. This way Major Caldwell." The aide led him through the door into the office.

President Lincoln with his lean, towering height and deep-cut eyes dominated the room. His somber face would command respect in any room, Trevor noted.

"Mr. President." Trevor saluted.

"Well, Major. Congratulations are in order for you."

"Sir?"

"Sit down." The president stroked his whiskers and motioned to the nearest chair, then sat down himself.

Trepidation and excitement blended together in the pit of Trevor's stomach as he sank onto the chair cushions.

"That was quite a feat you pulled off, Major. You're more than deserving of an accommodation, but I'm afraid that at this time, all I can offer you is my own personal congratulations."

Trevor stared at the president in confusion.

"I'm sure there's a good story behind how those papers got to me, and maybe someday we'll have to discuss it. For now, I want to thank you for your sacrifice in seeing those documents safely delivered."

Trevor couldn't believe what he was hearing. The papers were safe? The president himself had them. Not Brianna?

"How?"

"When your horse was delivered to McClellan's men, he had those documents rushed straight here to me. Quite a good bit of Yankee know-how sending your horse on to the unit outside Chattanooga."

In a flash Trevor understood. He hadn't made it to the unit to deliver the papers, but his steed had. From there, the horse had been ridden to Washington.

If Brianna hadn't shown him a few shortcuts through Tennessee—shortcuts a Union soldier wouldn't know about—then the horse would have beaten them to the capital. As it was, he and Brianna had gotten in before the horse and papers.

With the force of a blow, it hit him. Brianna had been telling the truth all along about the papers. *He'd been wrong.*

President Lincoln stood, signalling their meeting was over. He held out his hand, and Trevor clasped it.

"Thank you, Major."

"No, Mr. President. Thank you."

"Pardon?"

"Thanks to you, I owe my wife an apology."

President Lincoln smiled. "Seems we men are

forever needing to do that."

"Yes, sir."

Trevor left the office in a rush. He had to tell Brianna. He had to make it right.

Once at the house, Sarah wasted no time in informing him that Brianna had gone to visit "that bossy woman." He knew it could be no other than Aunt Harriet. Taking the stairs two at a time, he ran outside. He swung into the saddle, applied a kick to the horse's side, and galloped off in a cloud of dust.

Aunt Harriet swung the front door open before Brianna reached the steps. The door banged against the wall.

"Well, land's sakes, girl. What took you so long?" Aunt Harriet tapped her cane on the floor in a show of impatience. "Well?"

"I got here as soon as I got your message," Brianna hastened to explain.

"Humph."

Brianna stepped into the house, shutting the door behind her.

"Not soon enough," her aunt muttered as she strode into the parlor. She sat down with a sniff, then propped her feet on the footstool, her cane across her knees.

"Is something wrong?" Brianna eased down in the chair across from her aunt.

"You tell me, girl. Have you patched it up with that handsome major yet?"

Brianna felt her cheeks grow hot under her aunt's scrutiny.

"I thought not."

"Aunt Harriet—"

"There's no excuses. You and that man deserve to be happy. And I can't be happy until I know you two have stopped your spatting." She caught up her cane and thumped it on the floor with vigor.

"How about if I promise to talk to him tonight?" Brianna attempted to placate her.

Her aunt frowned a minute, then thumped her cane again. "See that you do."

"I will."

Brianna leaned forward and gave her aunt a quick hug.

"What was that for, girl?"

"Because I love you," Brianna laughed.

"Land's sakes, girl. You got me all distracted over your handsome major so that I forgot what I called you here for."

Brianna coughed to hide the grin that surfaced.

Aunt Harriet reached over and picked up an envelope from the little table beside her.

"What's that?"

"It's got your name written on it." Her aunt held it out.

Brianna took the envelope from her, turned it over, and stared at the too-familiar writing sprawled across the paper. She gasped and tightened her hand over the envelope.

"It's . . . it's Ethan's writing," Brianna stammered.

"I thought so."

"But—"

"I thought you might be wanting it." Her aunt patted her hands.

"Where did you find it?" Brianna's voice came out in a whisper.

A chill of gooseflesh crept over her arms. It was as if Ethan were reaching out to her from the grave. She shivered against the thought.

"I was looking for a book this morning. I pulled out Ethan's old dog-eared copy of *Three Plays of William Shakespeare*—"

"Third," Brianna repeated his clue. *"Three Plays* . . . third."

"What?"

"Umm, oh, nothing."

"And anyhow, that fell out," her aunt concluded.

"Ethan's letter." Brianna smoothed the envelope with her fingers.

"Go ahead," Aunt Harriet cut in. "Open it."

Brianna turned the envelope over and over in her hands.

"Land's sakes, girl. It won't bite. Open it."

As Brianna tucked a fingertip under the corner, a knock sounded at the door. She jumped and gripped the letter defensively.

Both women turned at the entrance of a servant.

"Ma'am, there's a man here with a message for Miss Brianna. Should I show him in?"

Aunt Harriet looked from the servant to

Brianna. "Yes, show him in to us."

Quickly, Brianna shoved the envelope into her pocket and jumped to her feet.

A thin, young man entered the parlor. "Miss Brianna?" he asked, looking from one woman to the other.

"Yes." Brianna took a step forward.

At least he wasn't wearing a Union uniform, she thought in relief. He couldn't be here to arrest her.

She looked at him closely. The young man stood with a bow-legged stance that made her think of a sailor she'd once gotten some naval information from. He wasn't anyone she recognized from her spying missions, but he had the nervous look of a man hired to deliver something of importance. A shudder of premonition ran down her spine.

"He said I's supposed to give you this. Only to you." He extended a folded piece of paper. "Here."

"Who did?"

He shoved the paper into her hand. In the next instant, he turned and ran from the parlor.

"Wait. Who sent you?" Brianna called after him.

She dashed from the room, but he was already out the door and out of sight. The front door swung closed with a click.

"Land's sakes, girl. What was that all about?" Aunt Harriet peered around Brianna's shoulder.

"I have no idea."

"Well, what's that?" She touched the corner of

the note.

"I don't know." Brianna slowly unfolded the paper.

The words leapt out at her in familiar script. No, she covered her mouth with her hand. It couldn't be true. It couldn't . . . be. . . .

The room whirled around her. Brianna clutched the note in her hand and continued to stare at it in disbelief.

Ethan couldn't be alive. She'd held him in her arms while he'd breathed his last breath. Rose had pronounced him dead, too. Rose had even arranged his private burial.

Brianna swayed on her feet. Aunt Harriet caught her shoulders and steadied her.

"What is it, girl?"

"It can't be," Brianna repeated.

He's alive. She reread the words. Ethan was alive and wanted to see her right away. Tears of joy sprang into her eyes, and she blinked them away.

She'd felt in her heart all along that he wasn't dead. She'd been right. The note was in his distinctive handwriting. He'd even used their childhood code. No one but she, Papa, and Ethan knew that code.

Alive, the word sang through her mind. There wasn't time for crying. She had to get to Ethan.

Brianna spun around and almost collided with Aunt Harriet.

"What in tarnation is this all about?"

"Aunt Harriet." Brianna stared at her aunt in

surprise. She'd forgotten all about her. "I'm sorry, but I've got to get to the glen."

"What—"

Brianna gave her a peck on the cheek. Turning, she caught up her skirt, opened the door, and ran down the steps.

He's alive. He's alive. The words kept resounding over and over in Brianna's mind as she ran the short distance to the glen she and Ethan had played in.

At the edge of the glen, she slowed to a walk. The surrounding trees blocked out the sunlight, and she walked through the semidarkness to the clearing.

"Ethan?" she called out in a loud whisper.

Brianna swallowed and stood waiting.

"Ethan?" she called louder.

He stepped out from behind a tree into the clearing, and she gave a cry. She couldn't have moved if her life depended on it. She just stared. He stood tall and proudly before her. Sunlight glinted off his blond hair. As a smile lit his face, his eyes twinkled, and he held out his arms.

"Bree."

The sound of his voice freed her from the shock that had held her frozen. She practically flew across the distance separating them and threw herself into her twin's arms.

"It's really you." She hugged him tightly.

"And who else would it be?" he teased.

"But what are you doing here? I thought . . ."

she stopped and buried her head in his shoulder.

"There, Bree. Love?" Ethan pushed her away slightly and looked into her eyes. "What's wrong? Did you miss me that much?"

She hugged him tightly again and whispered, "I thought I'd lost you."

"Never. But I have to leave again soon. Come with me?"

"What?"

"Sail with me to England? How about it, Bree?"

It took all of Trevor's control not to lunge out from behind the tree that concealed him from the view of the two lovers. He'd followed Brianna's fleeing figure from Aunt Harriet's, but hadn't been able to catch up to her in time. When she'd thrown herself into the other man's arms, he had stopped dead still as if struck by lightning.

Trevor clenched his fist around an outstretched limb. He could barely breathe for the crushing weight within his chest. *His Brianna. Held lovingly—willingly—in another man's arms.* He wanted to drag her away from her lover, but the sense of betrayal cut too deep. This was the last time he'd risk believing her. She'd never treat him this way again, he vowed.

"Very touching." Trevor stepped into the glen.

Ethan and Brianna sprang apart at the harshly spoken words. Together they turned.

"Trevor," Brianna cried out.

"No wonder you wouldn't quit spying. All this time you had a lover you were meeting as well."

Ethan took a step forward, hands clenched into fists at the insult.

Trevor drew his pistol and pointed it dead center at Ethan's chest.

Chapter Nineteen

Brianna screamed and reached out for Ethan.

"I could kill you both here and now." Trevor held the pistol steady on Ethan. The dappled sunlight shimmered off the brass buttons of his blue uniform.

Trevor's eyes met Brianna's. His were dark with suppressed fury.

She gazed into his face a minute, unable to move or speak. This must be what an animal felt like before the kill. She suppressed a shudder. He wouldn't shoot her; she knew it. But shooting Ethan was another matter.

"No, Trevor." Her voice cracked. "Please, listen to me."

She took a step forward. At the coiled tension in his body, she stopped. She didn't want to provoke him into anything.

"I'm through with your lies," Trevor continued, his voice filled with a dead calm that frightened her as much as the gun.

Brianna stared transfixed as his finger tightened

on the trigger of the pistol. The gun stayed steady in his grasp.

Her mind screamed out to stop it, but not a sound passed her lips. She wanted to lunge for the gun, but her feet wouldn't move.

"Oh, hell." Trevor threw the pistol to the ground. "You're not worth it."

He spun on his heel and vanished into the surrounding trees.

It was over. Brianna faced the area of thick brush and trees where Trevor had disappeared.

Ethan pushed her to the side. "Stay here. I'm going after him."

"No." She grabbed his arm.

He continued forward, and his momentum lifted Brianna off her feet. She held to him tightly, trying to force him to a stop.

"No. Ethan. Please?"

He paused and looked down at her in puzzlement.

"Bree, I won't let him—"

She dug her fingers into his arm. "No. I won't allow it."

"Why ever not? I can take care of myself nowadays. Don't worry about—"

"Ethan, he's my husband."

His jaw slackened. "Husband? You're married? To a Yankee?"

Brianna bit her lip. "Yes." She released her hold on Ethan. He wasn't leaving. Right now, he was too shocked to chase anyone.

"That settles it. You're definitely coming with me

to England. We sail in less than two hours." He caught her arm and turned toward where he'd hidden his horse in the trees.

"No." Brianna dug her heels into the ground and stood firm. "I can't come with you. I won't leave Trevor."

"Bree—"

She crossed her arms and raised her chin in defiance. "I love him. And I'm likely carrying his baby by now."

"I won't allow it."

Brianna snorted. "I really doubt if there's much you can do after the fact, dear brother."

"Bree? You can't be serious. You can't love a Yankee."

She looked up into her twin's face. "More than life itself."

"But, Bree, Papa will—"

"Papa knows. Papa's already met him. He helped care for Trevor when he was wounded in Chattanooga. He gave me his blessing when we left to return to Washington."

Ethan gaped at her in disbelief.

"Can't you do the same? Ethan, I do love him. And I know he loves me."

She watched the battle going on in her twin. Silent, she gave him time to fight it out for himself.

"You really love him? Sure you won't get over it?"

"As sure as I breathe."

"Is he good to you? Does he care?" Concern edged his voice.

"More than I knew." Brianna stared off to the trees where Trevor had disappeared. He'd left in a fit of jealousy.

"You really think you're . . . that you might be . . . with . . ." Ethan trailed off in embarrassment.

Brianna smiled, and it spread into a grin. "Likely so. You'll have a nephew or niece to brag about before the year's out." She wrinkled her nose. "And if I know Trevor, he's already decreed it'll be a boy."

"Yee haw," Ethan gave a cry.

He swung her up into his arms and around in a wide circle.

"Put me down. You're making me dizzy."

"You've always been a bit dizzy, if you ask me," he teased.

"I still can scarcely believe you're alive."

"Bree, have you gone daft?" Ethan slowly lowered her to the ground.

"Sometimes I've thought so. Thanks to you." She hugged him close.

"What do you mean by that remark?"

"You're supposed to be dead."

"Do I look dead? Bree?"

"No, you look wonderful." She squeezed him so tight that he yelped.

"What was that for?"

"For being alive." Brianna tilted her head back and looked up at him. "To me you died. I held you in my arms until you stopped breathing." Her voice broke. "Rose even declared you dead to me."

"Silly goose. I never died. Maybe I passed out," he modified. "But I didn't die. I can assure you.

Weren't you told that I'd left the country?"

"No, I was told you'd died." Bitterness tinged her statement. "Why, Rose even buried you and showed me your grave."

"Buried? Not likely." He grinned down at her. "Do I look like some haint or apparition to you? Poor Rosie thought I'd likely die as live when she had the doctor brought in."

"She lied to me."

"Oh, Bree." Ethan dropped his chin onto the top of her head. "Try not to blame her. Thanks to her, I am alive. Rose took care of me. I came to in a doctor's house. As soon as I was well enough to travel, I left on a ship for England—"

Brianna snapped her head up. It connected with Ethan's chin with a crack. She gingerly rubbed the top of her head with one hand.

"A boat?"

"Actually it was a big ship. And please watch my chin." He rubbed his palm back and forth over his chin.

"You were on a boat. Very well, a ship," she corrected. "And I was seasick." She stared into his face, waiting for his reaction.

His jaw dropped open and stayed. "You . . ." He worked his mouth muscles, then shut his mouth.

"Uh huh," she nodded, this time being careful of his chin.

"Then, you felt—"

"Uh huh. But I couldn't understand it because you were dead. I even thought your spirit couldn't find rest because," she paused. "Because . . . of me and Trevor," she rushed on. "I thought I was losing my mind. First the seasickness, then the shoulder pain and fever—"

"I took the fever on the ship."

"Then the seasickness again."

"Bree? When was that?"

"About a week ago."

"We hit rough water almost a week ago. It was a few days out of Virginia on the way back here."

"Well, that explains it."

"Bree, I'm sorry you went through that."

"I should have known," she chided herself. "If I hadn't been so distracted by Trevor, I would have realized what was going on sooner. I was going to question Rose, but—"

"She's the one who sent me to England to try and raise support for the South."

"Why?" Brianna murmured. "Why didn't she tell me?"

"I thought you knew, otherwise I would have gotten a message to you sooner," Ethan apologized. "I reckon she figured the less who knew, the better it would be. And, she figured that way you'd take my place," he added sheepishly.

"She was right about that."

"I heard you did pretty good."

"I did—at first. Then I got caught. By Trevor."

Ethan whistled.

"So I guess we're even." She pinched his arm. "You worried me half to death, and I got a husband."

"A Yankee husband," he muttered.

"A Yankee." She smiled, wrinkling her nose at him.

"Whatever happened to Grant Lewis?" he asked, his hand clenching into a fist.

Brianna caught his hand. "Why, nothing. Don't worry," she assured. "Grant's fine."

"Bree?" Ethan grabbed her by the shoulders. "Didn't you find my letter?"

"Would you believe Aunt Harriet found it today? I have it here in my pocket." She reached for the sealed envelope. "I haven't had the chance to read it. Your message came and—"

Ethan shook her. "You haven't read it?"

"No. I rushed here first."

"Bree, Grant is the traitor. The jackal who betrayed me. He was selling information to both sides." He closed his eyes and threw his head back. "And I don't have the time to go after him."

"I'll take care of him." Brianna's voice was as cold as ice. "Don't worry. He'll get what's coming to him. I'll see to it."

"But, how?"

"I'll tell Trevor. Having a Yankee officer in the family is good for something."

"I guess it doesn't matter which side gets him, so long as it happens."

"Oh, it will happen. Will you come and meet Trevor? This time properly?"

"Bree, I can't this time. You know I can't go riding into town. Besides, the ship sails in under two hours, and I have a long ride." He drew her within the circle of his arms. "I'll miss you. Sure you won't change your mind and come with me?"

"I'm sure," she murmured against his chest.

He drew back and kissed her on the nose. "Then, I'll see you in a little over a year when I come back. Say, what's the name of the chap you married?"

"Trevor Caldwell."

"I reckon he's passable if you love him."

He chucked her under the chin and strode to where he'd hidden his horse. Waving farewell, he swung up on to his mount and rode out.

Brianna watched the space where he'd left for long minutes after he'd gone. She'd miss him something terrible, but at least this time she'd know he was alive.

She balled her hands into fists. Grant Lewis had an overdue debt to pay, and she planned to see it paid in full.

Trevor would know to handle Grant. The Union likely wanted him as bad as the South. However, before Trevor would listen to her about a traitor, she'd have to explain what he'd witnessed.

The fool, he should have noticed the similarities between her and Ethan. How could he miss it? Brianna smiled.

Trevor had been jealous. Admittedly, he'd also been furious, but that would pass when he realized whose arms she'd been in. To prove it, all she had to do was show him the miniature of her and Ethan. That would do the job. If it didn't, Aunt Harriet could confirm it. Trevor would believe her aunt. He knew the woman was positively smitten with him.

The smile remained on her face throughout the short walk back. She spent the time imagining just what Trevor would do once he realized the truth of what he'd seen. Today, she'd get him to admit he loved her. Again. Only this time he'd damned well remember.

"Brianna."

Almost to the steps of the house, she spun around to face the caller. Her breath left her in a rush. Grant Lewis stood calmly before her.

The blood chilled in her veins, then heated with white-hot anger. She tried to quell her emotions enough so they didn't show on her face. Licking her lips, she forced a smile.

"Why, Grant, what brings you here?"

She shoved her hands into her pockets, and the envelope crackled. It sounded noticeably out of place in the quiet afternoon. She sucked in her breath sharply and stared at him.

Her expression must have given her away, because Grant's eyes narrowed on hers, and he leaned forward.

"What have we here?" He snatched her hand out of her pocket.

The envelope fluttered to the ground. Brianna reached for it, but Grant beat her to it.

As he turned it over, she grabbed for it. Her hand came away with the ripped top of the envelope.

Grant stepped back and unfolded the paper. Skimming the words, he grabbed Brianna by the arm and yanked her to him.

"Let's go inside and talk."

He pulled her along with him as he mounted the steps and entered the house.

Brianna looked around desperately searching for Trevor or Sarah. The house was empty.

Where was nosy Sarah when one needed her? Probably shopping, or off gossiping. And where was Trevor?

"So, now you know the truth." Grant turned her to face him.

Brianna glared at him. "You betrayed Ethan and—"

"I'm really sorry about him. I hated to turn in a friend, but the Union was offering a lot of money."

"You betrayed Ethan for money? You—"

Grant yanked her to him so hard that the breath was knocked out of her when she hit his chest.

"I did it for you. And now, I've got more than enough money for us."

"Me?" Brianna sputtered. "You did it for yourself. Don't you dare try to blame this on me. There's nothing between us; you know that."

"Oh, yes there is, my dear. That's why you're leaving your husband for me."

"Never."

"You can come with me, or die right here."

Grant's face tightened with the threat. She had no doubt that he meant it.

Brianna raised her right leg back and brought it forward, but before it connected with him, Grant twisted her around. He held so tight she could scarcely breathe.

"Oh, no, my dear. You're coming away with me

like you should have done long ago. Caldwell will never have you. You belong to me. You always have."

"You fool." She struggled against him. "I won't go willingly."

"That's fine, too. I'll enjoy the fight much more than you will, Brianna. I promise you."

He dragged her to the table and threw the envelope down on to the wooden top.

"Now, I want you to write a note to your dear husband." He ground the last word out, hatred coloring his voice. "Tell him you've run away. With me."

"I won't do it."

Grant jerked her arm up. Pain shot from her wrist to her shoulder. Brianna bit her lip to keep from crying out. She wouldn't give him the satisfaction.

"Very well, my dear. I'll write it myself."

Grant shifted his hold and caught her around the throat with his arm. He tightened his hold until Brianna ceased struggling. She held onto his arm with both hands, trying to gulp in enough air.

"That's a good girl."

With his free hand, he scribbled a message to Trevor.

"Do you want to hear it, my dear?" He didn't wait for an answer. "It says that you've left Caldwell for me. You really should have, you know."

"Trevor won't believe it," she argued, her voice scratchy and hoarse.

She hoped her doubt didn't show. After the scene

he'd come upon in the clearing, she wasn't sure.

"You'd better hope he does. Because if he comes after you, I'll kill him."

Grant spoke the words with a calm certainty that chilled Brianna. She had to find a way to let Trevor know what Grant truly was. There had to be a way.

A possibility dawned in her mind. Ethan's letter. Grant had put it in his pocket. Perhaps. . . . Years ago, one of Ethan's friends had taught them pick-pocketing. She only hoped her skills weren't too rusted.

She lowered her left hand and carefully brushed Grant's jacket pocket. Her fingertip caught the edge of the letter. She closed her fingers around it and slowly withdrew the folded paper.

As soon as the letter cleared Grant's pocket, she released it. Trevor would be sure to see it on the floor. If she could just keep Grant from seeing it.

"I don't know why you married him," Grant continued. "I can give you so much more."

"With money that's stained with the blood of others," she accused.

Grant shoved her toward the door. Brianna stumbled and grabbed the wall to catch herself. In an instant Grant was at her side again.

"It spends the same, my dear."

He ran a finger down her cheek, and she turned her head away from him.

"Not to me," she said with disgust.

He caught her arm in a cruel hold. "We'll see what you say when you're hungry or thirsty. Shall we go?"

Brianna gripped the edge of the door. She wasn't about to go along meekly. She'd fight him. If she could stall long enough, Trevor would come.

"Maybe you'd rather wait for your husband to return?" Grant asked, gesturing to her grip on the door.

He smiled, his mouth in a thin line, so unlike the smile she was used to seeing. He held up a pistol in his hand. "And I'll put a bullet in him as he walks through the door."

"No," Brianna gasped.

Grant caught her arm again. He tugged her toward the door.

Brianna sent one last desperate glance around the foyer. The note lay on the table, and the letter on the floor.

Please, let someone find them both, she prayed.

Trevor, please come for me, she silently cried out to him, hoping in some way he'd hear. Trevor had to come after her. He had to.

She knew, as sure as she breathed, that Grant wouldn't let her live for long.

Chapter Twenty

Trevor reined his horse in and dismounted. He tied the stallion to the post, then strode to the door.

He'd ridden halfway to the other side of Washington and back, trying to wear out his anger. It hadn't worked. His temper was still barely below a boil. In the end, he'd decided to return home and have it out with Brianna once and for all.

He slammed into the house, only to be greeted by silence. Taking the stairs two at a time, he shoved the bedroom door open.

"Brianna."

No answer.

He looked around the room. Nothing was out of place. No sign of either packing or a temper tantrum. It was a far sight different than the last time she'd left him.

He strode out of the room and down the steps. At the foot of the stairs, he stopped.

"Brianna," he shouted.

His voice echoed through the empty house. She wasn't there. Damn her. Had she not returned from her rendezvous with her lover? Or had she left again?

Pain sliced deeply through him at the two possibilities.

Trevor slammed his fist into the wall. He still wanted her. No matter what. He still loved her.

Calling himself a fool did no good. His heart held firm to the love inside. Turning, he surveyed the room. Had she left any kind of evidence that she'd even come home at all?

The note propped up on the table cried for his attention. Trevor crossed to it and grabbed it up. He read the brief message, then closed his eyes against it.

"No," he violently denied the words.

Doubling his fists, he crumpled the note into a ball and threw it against the wall. It bounced and rolled into the corner.

"No," he repeated.

He took a step toward where the note lay, taunting him, and he stopped.

His eyes caught a flash of white at his feet. Bending, he picked it up. Slowly he unfolded the letter, not wanting to open himself up for another barrage of hurt from Brianna.

At first the words made no sense. It wasn't a lover's note. Far from it. The firmly slanted script listed dates, amounts of money, facts. Definitely not a lover's missive. The letter held evidence against a traitor to both sides of the war. It contained irrefutable, damning evidence against Captain Grant Lewis.

At the bottom of the letter, the signature read

Ethan Devland. Trevor stared at the name. How had Brianna acquired the letter? He turned it over in his hand while something nagged at his mind.

The picture of Brianna and her lover in the clearing bothered him. Something about it was all wrong. The man's red-gold hair, challenging clear blue eyes, lightly freckled cheekbones—where had he seen them before? The features were achingly familiar to him.

Realization hit Trevor with the force of a punch to his gut. The picture in the woods cleared for him, and he knew Ethan Devland lived.

The man he'd caught Brianna having a rendezvous with had been her twin brother—Ethan Devland—not a lover. But she'd told him her brother died. Trevor vowed to get the truth of that story from her later.

Trevor tightened his fist around the letter. The feel of the paper in his palm brought his attention back to the present. Ethan Devland had gathered proof of Grant Lewis's activities and given it to Brianna.

Surely Grant now knew that as well. He had been exposed and knew it, and now had Brianna in his grasp.

Trevor ran into the study and jerked open the desk drawer. He pulled out the spare pistol stowed inside and stuck it in his waistband. Throwing the letter onto the desk top, he spun around and tore out of the house like a man possessed.

He had to catch up with them. Grant would surely kill Brianna if she so much as breathed a word against him. From past experience with her, Trevor knew Brianna couldn't keep her mouth safely shut for long.

Trevor threw himself into the saddle, tucked the pistol into a saddlebag, and sent the stallion charging down the street. If Grant were on the run, fearing discovery, there was only one likely route. He had to go by boat. The secluded, little-known harbor of Sheraton lay less than an hour's ride away. The cove was well known for catering to anyone with money and no loyalties.

Fear rose up in his chest, and he tapped it down. If Grant made it that far with Brianna, he would make his escape, likely as not leaving Brianna dead. Trevor clenched the reins between his fingers. He'd stop Grant or die trying.

At a fork in the road, Grant slowed the horse to a walk. He tightened his hold around Brianna's waist and nuzzled his face in her hair.

Brianna snapped her mouth closed on the scathing comment she'd been about to make. She brought her shudder of revulsion under control with a great deal of concentration.

Fighting Grant had gotten her nowhere. She had a bruise across one cheek to prove that fact. Her first lesson for disobedience to her captor's orders. The small cut at the corner of her mouth proclaimed her second lesson. One thing Brianna wasn't was a slow learner. She wouldn't fight Grant again—not until she was sure she could win.

She gritted her teeth against the feel of his lips on

her neck and made plans. If he believed that she'd given in, cowed down to his superior strength, perhaps she might be able to catch him off guard.

Purposely she let her shoulders sag in a pretense of defeat. She willed all show of defiance away. It was the only chance she had. She refused to think on just how slim a chance it actually was.

No matter the fate, she refused to give up. One thing Ethan had taught her as a child—the Devlands weren't quitters or cowards.

Brianna sucked in a startled breath as a flash of ten-year-old memory struck her. That wasn't the only thing her twin had taught her. She smiled a sly, secret smile. He'd also taught her how to perform the same riding tricks as the travelling circus performer they'd idolized. By the time the entertainer left Chattanooga for Nashville, she and Ethan were putting on their own circus for Papa. Could she still do the trick? Dare she risk it?

Absolutely.

She groaned aloud and covered her mouth with her hand. "I think I'm going to be sick."

As she'd hoped, Grant instinctively removed his arms from around her waist. It was all she needed.

She lunged, shoving with all her might. In the next instant, she tumbled off the horse and rolled to her back. Closing her eyes to the merest of slits, she held herself perfectly still, peered through her lashes, and waited.

As she'd predicted, Grant pulled the horse to a halt and rapidly dismounted. He stomped toward her. A dark look of rage colored his face.

Brianna forced herself to lie not moving and wait for him to come to her. It was about the hardest thing she ever had to do.

Grant came to a stop and reached down for her. *Now,* her mind shouted.

She kicked him with all of her might. Grant gasped as the breath left him, then doubled over from the force of the blow.

Brianna rolled to the side and scrambled to her feet. Without even a glance back, she grabbed her skirt in her hands and ran for her life.

"Run, my dear. Run." Grant's voice echoed after her, overloud in the deserted area. He gave a hollow laugh.

Grant's laughter chilled her blood, spurring her on.

"Brianna," he called out, taunting her. "Wilkens ran, too. And when I caught him, I slit his throat. From ear to ear. You hear me, Brianna? Ear to ear."

His confession almost stopped her. Wilkens? Grant had killed Wilkens. The little butler hadn't been a traitor, only a poor victim.

She swallowed down her sadness and shock at Wilkens's death. If she stopped to think about it, she'd end up the same way. She dashed off the roadway and through the bordering wooded area. Gulping in draughts of air, she continued running. She ignored the burning in her chest. She just ran.

A fallen log blocked the overgrown path, and she jumped it in one hurdle. Ignoring the pain in her side, she pressed on. She had to escape. She had to.

Sounds of pursuit echoed all about her. She

pushed the horror of capture aside. One foot in front of the other, she ordered her body. She'd run until she dropped, rather than give in.

Her heart pounded in her ears, and she gulped in air. The burning in her chest increased. The pounding of her heart grew louder and louder, then merged with the thundering of hoofbeats.

A horse came alongside, and Brianna screamed.

Strong arms pulled her off her feet. She lashed out at her captor, kicking and clawing at him. The horse shied, then stopped.

"Brianna. It's me."

At the familiar, beloved voice, she went limp.

"Trevor?"

He released her and dropped down beside her. As he loosened the reins from his wrist, his horse shied.

"Yes, my sweet. I'm here."

She sagged weakly against him, clutching his shoulders. "Trevor."

"You're safe," he murmured against her hair, raining kisses across the top of her head.

She jerked away from him. "No. No. Grant's coming. He's going to kill me. He's promised to shoot you."

"It's all right—"

A rustle in the brush a few feet away sent Trevor's horse into a wild gallop out of sight. He took a step after his mount, but Brianna stopped him.

"Trevor." She grabbed his arm and pulled. "We've got to get away from here. Grant will—"

"It's all right. I'll stop him. I know everything," he paused. "Well, almost everything. I found the note."

"I didn't run away with him. I didn't," she insisted. "You've got to believe me."

"I know, my sweet."

Trevor drew her back into his arms. He held her as if he feared she'd vanish if he dared release her. Brianna rested her head on his chest. The beat of his heart was reassuring under her ear. She felt so safe. So very protected.

The click of a pistol behind her shattered her sanctuary.

"How touching," Grant sneered. "But if I were you, Caldwell, I wouldn't believe the lying bitch."

Brianna jerked away from Trevor and whirled to face Grant. He held a pistol pointed at them. His hand shook, wavering the gun back and forth. The movement worried her far more than if he'd held it steady.

"Come over here, my dear." Grant motioned to her with the pistol.

She stood where she was. There was no way she was getting within arm's reach of him. She glanced to the side. Trevor stood so stiffly beside her, he could have been carved of stone.

Trevor held himself still, resisting the impulse to charge at Grant. If he did that, Grant would likely shoot, and Brianna was in the line of fire. He'd die before he'd allow anything to happen to her.

He called himself every kind of a fool for leaving his own pistol with the horse. Now they were both long gone. How was he going to get Brianna out of this mess? He hoped reassurance and not the fear he felt for her showed on his face.

Brianna bit her bottom lip. Her eyes never left his.

"I said come here," Grant ordered.

Brianna ignored him. There had to be some other way. If he got ahold of her, he'd use her against Trevor. She wouldn't let him do that. She threw a glance around her. To the right the ground fell away sharply. She returned her gaze to Grant and the gun.

"What's the matter? Thinking of changing your mind on me? Remember the money. I can give you everything you want."

"You have nothing I want." She glared her hatred.

"Don't believe her, Caldwell. You should have heard what she was whispering in my ears just a few minutes ago," Grant taunted.

"You're lying." Brianna took a step forward, fists clenched.

"Huh uh." Grant waved the pistol at her. "Now, come on over here nicely. And we'll take up where we left off."

"We left off with me kicking you in the—"

"Move. Now. Before I shoot you where you stand, and him along with you."

Trevor moved forward, and Grant shifted the gun to him.

"Oh, yes, Caldwell. Take one more step." His grip on the gun tightened. "Now I can kill you like I should have that night at the ball when you interfered."

"No." Brianna dove for Grant, intent on stopping him from shooting Trevor.

The gun discharged just before she hit the ground, and she shut her eyes against the horrible picture the sound brought. A ragged sob tore through her. *Trevor.*

Biting her lip, she raised her head and looked up. Her mouth dropped open. Grant stood, frantically looking around for his missing pistol, while Trevor came straight toward her after Grant. She rolled out of the way as quickly as she could in skirts.

Trevor and Grant locked in combat. There was no red-stained wound on Trevor.

She wanted to cry out in joy, but knew the jeopardy the distraction could bring to Trevor. She choked back all sound except her shallow breathing.

The two men grappled, too close together for body blows, each trying to trip the other. Trevor had the advantage of height and muscle, but Grant fought with the violence of a madman.

As they neared her, she rolled to the side and watched in fixed horror the battle. Trevor would win, she told herself. He had to. If he didn't. . . .

She cut off the thought before it could complete. No, she wouldn't allow Grant to win this fight. Desperately, she glanced around the ground, searching for Grant's pistol. It lay in a clump of dirt, near the cliff, a couple of feet away from where the men fought.

Brianna crawled, trying not to distract the fighting men. Slowly, she inched toward the gun, keeping her eyes on the fight. She drew dangerously close to both the men and the pistol. Eyes pinned on the fighting, she froze.

Grant pulled back and scored with a punch to Trevor's midsection. She clenched her hands into impotent fists. Grant stepped back to land another blow, but Trevor dodged, landing an upper-cut to his chin.

Grant staggered backward and teetered, less than a foot away from Brianna and the edge of the cliff. Before she could roll out of the way, he snaked his arm out and grabbed her ankle.

"No," Trevor cried out.

Grant merely smiled and dragged Brianna with him over the edge of the cliff.

Chapter Twenty-one

Trevor threw himself at the cliff's edge. He caught Brianna by the wrist.

For an interminable minute, she hung suspended in air. Grant clung to her foot while Trevor hung on to her arm. She felt as if she were being torn into two pieces.

Brianna kicked against Grant's viselike grip on her ankle. Her foot connected with solid flesh.

Grant cried out, releasing his hold on her leg. His scream of rage echoed up the cliff face as he plummeted to his death.

Trevor pulled Brianna up to firm ground and held her close. She shivered in his arms, trying to shut out the horror of what had happened.

"It's over, my sweet." Trevor brushed her tangled hair back from her face. "It's all over."

Brianna clung to him, trembling in his arms.

Trevor murmured soft words of comfort. He drew her away from the cliff edge. His own arms trembled with thoughts of what might have happened.

Brianna raised her face to look into his. Her lower lip trembled, and tears glittered on her lashes.

"He's dead?"

"Yes, my sweet darling. He'll never touch you again."

"You . . . are . . . are you hurt?" she stammered, afraid of his answer.

Blood smeared over his jacket front, and two buttons were missing. She gingerly touched his chest where the scratched, bare skin showed.

At Trevor's sharply indrawn breath, she pulled her hand back.

"You're hurt. What—"

"No. It's only the power you have in your touch."

"Trevor?" The question shone clearly from her eyes.

"Oh, my sweet." He closed his arms tightly around her. "I could have lost you. I'd rather die myself."

Brianna smiled. "I love you." She tipped her head back, her love for him shining in her eyes. She didn't care if he saw. As a matter of fact, she wanted him to see.

"Oh, I love you, Brianna. You're my life. I was terrified you'd die without me ever having the chance to tell you. Without ever knowing of my love."

"I knew. You told me weeks ago."

"When?" He gazed down at her in perplexity.

"The night you made love to me in the slave cabin in Tennessee."

He frowned at her. "I what?"

"You did. And you told me you loved me."

"I didn't. I couldn't have made love to you and ever forgotten."

"Well, you did. But I'll make you remember that

night if it takes a thousand nights of lovemaking," she vowed.

"Can we start tonight?" He smiled at her, his mustache tipping up in an alluring tilt. "I warn you, I have a very poor memory."

"And I have forever to help you remember."

"Forever," Trevor murmured against her lips, "Rebel mine." His mouth claimed hers in a kiss to seal their love.

Epilogue

June 1867

Soft strains of music filled the church. Smiling to herself, Brianna took in the scene around her.

Ethan, alive and well, stood before the minister. Beside him Selina, dressed in the same ivory gown Brianna had been wed in, beamed up at him, her hand possessively on his forearm.

To her right sat Papa with his arm around Betty Preston Devland, his wife of four years now. Brianna's smile widened. Her family. Together.

Trevor caught up her hand, placing a kiss on her palm. At the touch a tingle ran the length of her arm, and she sighed in pleasure. He still had the power to affect her this way. Even now. And here in a church. Turning, her eyes met his and were held fast.

Trevor leaned down, his lips lightly brushing her cheek. "Happy?"

"Very," she whispered against his cheek, "Senator Caldwell."

"Your papa can be very persuasive. I'm still surprised I was elected."

"I'm not. How could any voter resist you?"

He rested his hand on her swollen abdomen. Beneath his palm the baby gave a healthy kick. Trevor grinned down at her. "I think he's eager to greet the world, don't you?"

"Not before this wedding's over."

Trevor's chuckle resonated in her ear. "If I recollect, babies tend to be born when they want."

"That they do."

She bit back her own laughter at the memory of her first time and glanced across her husband to where two cherubic-looking four-year-olds sat, dark heads bent together in hushed whispers. Likely as not, the twins were planning something. Jefferson and Mary, named so for the Confederate president and the Union president's wife, were rarely as angelic as they appeared.

"Shh" sounded behind her, and Brianna turned to meet Aunt Harriet's twinkling eyes. The old woman blinked back happy tears.

"I'm glad to see that girl finally ran him to ground." She pronounced her approval of Ethan and Selina's union.

Brianna turned back to the ceremony, holding back a giggle.

Once again, Trevor's breath teased her ear. "I, Trevor Caldwell, take thee Brianna."

A shiver of pleasure and remembrance coursed through her.

Trevor bent low and whispered the rest of the wedding vows for her ears alone.

The minister intoned, "You may kiss the bride."

Ethan swept Selina into his arms, kissing her

thoroughly, leaving no doubt in any of the guests' minds of his love for her.

A moment later, Trevor caught Brianna by the shoulders and drew her gently into his embrace. Slowly his head descended until his lips were a mere breath from hers.

"Forever, my sweet," he whispered before taking her lips in a kiss more reeling than life.

It was a kiss to remember always. It was a kiss to promise forever and into eternity. Like their love.

DISCOVER DEANA JAMES!

CAPTIVE ANGEL (2524, $4.50/$5.50)
Abandoned, penniless, and suddenly responsible for the biggest tobacco plantation in Colleton County, distraught Caroline Gillard had no time to dissolve into tears. By day the willowy redhead labored to exhaustion beside her slaves . . . but each night left her restless with longing for her wayward husband. She'd make the sea captain regret his betrayal until he begged her to take him back!

MASQUE OF SAPPHIRE (2885, $4.50/$5.50)
Judith Talbot-Harrow left England with a heavy heart. She was going to America to join a father she despised and a sister she distrusted. She was certainly in no mood to put up with the insulting actions of the arrogant Yankee privateer who boarded her ship, ransacked her things, then "apologized" with an indecent, brazen kiss! She vowed that someday he'd pay dearly for the liberties he had taken and the desires he had awakened.

SPEAK ONLY LOVE (3439, $4.95/$5.95)
Long ago, the shock of her mother's death had robbed Vivian Marleigh of the power of speech. Now she was being forced to marry a bitter man with brandy on his breath. But she could not say what was in her heart. It was up to the viscount to spark the fires that would melt her icy reserve.

WILD TEXAS HEART (3205, $4.95/$5.95)
Fan Breckenridge was terrified when the stranger found her near-naked and shivering beneath the Texas stars. Unable to remember who she was or what had happened, all she had in the world was the deed to a patch of land that might yield oil . . . and the fierce loving of this wildcatter who called himself Irons.

Available wherever paperbacks are sold, or order direct from the Publisher. Send cover price plus 50¢ per copy for mailing and handling to Zebra Books, Dept. 4237, 475 Park Avenue South, New York, N.Y. 10016. Residents of New York and Tennessee must include sales tax. DO NOT SEND CASH. For a free Zebra/Pinnacle catalog please write to the above address.